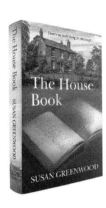

The House Book Trilogy

The House Book

Oakwood Grange is an old house complete with its own history in the form of the House Book, and it has new owners, but an incident from over 300 years before refuses to be laid to rest. Admittedly, there are a few odd little happenings and weird carved symbols about the house, but common sense tells Janie Whittaker there's really nothing to worry about – everyone knows there's no such thing as witchcraft.

An Uncertain Legacy

Elisabeth Osborne is different – in ways that are dangerous for a young girl in the 17th century when witch-hunting is still commonplace. Knowledge of herbs and the body are one thing but then there are the visions and much more besides... Unsettled until she finds the reason for her unusual powers, Elisabeth's adventures start in France before taking her to England where she finds herself in a house she has only seen before in visions – Oakwood Grange.

Recognition

Elisabeth is an old woman looking back on her life. She has long since come to terms with what she is and recognises that her presence at Oakwood Grange is more important than she first realised.

RECOGNITION

SUSAN GREENWOOD

For all those who encouraged me
to write the final part.

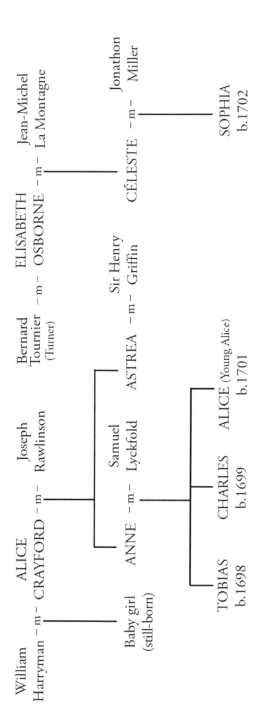

Family Trees for Alice and Elisabeth: 1717

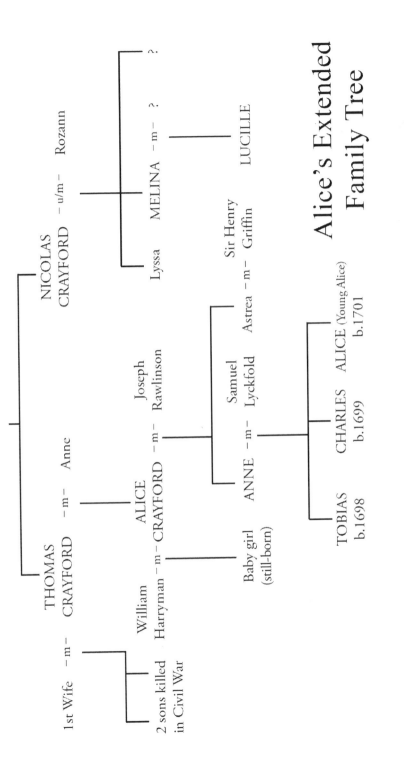

Alice's Extended Family Tree

PROLOGUE
October 1725, Oakwood Grange, West Sussex

I thought I saw her last evening, just before daylight went completely.

A flash of tortoiseshell fleetingly on my windowsill. Reality is a little slippery now so I may have imagined her, or dreamt her, but it makes no odds, she'll be here when the time is right. Although now seems too soon.

Not for me though, my poor body has been aching for release for some time now and I'm so cold I can no longer feel my hands and feet. But today is not the day.

Hopefully, there'll be a change in the weather very soon. The day I wake to see the ground sprinkled with a light frost and leaves swirling from branches bent over in the teeth of a strong wind – then I'll know. Or perhaps I won't even wake to see it – but that will be the day.

The signs have never let me down before.

~ 1 ~

8 years earlier, Summer 1717

'Tell me about Aunt Aphra.' Tobias perched himself on my bed, crunching his way through an apple. It has become his habit to keep me company in the afternoons since I've been forced into bed rest.

I shifted my feet sideways to give him more room and motioned for the extra pillow for my back. I could hear Aphra's voice in my head laughing, "Well, go on, tell him. He's not a child any longer."

I sent her away. 'What do you want to know?'

'What she was really like. Mother's rather vague on the subject and it's not everyone who's got a famous literary relative entombed in Westminster Abbey.'

'Well, for a start, she was your mother's godmother, not a relative – no more than I am – and your mother was only young when Aphra died.' That was no lie, but the real reason for Anne's reluctance I suspect lies in the fashionable notion that everything to come out of Charles II's reign, including Aphra and her plays and poetry, is now considered far too licentious for today's taste. Society has since made sure that women know their place and are still not expected to enjoy life in the same way as men. 'But we were a little trio – your grandmother Alice, Aphra and I – closer than some sisters I know. We were different in temperament and personalities certainly, but firm friends until death separated us.'

'Describe her to me.'

I had a vision of her as she was in her prime and not as I'd last seen her. It made me smile. 'Someone else who knew her well once said she was "pretty, witty and clever" and she was certainly all those things as well as irreverent which, of course, made her extremely good company. Men loved her and she loved them. She lived her life the way she wanted to without worrying too much about what people thought or said and you, Tobias, from what I've heard recently, would have got on very well with her.'

'Ha!' Tobias threw the apple core out of the window and wiped his mouth on the cuff of his jacket. 'I take it my darling mother has been complaining again about the company I keep?'

I didn't answer. 'Anyway, if you really want to know about Aphra, there's an Anthology of her work in that drawer over there, and if you can find time to read it between estate business and meeting friends, then it'll give you a good idea of what she was like, for she wrote as she lived. Just be careful with it. It's one of my treasured possessions.'

He slid off the bed, made his way to my desk and took out the leather-bound book. Opening it up he read the inscription and turned back to give me a knowing smile, so reminiscent of his grandmother that my heart gave a little lurch. Alice would have been so proud of the man her young grandson has become.

'Don't get sticky finger-marks all over it, and it's probably a good idea to keep it in your room, out of sight. I don't want to be accused of leading you astray.'

He closed it smartly, wiped his hands on his breeches and came back to my bedside. 'I'll be off now then.' Planting a swift kiss on my forehead he waggled a finger close to my face. 'Now make sure you don't get up to anything dangerous while I'm gone, Aunt Elisabeth – you know what you're like. I'll tell Mother if you...'

'Oh, get out you fool.' I pushed his stupid, grinning face away. 'And take care of that book!'

Tobias keeps me feeling alive. His life is just starting as mine is nearing its end, but the bond that was forged on the day I delivered him 19 years ago means that I feel as close to him as I do my own grandchild. This sudden interest in Aphra has taken me by surprise and I wonder where it will lead. Just recently, lying here with nothing much to occupy my mind, I've been feeling a little maudlin, lamenting the fact that there's no one left alive who remembers the person I used to be. It's as though all that history just ceases to be. Perhaps Aphra will fire Tobias's curiosity and the three of us will be able to live again, however briefly.

Hearing familiar footsteps along the landing I anticipated the knock. Anne stood in the doorway, the little frown which is in danger of becoming permanent making her look older than her years. 'I'm sorry Aunt Elisabeth, I'm looking for Tobias. I thought he might be here.'

'He was, my love, but I heard him go down the back stairs only a few minutes ago. I think he was going to see Gabe about something.'

'Oh, alright, fine...' She lingered on the threshold a little longer. 'It's just that we haven't seen him today and I have a suspicion he didn't come home last night. Cook says he turned up for an early breakfast and went straight out again. Did he seem alright to you?'

'He was fine. Come here Anne, and tell me what's worrying you.' I patted the bed and she came obediently. Sitting on my bedside stool, she laid her head down, hoping I'd stroke away the fears as I've always tried to do. 'I have no idea what he was doing last night but he was in very good spirits this afternoon and, as far as I'm aware, he's been on the farm all morning.'

She looked up at me through eyes on the verge of tears. 'Aunt, you know why I worry.'

And I do.

I have attended every birth in this household for the last forty-odd years but none was more stressful than when Anne was born, for Alice had already suffered two miscarriages and a still birth. I remember cleaning and swaddling the baby before handing her over to a relieved and beaming mother. It was just the two of us in the room.

'What is it, Elisabeth? Is everything as it should be?'

Alice had caught me by surprise. 'Yes, of course. Just look at your beautiful daughter, how could anything be wrong?' I sat on the bed and we both stared at the funny little bundle.

'I thought I noticed something when you were wiping her. She has got everything, hasn't she? I daren't look.'

Lying to Alice was not something I was used to, but this wasn't the time to confess anything more than a vague unease. I'd double-checked the baby's airways and everything seemed in order. It was years later when Anne had distressing bouts of breathlessness and agonized coughing fits that I recalled what I'd felt the day of her birth.

And I had the same experience at Tobias's birth. Alice took one look at me and knew what was probably in store for her first grandson. It did not bode well for someone expected to take over the running of a large estate.

'He seems to be coping well though, Anne. When I'm up and about tomorrow, I'll make some more liquorice and linseed infusion and insist he drink it every day. He says it helps.'

'You won't, because you won't be 'up and about' tomorrow, for goodness' sake. What on earth are you thinking?' She sat up quickly and the frown deepened. 'It wasn't just a faint, I'm not stupid and I know you sent Mary out looking for foxglove.' She fussed unnecessarily over my bedding and pillows, then softened and reached for my hand. 'Just stay here another day or two, please, then take things easy for a while. We can't afford to lose you.'

She left and I immediately regretted the way I'd dismissed her fears. It has become second nature for me to play down her fussing, but this time she has good reason. Whilst her affliction disappeared early on, Tobias's has become worse. He has the appetites of a normal healthy young man but, for him, long evenings spent carousing and smoking are not to be recommended. And given Mary's latest gossip about unbridled physical activity with certain willing village girls…it's probably time to have a word. Better, too, that it should come from me as both Anne and Samuel are so straitlaced and concerned with their social standing that I imagine the conversation would not go well.

~ 2 ~

Summer 1717

'It's ironic, isn't it? My sister is named for grandmother Alice, but from what Mother tells me and from what I remember, I can't imagine they'd have had much in common.'

Tobias was sitting on the windowsill and I was next to him in my chair, a permitted halfway house before being allowed downstairs. It was a hot day; the windows were flung wide and the air was alive with insect noise. The view from this window is glorious; it stopped me in my tracks many years ago and it still has the power to calm my soul no matter what the season.

'True enough, the likeness ends with their looks. Your grandmother certainly had no time for needlepoint or dancing and nothing much kept her from the farm when she was young, but that's not to say that she neglected her studies. Her mother was the daughter of the architect who built this house, did you know that? – and she made sure Alice had the sort of education usually reserved for sons. No one could match your grandmother when it came to numbers.'

Tobias gave a little laugh. 'I have to thank her for that. Making times tables fun is one of the best memories I have of her. What was I then – 6 or 7?'

'About that. I remember you sitting at the kitchen table and getting little sweet treats if you got them all right, which you usually did. Yes, she was so proud that you took after her and not your mother in that respect.' We were both lost in the memory for a short while.

'Is it true she ran this place all by herself until Grandfather came along?'

The short answer to this was 'yes' but I needed to tread carefully at this stage.

'She more or less ran this place after her mother died. There had been two, much older step brothers but both had been killed in the Civil War so she was the sole heir. At 15, she took on the management of the house and then, a few years later when her father became too infirm, she ran the farm too. She had good loyal staff, of course, and the estate was smaller then, but still it was a big undertaking.'

'I can't imagine how she did it. I mean, I find it hard enough and...'

'...you're a man? Yes, well, Alice had a lot of that to contend with. While her father was alive it was assumed he was in charge, but all the time she was learning more and more and the farm manager, Durling was his name, was very supportive. In those days, more so than now even, this farm was really one big extended family, much of the workforce had been born on the estate and they all wanted her to succeed.'

'Which she did, on her own. And she was what – about my age now?'

'As you will make a success of it, too.' I shelved my intention to speak to him about taking more care of himself at this point. It could wait.

Tobias gave a little noncommittal shrug. He hopped off the windowsill to fill my water glass and I half expected him to leave then, but he surprised me.

'So, changing the subject slightly, you've never spoken about how you and my grandmother came to be friends and how on earth she got to know someone like Aphra Behn? I mean, I've started reading her work and it's, well... surprisingly graphic for a female writer. Did Alice have a secret life in London that no one ever knew about?'

Ah, there it was at last. The question no one had directly asked me before. I find children are mostly accepting of the *status quo* and largely incurious about their parents' early lives. In that regard, Alice's daughters were no exception. Of course, that often changes once the parent dies and regrets set in. Still, at least there's the chance now that her grandson will get to know her better. The question I needed to ask myself was whether or not Alice would want me to tell Tobias everything.

No, not everything. Definitely not. 'I suspect you don't know that Alice was married before she met your grandfather.'

He looked up sharply, his expression surprised, but mainly confused. 'Mother's never mentioned that. She must know, surely?'

Alice was with me now, as if looking over my shoulder. I'd been wondering if she would turn up to give me permission. 'I'm not sure. It should be in the House Book where everything is recorded, but then Alice was the one to do all the recording, so I don't know.'

Tobias ran a hand through his thick, wayward hair and let out a long breath. 'What happened to the marriage? Do we have relatives we don't know about?'

'No, nothing like that. There was a child but she was stillborn, and her husband, William Harryman, died young in the cold winter of 1670/71. Anyway, I mention the marriage only because it's relevant to your original question of how we three came to know each other and became such stalwart friends.'

I sensed Alice retreating and took that as a sign I could continue.

'Alice and Aphra had a friend in common, Colonel Thomas Culpeper, but they didn't know of each other's existence until 1667. Aphra was a sort of foster sister to Thomas at his family home in Kent, and Alice knew him because their fathers were close friends, and he was a frequent visitor here.'

'And you knew this Thomas as well?'

'I got to know him through Aphra.'

'In Kent? I thought ...'

'If you keep interrupting me, Tobias, I'll lose my thread. Just listen, would you please?' Patience was never one of his virtues but the pause did give me time to choose the next words. 'Aphra and I were both living in London at the time and Aphra had got herself into a bit of bother. In short, she was owed a considerable amount of money by the Court and had taken out a loan to cover her debts, fully expecting to be paid at some point for her services to the King.' I saw Tobias raise his eyebrows and struggle to keep quiet. 'I doubt we're thinking of the same services – although, given the opportunity, I'm sure she wouldn't have turned him down. She was great friends with Nell Gwynn after all. No, and this will no doubt surprise you too, the payment was for her role as a spy during the Dutch war and if you want to know more about that, I'll tell you later. Anyway, the point is, the Court acted shamefully, never paying up and she was on the point of being arrested for non-payment of the loan when Thomas arranged for her to hide somewhere where the law and the lender couldn't find her and throw her in prison.'

'Here?'

'Yes, here. Somehow, he'd managed to persuade Alice and William to give us shelter by suggesting Aphra was in danger from a man – the truth, but misleading all the same. And I was to accompany her as a companion but also a calming influence; she could be a little volatile on occasion.' I was getting wrapped up in the past, explaining more than I needed to. 'That's all by-the-by now. What happened though was that we three women became close very quickly and I have to say that your grandmother blossomed while we were here. There was our shared love of literature and music, plus the fact that we all spoke French quite well.'

'Quite well? Aunt – you're French!'

'Half French, and I was really referring to the others. So…after a while it became obvious that Alice was not keen for us to leave and in the end I stayed here on and off for about two years, sometimes for long stretches as Alice was suffering with her pregnancies, and Aphra tended to flit between here and London trying to settle her affairs, which she did eventually.'

'And this William, what was he like?'

I felt my mouth turn downwards as I gave a little shake of the head. 'Unpleasant, jealous, devious – should I go on or have you got the picture?'

'No, Aunt, you've made that very clear.' He grinned. 'Surely the man had some redeeming features, or else why on earth did she marry him?'

'I grant you he was a handsome man and, frankly, Alice was young, naïve and had no experience of men when her father arranged what he thought would be a good match for her. Her father was desperate, I think. He knew he was dying, you see.'

'Go on then. Tell me what he did to upset you so.'

Perhaps I was stupid to go down this road but there was no sign to make me turn back now. Alice would know I wasn't likely to explain to her grandson how William had fought to control his wife, was incapable of a normal loving relationship, raped her when drunk and fathered a child with a young milkmaid. Fortunately though, there were plenty of other reasons.

'This has always been a Royalist household, you know that. So, ask yourself this Tobias, why would an ex-Parliamentarian, a follower of Cromwell with definite Puritan tendencies, marry into this family even after the Restoration? I see by your face that you've probably worked it out for yourself. Unfortunately for William, Alice's father may have had doubts, for he'd placed the whole estate in a trust for his daughter which meant it was unlikely her husband was ever going to get his hands on it.'

'Did my grandmother dislike him too?'

'Your grandmother made more allowances for him that any other woman I know, because she always saw the best in people. I don't want to lay bare all the personal reasons, but one incident made sure that she would never see him in the same light again. She was suffering with a pregnancy at the time and in no condition to object, when William insisted on managing the farm, including the accounts which Alice had always seen to. It did not go well. Very soon, the trustees were so horrified that they insisted he have nothing more to do with the farm and Alice discovered he'd been using estate money to renovate some properties he owned in

Chichester. That's when she really saw the man for what he was.'

Of course, there was another incident which upset Alice far more, but the less said about that, the better.

'So, did she kick him out?'

'No. Legally she was stuck with him and shortly afterwards William became ill – and not just physically – he became very odd, imagining things and rambling. Alice cared for him until he died a couple of years later.'

'No wonder she wasn't keen to talk about that period in her life.' Tobias stared out of the window into the far distance. 'I expect she just wanted to forget about it.'

If only that were true. 'You mustn't think though that that experience completely quashed her lust for life, because it didn't. Underneath that gentle, comfortable exterior that you knew, your grandmother was a woman of the world who loved literature, was well-versed in political thought and who, for a time before she married your grandfather, loved to visit us in London to see Aphra's plays as well as Mr. Shakespeare's. So, probably not the country mouse you might have imagined.'

Tobias grinned. 'Tell me more.'

'No.'

~ 3 ~

49 years earlier, January 1668

'Alice, really, I know of no husband who wouldn't be happy to see his lovely, young wife looking her best in a beautiful gown.' Aphra was sorting through her trunk for something suitable as she spoke. 'But if that's what you're worried about, you can always change back before supper.'

Elisabeth exchanged a sideways glance with Alice. 'I think I might have just the thing in my room Aphra, let me go and find it.'

The trunk lid closed with a bang and Aphra sat on top, hands on hips, lips pursed dramatically. 'What are you suggesting, Elisabeth? That my gowns are somehow too decorous – or that they're too big for her?'

'Both, now you mention it. And don't look at me like that, you know it's true. I'll be back shortly.'

Elisabeth left with a grin, delighted that Aphra was once again the happy, mischievous companion that had been so absent of late. Today was going to be spent enjoying themselves, a rare indulgence for Alice, but even she had agreed it was far too wet to do the rounds on the farm. William was away all day in Chichester.

The morning had already been spent styling Alice's hair. Thick and curly, it now fell in long chestnut ringlets with pretty tendrils framing a freckled, heart-shaped face. 'Is that really me?' she'd asked, bending forwards to see herself in the mirror.

'Yes, you're the mistress of this house, not some housemaid.' Aphra had already tossed Alice's coif across the room.

'What about this?' Elisabeth was back with one of her favourite gowns. Only Aphra knew the significance of this pale blue silk, a physical reminder of the short time Elisabeth had spent with her late husband.

'It's beautiful.' Alice bit her lip and smoothed her hand over the silk. 'I've never seen anything so exquisite and this lace – oh really, I can't wear this…'

'It's French couture at its finest, that's why, and yes you can.' Resistance to Aphra was futile.

The morning concluded with the three of them taking the various parts in what was to become Aphra's first play, *The Forc'd Marriage*. It was chaotic and their laughter so loud that Mrs Lynd, the Cook, found herself singing as she went about her work. It had been some time since she'd felt like doing that.

Lunch was served in the formal dining room at Elisabeth's request. 'Oh, Miss Alice, if only your dear mother could see you now.' Head on one side, Cook tilted Alice's chin and beamed at her. 'You look beautiful.' As with all the older members of staff, she'd never got the hang of calling her 'Mistress' having held her as a baby. The familiarity was a running sore for William.

It was a long lunch with Aphra assuming charge of the wine decanter and the laughter becoming ever louder as her impromptu rhymes became ever bawdier. Work in the kitchen ground to a halt as maids giggled with their ears to the door and Cook let them have their fun until the scraping of chairs signalled the end of lunch and then it was back to work. There was much to do and little time left to do it before supper.

'Well, that was fun.' Aphra flopped down onto the little sofa in her room whilst Elisabeth and Alice lay on her bed.

'I should get out of this lovely gown before I do it some damage…
but I might just stay here a little bit longer.' Alice closed her eyes.
'My head's feeling a bit all over the place.'

'You only had two glasses of wine.'

Elisabeth propped her head on one hand. 'Yes, and I only had
two glasses too so it's a mystery how we managed to get through
so much, Alice.'

'That is a lie, Elisabeth Turner, I distinctly remember topping
up your glass more than once.' Aphra kicked off her shoes. 'Anyway,
lovely though your wine is, Alice, I was introduced to much more
potent stuff when I was in Surinam and that's probably why I'm
better at holding my drink.'

'Where on earth is Surinam?' Alice turned on to her side to look
at Aphra, who, with feet tucked beneath her, was more than ready
to tell her story.

Elisabeth had heard it all before and hoped this would be the
abridged version – and not just because of the time it took to tell.
Thankfully, it was.

'Oh, look, it's getting dark already.' Alice slid off the bed. 'I must
go and change, Elisabeth.'

'Why?' Aphra uncurled her legs.

Elisabeth shot her a look over Alice's head to warn her off. She
knew perfectly well why.

The reply was a raised eyebrow. 'Well, for goodness' sake, don't
hide your lovely curls under a coif – it would be a sin.'

Alice kissed them both on the cheek. 'I won't, I promise. Thank
you both for today, it's been such fun. I'll leave this gown back in
your room Elisabeth, if I can find Jennet to help me out of it.'

'Sad, isn't it?' Aphra got up to stretch her legs once the footsteps
had disappeared down the corridor. 'Any normal man would be
delighted to see her looking like that.'

'Mmm, but best not to interfere. It's the life she's chosen and as long as she's content…'

'But she isn't, is she? Otherwise why the need to keep quiet about what we've been doing today? And anyway, why should anyone settle for content; why not happy?'

'Because very few women are.'

'You are.'

'I'm fortunate to be independent and financially secure. And you will be too once your plays are the toast of London and now it looks like your current little problem may soon be solved.'

'God willing…'

'Just don't make life awkward for her, that's all I ask. He already thinks we're a bad influence and he's jealous to boot. I'm going to help her out of the dress; I suggest you have a little nap.'

'An excellent idea. See you at supper.'

Perhaps if William had not returned home already drunk and boorish, or had taken the time to compliment his wife on her appearance instead of scowling, supper may have passed without incident. As it was, neither of those things happened, and as the wine flowed, Aphra and William's mutual antagonism got the better of them until the pretence of good manners was completely abandoned.

~ 4 ~

Summer 1717

I heard Samuel's measured tread on the landing and waited for him to knock and poke his head round the door. Anne had already warned me that he had instructions to make sure I was being sensible.

'Your white knight is here to ferry you downstairs, Elisabeth. Are you ready?' He entered with a flamboyant bow and a wide smile. Resting one hand on the back of my chair, his lips brushed my cheek. 'I must say you're looking considerably better than the last time I saw you.'

'It was a faint, Samuel, Anne's making too much of this. I'm not at death's door – not yet, anyway.'

Samuel Lyckfold is a large man, a magistrate who has no trouble commanding respect when at the bench but who willingly relinquishes authority at home. As he has no interest in farming and this is Anne's family home, he's wise enough to offer advice only when asked.

'Whatever it was, I'm not to let you out of my sight until you're safely downstairs. There's a daybed waiting for you in the morning room.'

'Well, it'll have a long wait. I'm going to the kitchen to see Mary, I'll be quite safe there.' I would normally take the back stairs just next to my room as they lead directly to the kitchen but they are steep and too narrow for two abreast, or at least Samuel and one other. It's 50 years since 'that night' and the memory of it is forever linked with those stairs but it never crossed my mind to change rooms. Alice offered but knew I wouldn't accept.

There was no one in the kitchen when we arrived but Samuel drew a chair up to the fire for me and I was happy to wait for company. 'That's lovely, Samuel, and please don't think you have to stay, I'm sure you've got plenty of work to do. The others will be back soon, I dare say.' He patted my shoulder, no doubt relieved, and made for the door before I could change my mind. I must have dozed off for I woke with a jolt as Anne's youngest careered through the door.

'Tante Élisabeth, I'm so pleased you're up.' She gave me a swift hug. 'You've got to help me design a ballgown. I'm so excited, we've been invited to Frances Armitage's birthday party and I'll definitely need something new, because nothing fits me properly anymore.' She looked down at what was once a flat chest, not that long ago. 'I have some ideas, of course, but no one knows more about fabrics and trimmings than you do so ...'

Anne followed her in to the kitchen. 'So, this is where you are, I've been looking in the morning room. Alice, for heavens' sake will you stop going on about this party. Aunt Elisabeth is still recuperating and there'll be plenty of time later to talk to her about that. Go and tell your father that we're back.' She heaved a sigh once we were alone.

'What's the matter?'

'Oh, it's nothing, just this party. I'm not looking forward to it.'

'Because of Tobias?'

'You see?' She went to close the door and lowered her voice. 'You know already what I only have a vague suspicion about. What's he said?'

'I'm sure I know no more than you, Anne. He's very taken with Frances.'

'Yes, well there's the problem, because she's more or less engaged to Richard Hadleigh and there's a good chance it will be announced at the party.'

I didn't say anything.

'You know what he's like, especially if he's had a drink or two ...' She was cut short by a commotion as Cook and Mary dumped heavy baskets just inside the garden door.

'Oh, Mistress, I'm so sorry, I didn't know you were there...'

Anne quickly plastered a smile onto her face. 'Don't be silly, come on in. I'm just going and Aunt Elisabeth's been waiting for you.' She gave me a look that suggested we were going to revisit this conversation later.

I get on well with Cook and Mary. For close on 30 years, we've seen this family through births, weddings and funerals together and there isn't much we don't know about each other. I have a suspicion that Mary may indeed know more than most, but it will never be spoken of.

'Look, Madam, what do you think of these?' Mary offered me her basket full of bright green leaves.

'They look perfect Mary, and they're completely dry. Did you get them from the bank over by the wood?'

'Yes, but I think the Mistress saw me collecting some the other day. I am sorry.'

I patted her hand. 'Oh, don't you worry about that. Now, tell me, the flowers were out but not gone to seed?'

'Yes, and I avoided the pink ones like you said. So, shall I get on with it then?'

We glanced at Cook who gave her the nod and she scurried off into the scullery.

'I know you know what you're doing but ...' Cook tailed off. I could see her chin wobble as she heaved jars and bags of produce noisily onto larder shelves. 'But you don't fool either of us, just so you know.'

The clattering and banging carried on as I rose and followed Mary to the scullery. She's been a careful pupil over the years and I've already told her what's required, but great care has to be taken with foxglove preparation and my sixth sense is the only thing I trust when it comes to something like this. And I have to get it right. I've already had glimpses of what lies in the future for this family and if I am to fulfil my deathbed promise to Alice, then I need to help my ailing heart.

I returned to my room after lunch for I have much to think about and it's the only place where peace and quiet can be guaranteed.

Frances Armitage may be a little younger than Tobias but is far ahead of her contemporaries when it comes to everything else – and she's ambitious, but I'm not one to criticise her for that. I'm sure she's attracted to Tobias; blessed with good looks and charm, he's never lacked for female attention, but he won't be inheriting a title or rolling acres of parkland. It will no doubt have amused her to keep him dangling, and he may not be the only one.

Is it likely the disappointment will trigger an attack? It may, especially if drink is involved, although it's obvious Anne also fears Tobias's disdain for the social niceties should the engagement come as a surprise. I'm confidently expecting another request for a 'word in his ear'.

* * *

'I already know about the engagement.' We were walking in the garden a little way from the house. Tobias drew back his arm, expertly sliced the heads off a stand of meadowsweet with his cane then turned to face me with a mirthless grin. 'So you can tell Mother she can enjoy the party without worrying whether or not I'll ruin their chances of ever being invited anywhere again.'

'She was worried for you, Tobias. Don't be mean-spirited.' He shot me a look which was meant to indicate he knew better, but I let it pass and linked his arm. 'In my opinion, if Frances Armitage doesn't have the good sense to see what an impressive catch you are, then it's her loss.'

This time the grin was genuine and he squeezed my arm. 'You're biased, it doesn't count. But you're right all the same.'

'How did you find out?'

'She told me herself, and she told me why.'

'I think I can guess why. The title and everything that goes with it...?' Just one more question and then I'd know for sure. 'What's he like, this Richard Hadleigh?'

Tobias shrugged. 'Not my sort. Spends much of his time in London, by all accounts.' He was studiously avoiding my eye, the only confirmation I needed.

'Well, you'll need to be very careful then, won't you? Both of you.'

He opened his mouth to speak but changed his mind just as quickly and we continued our walk in silence until we reached the field gate.

'Are you tired, do you want to go back?'

I smiled up at him and shook my head. 'Do you know, I don't feel a bit tired. I can't manage the hill, but let's go as far as the bench by the pond. This is doing me the world of good.'

'It was her suggestion you know, not mine. She reckons he's got someone in town.'

'Well it's a poor way to start a marriage. And what about you?'

'I'll be all right.'

'That depends though, doesn't it?

'On...'

'On the relative strength of your feelings for each other. I have experience when it comes to affairs outside marriage, Tobias, and you need to know what you're letting yourself in for. And don't give me that look. I, too, was young and pretty once.'

Tobias stepped in front of me, walking backwards, eyebrows raised and with his silly grin in place. 'I wasn't doubting how beautiful you were – still are, if you must know – I'm just surprised about the affair. Desperate to hear all about it though, shall we sit a while?'

I laughed. It briefly crossed my mind to tell him about my first intimate experience with a young, charismatic priest who taught me more than any fifteen-year-old should know, but I abandoned the idea just as quickly. That little episode will die with me now that Aphra and Alice are gone.

'How old is Frances?'

'18, going on 19.'

'Well, I too was 18. This was in Paris, of course, a few years before I came to England. François was a friend of the King and in Louis XIV's court having at least one mistress was quite the norm. Anyway, François was a few years older than me, but not many, and was newly married to the woman who'd been chosen for him when they were both infants. That was very much the thing in those families.'

'Hence why there were so many mistresses.'

'Exactly.'

'You certainly moved in elevated circles, Aunt Elisabeth.'

I ignored that. 'I shall not regale you with the details, Tobias. Suffice it to say that we were very much in love but there were difficulties on both sides. François respected his wife, who had no thought of gaining a lover herself as she adored her husband, and he didn't want to upset her. For that reason, our affair was kept secret from everyone, snatching moments where we could. My good friend, Marie-Louise, veteran of many affairs herself, always said that our tragedy was that we were too much in love, for in the normal way of things one partner tires of the other.'

'But that didn't happen.'

'No. François wanted to carry on as we were but I just couldn't do it. Very soon, he had young children, the demands of a wife and court life, and I saw him only when he could spare the time. It wasn't enough. I became jealous and resentful and I wasn't prepared for any children I might have to be called bastards. For me there was no solution other than to finish the affair, but be glad that we still loved each other.'

'How on earth did you manage that?'

'I'd already decided to come to England to find Mama's family so the distance made things easier.'

'And that was that. The end?'

'Yes, although I did see him one last time. A few years later he was badly injured in a riding accident and he asked his wife to send for me knowing he wouldn't last much longer. It was very sad.'

'I'll say. It's not exactly the same with me and Frances though, is it?'

'I don't know and I'm not asking you to tell me, Tobias. All I'm saying is that the relationship will not be equal and that will breed discontent for one of you – and could be dangerous.' I'd gone as far as I could. Ever since I first heard Frances Armitage's name linked with Tobias's I'd felt uneasy, and recent visions, although dark and indistinct, suggested trouble did indeed lie ahead for him. The sort of trouble that can't be fixed by herbal medicines and tonics but might necessitate intervention of the more arcane variety. If it comes to that, I hope my body doesn't let me down.

~ 5 ~
May 1671

Taking her usual walk, Elisabeth left through the kitchen garden gate beneath her bedroom window and crossed the field diagonally to reach the far-left corner. Then past the dew pond, still full, and left up the long, slow rise to the top of Windmill Hill where she stopped to catch her breath and take in a view stretching all the way to the sea. City life had its moments, but she'd never found anything to compare with the sheer exhilaration and feeling of well-being that follows from such a walk. She stood for some time facing into the breeze with eyes closed, one hand firmly on her bonnet and the other wiping wayward strands of hair from her face, before turning to continue her walk.

Deviating from her normal path but still on Oakwood Grange land, it was another half hour or so before she rounded a bend and came across him, just yards away on the edge of a wood. Standing quite still, the fox was watching her, and she froze on the spot. He sniffed the air. Eyes locked on each other, neither one moved giving her time to register his size and markings and wonder why he hadn't fled. There was no question he was male.

She chanced a step forward and he turned, flattened his body under the fence then paused just inside the wood. Another step, and they made eye contact once more as he glanced over his shoulder.

Seconds later he was gone, swallowed up by the gloom of the wood.

Unaware she'd been holding her breath, she let it out slowly in a long sigh. Never before had she been so close to such a magnificent wild animal for so long.

* * *

In the study, Alice was poring over accounts and making plans now that the bitterly cold weather was behind them. Still dressed in mourning black as convention demanded, there were now subtle signs that a new, more confident woman was emerging; one who had become quite particular about her hair now that she'd abandoned the coif. Aphra's comment was 'Not before time…'

Immediately after William's funeral, Elisabeth and Aphra had returned to support her – Alice never expected them to attend the service – and this period of catching up had benefitted all of them. It had been nearly three years since they were all together.

No longer pandering to her husband's puritanical world view, this new open-minded Alice wasn't shy of expressing her opinions on politics, society and much else besides. The woman she had always been was emerging from a drab stasis that had continued even after the final, fateful breakdown of her marriage. Playing the silent wife had become second nature, in part because her real life was spent on the farm but also because, by then, there was no point in provoking the pitiable, fearful figure William had become.

Elisabeth still considered herself responsible for his decline, but she was the only one.

The change in Alice delighted Aphra who now felt free to discuss the difficulties she was facing trying to get recognition as a playwright and poet. Although there was acclaim for her first play, The Forc'd Marriage, and she was not without some famous supporters, Aphra's grievance was against those who she knew would not criticise her work if she were a man. But literary figures in London tend to operate in the same way as a gentlemen's club, and Aphra, being neither male nor a wealthy aristocratic dilettante was at a distinct disadvantage.

Nothing was going to keep her away from London for long and soon only Elisabeth remained.

Alice looked up from her desk and sat back in her chair. 'Goodness, Elisabeth, you look radiant. Where've you been?'

Elisabeth flopped into the chair opposite. 'On the long walk, the whole circuit, coming back via the cottages. It was glorious and I plan to do it again tomorrow. Won't you come with me?'

She waved a hand over the accounts. 'I can't. The trustees are coming tomorrow and I need to make sure these are all up to date. Perhaps the day after?'

'Yes, let's.' Elisabeth untied the strings and eased off her bonnet. 'I saw a dog fox this morning. We stood and stared at each other for a while and then he was off. He was quite magnificent.'

'I wonder if it's the same one young Gabe's been seeing. A couple of early mornings last week he spotted it in the field near the kitchen garden and he's worried for his chickens.'

Elisabeth's stomach did a little somersault. 'He won't shoot it, will he?'

'Not if he can help it. Only if he finds it tearing his precious birds to shreds. Where did you see it?'

'Right up beyond the topmost field, the one with some cereal crop in it. Does the wood up there belong to the farm? There's an old fence round part of it.'

'It does, but it's so out of the way we've never really done anything with it. I think some of the villagers might use it for timber and foraging but it's a long way even for them. And we've got woods much closer for our needs.'

'Well, that's where he went anyway. I expect it's a different fox.'

* * *

That night he was in her dreams. Convinced she'd heard a shot Elisabeth woke in a panic, but it was still pitch black and the silence so absolute that she knew it couldn't be true. There were no startled birds fleeing their roosts. Sleep was then elusive; memories of that other night, when she'd woken just as abruptly, wormed their way into her brain. Screwing her eyes shut, she pulled the covers up tight and willed herself to think of something pleasant. In her head this would always be her room – and nothing was going to drive her from it.

Setting off after an early breakfast, she followed the same route as before but with only one aim in mind this time. As her pace slowed, her heartbeat quickened approaching the last bend, knowing he'd be there waiting for her. The clearest vision she'd had for some time told her it would be so and the excitement was growing.

But he wasn't there. Casting around in all directions, there was nothing to see, no rustlings, nothing. Reluctant to leave, Elisabeth sat on a bank facing the wood, elbows on knees and chin in hands, trying to figure out how that made her feel. Being different hadn't always been comfortable and the visions not always welcome, but did she really want to be normal? It would seem not, for there was no other explanation for the upset and disappointment she was feeling now that a vision had proved false.

Dispirited, she stood, brushed the back of her skirt, and took one last look at the wood. It was no more than a flash of rust, but she saw it and waited until he showed himself properly. Accepting the invitation, she climbed through the fence and followed him.

The wood was so dense that, even just a few yards inside, sunlight was struggling to make an impression and the vegetation so lush it was difficult to make out the track. Seeing the fox up ahead though, waiting at each turn to make sure she was behind, was enough to banish any doubts she had. Years ago, just such an experience with a different animal had been a defining moment in her life. This was going to be no different, she knew it.

By the time she reached a clearing, the fox had disappeared and she felt the first little flutter of fear; she was a long way from anywhere and wasn't convinced she knew her way out of the wood. Feeling faintly ridiculous she banished all thoughts of fairy tales, stood tall, swallowed hard and concentrated on this place where it seemed she was meant to be. No more than a few dozen yards in either direction it was a small space, but the sun was coming up fast over the treetops to the southeast, chasing away doubts along with the shadows and bathing everything in a golden light. Looking around for somewhere to sit, Elisabeth chose a felled tree trunk and set about unbuttoning and kicking off her boots in the hope that the sun would dry her dew-sodden feet. Her skirt too was wet around the hem and snagged where the odd bramble had done its best to make progress difficult. She spread it out along the log and idly tried picking off the little green burrs that Alice calls 'sweethearts'. She waited, unsure what she was waiting for.

With the sounds of the wood coming alive it was so perfectly peaceful and unthreatening she leaned back, eyes closed and raised her face to the sun. Aphra would be shocked. Elisabeth knew what she'd say – 'You're going to look like a peasant if you don't watch out' – and it made her smile.

A different sound, a rustling coming from the other side of the clearing, broke the mood and made her sit up quickly. Ferns were moving but she struggled to see anything more until two little bodies tumbled out of the fronds, rolling over each other, squeaking all the while. The entrance to the den wasn't obvious but soon another tiny face emerged immediately behind them, then another, and all four cubs put on such a show of play-fighting that she struggled not *to laugh. The tumbling grew ever closer at which point the largest cub stopped, alerting the other three to potential danger. The others fell back immediately but he stood his ground for several seconds, head on one side and his eyes on her face, before giving the signal to resume the game. She was left with the feeling of having passed a test.*

There was no vixen on that occasion.

* * *

Under normal circumstances Elisabeth would have rushed back, eager to tell Alice about the cubs, but until she understood more it would have to wait. It didn't sit well with her though; keeping even the smallest thing from Alice made her uneasy and her sixth sense told her this wasn't a small thing.

She didn't have to wait long.

The cubs were growing rapidly but now there were only three. The leader, already looking more like a grown fox with a full reddish-brown coat and an adult snout, had no fear of Elisabeth and regularly approached to within an arm's length, sniffing the air just like the dog fox had done on that first day. And by now the vixen had made an appearance.

Strolling into the clearing one day with a dead rabbit hanging from her mouth, and showing no surprise at seeing a stranger sitting on the tree trunk, she dropped the meal in the centre of the space. Soon the cubs were ripping apart the flesh, a tug-of-war game inevitably favouring the two strongest. The vixen looked tired and thin but stood whilst the new runt now demanded a milk feed to supplement any scraps it might find later.

Relieved from that duty, she sat facing Elisabeth, and an air of expectancy hung heavy about the clearing. Without moving her head, the vixen's left ear cocked sideways, aware of something beyond human hearing, and raised her snout to sniff the air. Elisabeth turned to look in that direction but saw nothing and, wary of what the vixen might do to protect her cubs, remained as still and unthreatening as she could. What happened next was the last thing she expected. Lowering her eyes, the vixen went down on her belly and crawled towards Elisabeth stopping a foot or two short before lowering her head to the ground.

Every instinct told Elisabeth to stand and lay a comforting hand on the fox's head – as if she were a dog – but she didn't. That couldn't be right. Afterwards, she couldn't remember clearly what she did do. She'd leaned towards the fox, she knew that, and most likely said something but couldn't remember what. It was only a brief moment that was soon broken when her cubs called and she loped off to join her family making their way back to the den, leaving Elisabeth wondering what on earth had just happened.

Deep in thought, she carefully retraced her steps out of the wood. There were no unusual noises and the scenery she knew so well by now was no different, but something in the air had changed. As if she wasn't alone.

* * *

Elisabeth devoted the next three days to Alice.

Even before being subjected to William's puritanical influence Alice was never one to be particular about her clothes, mainly because she never had much time for a social life outside the farm. It should be noted here that her husband's love of plain attire extended only to the outward appearance; his clothes were always of the finest quality.

It came as a complete surprise, therefore, when Alice announced her intention to buy a whole new wardrobe.

'Truly, Alice, I never thought I'd see the day.' Elisabeth was beaming. 'Sussex society is going to be agog when they see this butterfly emerge once the mourning period is over.'

'It will be a new me, I grant you, but emerging butterfly really is going too far. Anyway, there are two excellent seamstresses in Petworth, I'm told, but I need your expertise to prevent me from choosing something entirely unsuitable. Your outfits are always just right, and I know nothing about fabrics and trimmings and...'

'...and you don't need to ask me twice. When are we going?'

Elisabeth knew enough about the industry to realise that her presence would spark some professional jealousy, but was banking on her ability to source the fabric from her Huguenot friends in London to win them round. Having access to bolts of the finest woven silk usually reserved for courtiers was no doubt going to do wonders for the seamstresses' reputation, and profits. Elisabeth would even pass on her special rates.

On the day, Alice contributed to the discussions when asked but seemed perfectly content to let Elisabeth and the seamstresses get on with it. Three outfits were ordered and another three were to be finalised at a later date. Alice watched proceedings with the sort of smile that left Elisabeth wondering if this trip had been arranged solely for her benefit.

Enjoyable though it had been to immerse herself in the world of fashion and fabrics again, for it was surely her weakness, Elisabeth found herself longing to return to the wood and the fox family once more. She was back there the very next day whilst Alice was busy on the farm.

~ 6 ~

Late Summer 1717

'Which one is it?' Young Alice had her head in the cupboard next to the fireplace in my room. She will always be 'Young Alice' to me.

I craned my neck to take a look. 'Oh, I don't know. I haven't opened any of those trunks since your grandmother died. It's not the top one anyway; that was my Mama's and has mainly jewellery and trinkets in it. You'll have to get them all out but I can't help you lift them. Call Mary, she'll help you.'

After much heaving, when all three trunks had been dragged out of the cupboard, it was, of course, the last one which proved the most interesting.

Lifting my old red travelling costume from its cotton wrapping, Young Alice shook it out and held it high for a better look. 'This is just...beautiful.' In truth, I'd forgotten how fine it was and the memories threatened to overwhelm me for a moment; how sentimental I'm becoming in my old age. 'I wish I had your colouring instead of this.' She flicked her chestnut curls. 'I'm so jealous of Céleste and Sophia.'

It's true both my daughter and granddaughter have very dark hair, as mine once was, but I expect neither would appreciate my old clothes – or indeed be allowed to wear anything second-hand.

'I remember feeling very sophisticated and à la mode when I wore it, but with those big sleeves and wide hips it doesn't seem as flattering now as it did all those years ago.'

'Yes, but it wouldn't take much, would it, to alter the sleeves and change the skirt?'

It made me smile to see she was thinking as a seamstress but she mistook my expression and quickly checked herself. 'I don't mean...I wasn't thinking of ... asking you if I could have it, Tante, and I don't think I can wear that colour anyway. It's just that the fabric, lace and braid are all so fine and it just sits here in this trunk. It must have cost a fortune all those years ago.'

'I wouldn't know, my darling, but I expect you're right. It was one of a few outfits my first husband, Bernard, had made for me as a wedding present. He'd been couturier to Louis XIII so that tells you everything you need to know.'

Alice's eyes opened wide. 'You must have led a very elegant life in Paris back then.'

'Yes, for a short time, both there and in London, and it was exciting whilst it lasted but it wasn't really me.' I reached for her hand. 'This part of England is my true home and being accepted as part of your family has given me the greatest happiness.'

'Do you think Céleste minds you being here?'

'No.' I allowed myself a little laugh. 'Céleste understands perfectly that this has been my home ever since your grandmother insisted I move in after your grandfather died. Then when she died we talked about my moving to live with Céleste but by then your mother wanted me to stay and I rather suspect my son-in-law is quite comfortable with the arrangement. You don't want rid of me, do you Young Alice?'

She leapt up from the floor and flung herself round my neck. 'I'd fight them if they tried to take you away.' And just for a moment there was a spark of her grandmother. 'You belong to us.'

Gently removing her arms so I could breathe freely again, I nodded towards the open trunk. 'I think you'll find there's a matching hat somewhere if it hasn't completely disintegrated.'

She found the poor, squashed thing and plonked it on her head, bare plumes waving at odd angles, and danced around the room holding the costume up to her body. 'What do you think?'

'*Très jolie, ma petite,* but far too old and staid for you. However, if you look in that other drawstring bag, I think there might be something that suits you perfectly.'

Amid much excitement, it took very little time for Alice to strip out of her clothes and for me to help her into the pale blue satin gown which had always been a favourite of mine. Watching her twirl this way and that, I sensed her grandmother with me once again and even felt her hand on my shoulder.

'Your Grandmama wore that dress once and you look so like her, Alice, that it's as if I'm seeing her once again as a young woman.'

'Really? And did it fit her here, and here?'

'Well, she also had the tiniest waist, even without stays, but she was older than you when she wore it so she probably filled it out a bit more at the top.'

Alice made a little *moué*.

'You already have a lovely figure, Young Alice, you have nothing to complain about. And remember not to pout if you want to appear older than you are.'

She stuck out her tongue. 'What about that?'

'Very grown-up, darling. Now…let's get down to the matter in hand, pass me those sketches you've done. Which one do you like best? Or should we ask your mother?'

It was eventually decided. Anne and I were agreed on the most suitable design for a young girl and, as time was critical, a talented seamstress would find it a simple task to adapt the pale blue gown and give it fresh trimmings. I knew Alice was a little cross I hadn't supported her design choice but the loan of my sapphire pendant and earrings softened the blow.

Bernard, if you could only see how well I learned from the master. How proud you'd be to know I managed to preserve your beautiful clothes with lavender and cedar and careful wrapping so they could live again. Also, somewhere in the bottom of one of those trunks is your Design Book for Court Gowns and I think I've just found the perfect person to pass it on to.

It's been such a long time since I felt your presence and I miss you.

~ 7 ~

July 1671

Her name was Lucille.

Odd rustlings and the occasional snap of a twig had alerted Elisabeth to the girl's presence some weeks ago, but slowly she'd become a little braver and every now and again could be seen flitting between trees. A little dryad, always watching.

It was obvious Elisabeth was going to have to make the first move.

'Won't you join me? The foxes aren't playing today and I could do with the company.' Continuing to pick flowers, Elisabeth kept her voice low knowing it would carry in the stillness of the wood and that the girl wasn't far away.

Emerging from the trees with near-silent footsteps, she stopped at the edge of the clearing. Only then did Elisabeth turn to face her. 'Hello. I was beginning to think I was the only person who ever comes here.'

She was small but older than Elisabeth had imagined. Dressed simply in a green skirt and cream shift under a rough brown bodice, nevertheless she was striking-looking with a green head covering artfully secured in a long, thick auburn braid. 'I come here a lot Miss but I don't do any harm.' Her eyes were wide, her whole demeanour open and innocent.

'Of course you don't, it never crossed my mind.' Elisabeth nodded towards her basket. 'What have you been collecting?'

Relaxing just a little, the girl took a step closer, her eyes never leaving Elisabeth's. She offered the basket without looking away.

'I see you've got storksbill as well.' Elisabeth smiled, opening her purse to show her the same pink flowers, willing her to look somewhere other than her face.

Eventually she did. 'We call that crow's foot round here, Miss. You're not frightened to take it inside?'

'No, why?'

'Its other name is witch's foot. Some folks reckon it brings death if taken in the house.'

'Well, I've been using it for years and no one's died yet.' Elisabeth gave a little laugh but it crossed her mind that perhaps that may not be true. 'I'm using it to help someone who's got the flux. Why are you collecting it?'

'Same reason. It's for my great aunt, but she's old and she's got lots of things wrong with her, so it may not help.' She shifted the flowers to one side to show some other herbs. 'I'm going to try this lot too, what do you think?' The wide-eyed stare was back.

'Without knowing exactly what you're treating, it's difficult to say. You'd better be careful with the foxglove though.'

'Oh, I'll not be doing that. Chicken Nan's got her own way of using it.'

'Chicken Nan? Is she your great aunt? I met her a few years ago.'

'Yes, she told me. You're back at the Grange, aren't you?'

Astonished, it was Elisabeth's turn to stare, and the girl's turn to laugh. 'Everyone knows everything in this village.'

'In that case, you must already know my name but I still don't know yours.'

'Lucille, Miss.'

'Well, Lucille, I can likely figure it all out now. I expect Gabe still consults Chicken Nan when he needs advice about his hens. Am I right?'

A slight blush rose to her cheeks as her gaze slipped off sideways. The embarrassment less to do with gossip and more to do with Gabe, I felt. I now reckoned Lucille was 14 or 15 years old and I could remember all too clearly how first love felt. Fortunately though for Lucille, I knew Gabe to be neither promiscuous nor a predator. The hurt still remained somewhere deep inside me.

'She'd like to see you, Miss, if you can find the time. You'd have to go to her cottage though, she doesn't get out much anymore.'

Another surprise, but intriguing all the same. 'Yes, of course I'll visit if you let me know when it's convenient. And perhaps you can tell me if there's anything special she might need that I could bring from the farm?'

'I think it's just you she wants to see, Miss, after I told her about the foxes.'

'I'm sorry…?'

'The other day, I was watching you with the vixen…'

I waited for her to go on.

'…because these foxes here are special. They just know.'

'And what do they know, Lucille?' Her heart was beginning to race even though she felt she already knew the answer.

'What we are, of course.' Lucille gave her the same look a child gives when they know an adult is teasing them.

* * *

'That's very kind, please thank Miss Alice for me.' Chicken Nan sniffed the cheese and smiled. 'Is Jennet Sandford still looking after the dairy?'

'She pops in there every now and again to keep the dairymaids on their toes, but now she's housekeeper-cum-lady's maid she's too busy for anything else.'

'Well, she wet-nursed Miss Alice as a baby so it's a role she was

born to, I expect.' Nan placed the cheese in a cupboard and came back with a jug of elderflower cordial and two glasses. 'Freshly made yesterday, tell me if it's too strong.' She poured, then lowered herself into an armchair with a sigh.

Elisabeth took a sip. 'Perfect – just how I like it.' She smiled but wasn't prepared to open the conversation, and for a few seconds it seemed Nan wasn't going to either.

Tiny, crooked, and dressed entirely in black with a simple grey cap, Chicken Nan had the look of a jackdaw as she assessed her visitor through sharp little coal-black eyes. 'Well I'm glad to see you've dressed down for this visit. When you were here a few years ago, with that other one, the two of you looked as if you'd come straight from the King's court.' She gave a little throaty chuckle. 'But you're bonnier for it now in my eyes.'

'Well, thank you for that. You're not far wrong as it happens, but this time I'm well prepared for country life.'

'So I hear, and don't mind me Miss Turner, I don't do fancy talk.'

'I don't mind at all…. I'm sorry, what should I call you? Chicken Nan sounds so disrespectful.'

'Nonsense, that's what everyone calls me. Or just Nan if you prefer.'

'Nan, it is. Incidentally my name is Madame Tournier, but I'd like you to call me Elisabeth.'

The old woman's face lit up. 'Congratulations, I hope he's a good 'un'.'

'Oh, I'm sorry, I should have said straight away, I've been a widow for some years. I chose to be Miss Turner on my last visit because French people weren't always welcome just after the Great Fire and I didn't want questions. And yes, he was one of the best.'

Nan sat with her hands on her stomach, fingers interlaced and thumbs circling, a little frown between her brows. 'I'm sorry you lost him. You're not French though, are you?'

'I'm half French, my father was from Brittany. Mama was from Kent but I was brought up in Paris.'

'Interesting. You don't sound French.'

'I think that's good, isn't it?'

She gave a noncommittal little gesture and the two women exchanged a smile. Seeing her shift in her chair to find a more comfortable position, Elisabeth felt sure she was now about to approach the main reason for this summons. She got in first.

'When I saw Lucille in the woods she was concerned for your health. Is there anything I can do to help?'

Nan shook her head. 'I don't doubt your ability, Miss Elisabeth, not at all. But I'm at that time in my life where I've come to accept the inevitable, and there are days when I feel it can't come soon enough. Lucille, bless her, has not yet come to terms with that.'

Elisabeth understood completely. Her adored Bernard had tried to tell her the very same thing.

'She has the gift, of course, Lucille. She can turn her hand to all sorts of tonics and potions, but I'm guessing you've probably worked that out already.' There was no question in her voice. Elisabeth said nothing in reply but held her gaze. Leaning forward in her seat Nan patted her knee. 'There's nothing to be scared of here, my dear. You'll realise that once I've told you what I know.'

But Elisabeth was scared. Only the nursemaid who'd looked after her as a small child and her late husband knew the extent of what marked her out as different from everyone else. And the fewer people who knew, the safer she felt.

Nan settled back to tell her story.

'I'm sure Miss Alice has already told you that her family, the Crayfords, has worked this land for generations; most of the villagers work on the estate and folks round here know they could do a lot worse. Thomas Crayford, Miss Alice's father, was one of the best, but now his boys are dead and she's the last of 'em. We all hope she marries again now she's free o' that bastard.'

Elisabeth didn't react. Nan looked her straight in the eye for several seconds to let her know she knew what he'd done.

'Any road, that's by-the-by. Way back, when I was a young girl, Nicholas Crayford was a second son who'd joined the military and went to fight in France. I've no idea what they were sent there for but, anyway, he came back with a French girl in tow – a pregnant French girl at that. My mother always reckoned that Nicholas came back from the war a changed man. He'd been a bit of a firebrand in his youth, handy in a fight especially in drink, but now there was something else – vicious, always looking for trouble. And he was forever at odds with his older brother; the last row they had became so violent that the farmhands had to stop Nicholas for fear he'd kill him. And that older brother was Miss Alice's father.'

Elisabeth was a bit bemused by this. Whenever Alice had spoken of her family, she'd never mentioned an uncle. 'What happened, did they make it up?'

'No. Miss Alice's father had had enough. Nicholas left the estate before he was thrown off. He'd already rented a place in Thatchling for his French girl, Rozann she was called, a pretty little thing, and he went to live with her. They had three daughters before he drank himself to death. And Rozann's long gone as well.'

'Is all this common knowledge round here?'

'It was, but it's old news now. Jennet Sandford will definitely remember Nicholas though.'

'So... the three daughters?'

'At least two of them had the gift to some extent, although Rozann herself didn't. The eldest was quite beautiful but was terribly plagued by visions and things she didn't understand and couldn't control, and her mother was no help. Eventually, she drowned herself, frightened *she was mad – or possessed. The youngest girl died of a fever when she was young and the middle girl, Melina, married my sister's son.'*

'And Lucille is their daughter?'

Nan nodded.

'And Melina and your nephew?'

'They live in Thatchling and Lucille's their only child. Melina is held in great regard. She's the first person to be fetched when someone's ill and she births nearly all the babies round about.' Nan filled up their glasses and said, without looking up. 'I understand from Jennet that you're well versed in that department yourself, Miss Elisabeth. Didn't you attend to Miss Alice during her confinements?'

'I'm sure you also know that they didn't go well.'

'And not your fault. It was obvious she was never meant to give birth to one of William Harryman's babies.'

Quickly, Elisabeth's throat thickened with unshed tears and she bit her lip. The memory of that long night, two years ago, when for a time it looked as though she was going to lose Alice as well as the baby, had never gone away. It never would. And what followed was nearly as bad.

She was ready to leave and Nan knew it.

'I'm sorry, I didn't mean to upset you. But please don't leave just yet. The thing is… Melina knew someone special was going to come. Lucille has visions and they've been waiting for a sign.'

'The foxes?'

'As clear a sign as anyone could wish for.'

* * *

Making her way back slowly, Elisabeth's head was full of what she'd just learned and her mind was playing tricks on her; every villager's nod and glance now charged with a different meaning. Did everyone know? Sights, sounds and smells from that night assaulted her from all directions. Memories of sleep-bleary eyes trying to focus on the figure at her door, the sound of grunts and boots clattering on the back stairs as they dragged her out and into the cart, the stench of the foul gag in her mouth, the rank odour of unwashed bodies and those fingers that stripped, probed and pinched with such glee. She changed course quickly, striding off across the fields, failing to avoid the memory of William, clearly drunk, telling his men to bind her hands and feet to prepare her for 'ducking'. She was shaking and couldn't control it. Death would have come that night had it not been for the farm manager raising the alarm.

So, Chicken Nan appeared to know everything, including the accusation of witchcraft, and obviously believes there's some truth in it even though William's claims were ridiculous. Why would she want to kill Alice's babies? Questions with no clear answers raced through her mind. Why am I so unsettled? Haven't I seen Oakwood Grange in visions for as long as I can remember? Didn't I always know there was a reason I was meant to be here? Could that reason be because here there are others like me, and not just because of Alice?

Unwilling to put it off any longer she knew the time had come to tell Alice everything and trust she'd understand. But first she had to see Jennet.

She found her in the kitchen garden.

'Ah, Miss Elisabeth, you're back. Miss Alice has been looking for you, she's in the office.' She went back to picking peas. When Elisabeth didn't move she looked up again. 'Are you all right?'

How to simply ask if Alice knows about her uncle? Instead Elisabeth said, 'I've just been to visit Chicken Nan.'

'Oh, aye, is she managing?' She didn't ask why.

'Just about, I think, and she was very grateful for the cheese I took.' Another pause. 'She was giving me something of a history lesson about the Crayfords.'

This time, Jennet stopped picking and wiped her hands slowly on her apron. '*I bet she was. I expect you've met Melina in the woods then, have you?'*

'*Lucille, not Melina. Jennet, does Alice know she has relatives in Thatchling?'*

Jennet led her well away from the house. '*No, I'm sure she doesn't. Please don't tell her. It's not that there's any harm in her knowing, other than her father's not here to explain why he cut Nicholas off so completely, and she might think badly of him.'*

'*And would she be justified in thinking that?'*

'*No. I'm sure Nan told you what he was like. Nicholas never accepted being the second son; he wanted it all and lost no opportunity to cause trouble for his brother. I'm sure he thought bringing Rozann back was the ultimate embarrassment, and he never even made an honest woman of her. She spoke very little English at first and had to put up with being permanently pregnant until he had the good sense to die.'*

Elisabeth was surprised; she'd half expected a more sympathetic description than Chicken Nan's.

'*I heard there was a fight.'*

She nodded. '*After that, we all understood never to mention Nicholas' name or repeat any gossip about him. It was all round the village, of course, but Miss Alice wouldn't have known, she was only a bairn when Nicholas died.'*

'*And then did Rozann or her daughters ever ask for help of any kind?'*

'*Never. Rozann wouldn't have dreamed of approaching Thomas Crayford. She was a simple, country girl who brought up her girls in the same way, living off the land and doing odd jobs. Did Nan tell you about the girls?'*

'*Yes. Very sad.'*

Jennet came closer and lowered her voice. 'Miss Elisabeth, I've never said this before but I need to say it now. When you looked after Miss Alice the last time you were here, it was clear to me then that you know the old ways, like Melina – things that very few people know about now. And what the master did to you was...' She stopped mid-sentence on hearing footsteps.

The kitchen maid had come to collect the peas. 'Excuse me, Madam.' With a little bob to Elisabeth she reached across to pick up the basket. 'Thank you, Mrs. Sandford, that's such a help.' Jennet waited till she'd gone back indoors.

'...it was terrible. That's all. If he wasn't mad then, he certainly went mad afterwards.'

Elisabeth leaned in and planted a kiss on her cheek.

* * *

'How's Chicken Nan?' Alice linked arms with Elisabeth as they walked up Windmill Hill.

'Weary, I think, but still sharp as a tack. She thanks you for the cheese, by the way.'

'You could mix up some of your wonderful tonic for her, couldn't you? I'm sure she'd welcome it.'

This was something Elisabeth hadn't done since her last visit. It had somehow seemed insensitive so close to William's demise, but the little squeeze on her arm told her otherwise. There would be no better time than this.

'I could, but I doubt she needs my tonic. I met this young girl in the woods the other day, Lucille, do you know of her?'

Alice shook her head.

'We chatted for a while and as well as appearing to be an excellent herbalist, it seems she's related to Chicken Nan.'

'Really? I didn't know she had anyone in the village.'

'Well, I don't think she has. This girl comes from Thatchling

but she likes to forage in your wood up by the top field there. And I'm not surprised, I don't think I've ever seen such diverse plants anywhere as up there.'

Alice grinned. 'There should be no stopping you now then. I think Jennet and Cook will be first in the queue with a list of their ailments.'

Elisabeth swallowed hard, took a deep breath and turned to face her friend. Taking both her hands, she said, 'Alice, there's something very important I need to tell you.'

They sat on Windmill Hill for two hours until Alice knew almost everything there was to know.

* * *

'Does Aphra know all this too?' It was the first time she'd uttered a word for a while and Elisabeth was struck by how calmly she'd taken it all in. Perhaps she'd always had suspicions.

'No, although over the years she's been witness to a few occasions which have definitely made her wonder, I know that. But she's never questioned me and my guess is she's content not to know.'

'What about the aura?'

Elisabeth shook her head. 'Other than my old nursemaid and my late husband I've not seen it on anyone but you. It glowed all around you in beautiful shimmering colours as you stood at the front door on the very first day I saw you 4 years ago. I was so overwhelmed, first because you and this house had just stepped out of my visions, and then by the aura, that I probably came across as rather odd.'

Alice laughed. 'I didn't notice, but then I was rather awkward myself that day. You and Aphra looked so beautiful and fashionable, I felt very small indeed. What do you think it means, the aura?'

'I think it means that I can trust you to accept me for what I am, whatever that may be, and not be scared.'

A little frown creased Alice's brow as she hugged Elisabeth tightly, whispering in her ear. 'It goes without saying; of course you can.' But the physical force between them was so strong, the words were fairly redundant.

Elisabeth pulled away gently. 'And I think it means something else too. For my nursemaid I was the child she never had, and she had sole charge of me for five years. For Bernard, I was wife, daughter and nurse all rolled into one, making his last years the happiest he'd been for a long time.' Elisabeth paused. 'What I'm trying to say is that there's a reason I'm meant to be here, and it must be about you. I'm just not clear what it is yet.'

'You don't think it enough that you are the best, most steadfast friend I'm ever likely to have? That you nursed me and saved me from dying in childbirth?'

'And completely destroyed your marriage?'

'That's not true. Long before your last visit, I was only too aware of the sort of man I'd married.' She gave a little laugh. 'Aphra, of course, had disliked him from the very start and so too the servants and farmworkers. The trustees had already banned him from having anything to do with the estate because of incompetence and financial irregularities, stealing in other words, and we were barely speaking to one other. You must have noticed.'

'Of course, but I knew he hated me being here…'

'I was well beyond caring what he thought. I couldn't go through another pregnancy without you, and look what my selfishness did to you.'

'Please don't think that, but there is something about that night I have to ask you. The carvings on the bresummer over the fireplace in the study – did William do that?'

She waved the question away. 'He didn't know what he was doing towards the end.'

'Well, apparently he did because they're all symbols to protect him from witches, aren't they? What else did he do? Shoes and urine bottles up the chimney to stop me from flying in and killing him?'

'Elisabeth, stop it.'

'But that's what he believed, didn't he? That I was coming for him?'

She sighed. 'He was ill with an affliction of the chest which he couldn't shake off. Half the village had the same thing that winter but William believed in blood-letting and the doctor made sure he had little left by the time he'd finished with him. That's what killed him.'

'And what did you think at the time, when you heard I'd cursed him?'

Elisabeth knew this was a discussion Alice didn't want to have, but she couldn't rest until it was out in the open.

'What I thought was that he'd got off lightly with a scare, given what he'd done to you that night. I remember Aphra and Thomas Culpepper were all for doing something much worse to him. I believe you said it, Elisabeth, but I thought it was just words.'

She couldn't help the tears. They were running unchecked and the words she wanted to speak got stuck in her throat. They sat with their arms around each other in silence for the longest time.

But Elisabeth wasn't sure she was right.

~ 8 ~

Autumn 1717

Anne was finding the day of Frances Armitage's birthday party more than a little stressful. Although unconvinced myself by Tobias's masterly attempt to show how unaffected he was, at least I'd been able to inform Anne that he already knew about the engagement.

I couldn't help noticing though that his breathing was more laboured recently. Admittedly that wasn't unusual at this time of year, but even Gabe was concerned enough to warn him off spending so much time in the tavern if he wanted to be fit to take over managing the farm. 'I'm 63, ye know. I won't be here forever.' And when Samuel had made a similar remark over lunch, Tobias had taken himself off, slamming the door behind him. I've no doubt it was an intervention sparked by Anne, and one he won't be repeating. There seemed little point now in my adding to the discussion.

Young Alice, seemingly oblivious to the tension as only a 15-year-old can be, spent most of the day in her room, preparing herself for the evening. The dress was a triumph, so much so that even Samuel was overheard to say 'I expect that's set me back a pretty penny, Anne' until informed to the contrary. What she didn't tell him was that any saved expenditure had been spent on matching accessories. As the maids had spent all morning preparing and laying out Alice's things and were now attending to the rest of the household, I volunteered to do her hair. It kept us both out of the way.

Adding to the general melée, Tobias's younger brother, Charles, was down from Oxford for the sole purpose of attending the party. He is a younger version of Samuel, studious, already destined to follow his father into the law and, I suspect, secretly embarrassed about living on a farm; even one as large as Oakwood Grange that pays for his education. Tobias and Charles do not always get along.

I was rather glad I had the excuse of ill health to decline the party invitation. Apart from everything else, it would certainly not fill me with joy to sit with all the other old folk, moaning about their ailments.

* * *

The relief I felt on hearing the carriage returning in the early hours was short-lived. Downstairs in the kitchen the commotion and Anne's high-pitched voice already had me reaching for my shawl by the time Young Alice burst into my room. 'Tante, where's the linctus? Quick, tell me, it's Tobias...'

Swiftly trying to marshal my thoughts, 'Er...it's...in the scullery. Second shelf, on the left, I think. It's labelled, but I'm coming now... and get the crampbark.' She disappeared as quickly as she'd come and, although wide awake now, my legs were shaky as I groped my way in the dark to the top of the back stairs. Before I knew it, she was back with a candle and we managed the stairs together, arm in arm. The sound of wheezing grew louder and louder as we descended.

Tobias was sitting hunched over the kitchen table, the noise from his chest punctuated by coughing, his face pale and sweaty and a look of panic in his eyes. Samuel was pacing up and down uselessly at the other end of the room whilst Charles dodged round him, busy lighting as many candles as he could find.

Anne's tears were streaming as she struggled to get him to sit up. 'Aunt Elisabeth, we're out of crampbark and he won't listen to me...'

Alice was handing me the linctus and a spoon as I sat down next to him.

'Look at me, Tobias.' His eyes slid sideways, the whites clearly visible. 'Your Mother's right, sit up straight with your back flat against the chair.' I nodded to Anne, who stood behind him and gently encouraged his shoulders back. 'Here, take this...' I spooned a large dose of linctus into his mouth quickly and moved my chair to sit directly in front of him. I took both his hands in mine. 'Now, look at me – keep looking – you'll be fine if you do as I say. Slow your breathing right down. You know how to do this. Breathe into your belly and expand your chest. That's it, again and ag...'

A coughing fit had him curled over once more.

'Pass me a rag, Anne.' I mopped his brow and gave what I hoped was an encouraging smile. 'Again, come on Tobias, long, slow breaths.'

'I c-can't get any air...'

'Don't try to talk.' My old fingers were fumbling over the buttons on his waistcoat. 'Dash it all... Anne, can you do this ...'

A split second later it had been ripped open, buttons flying everywhere, and she'd loosened his breeches so I could lay a hand flat on his stomach. I couldn't see Samuel but I could imagine the surprise on his face.

'Good. Just give me one big breath in, Tobias, then let it go – and another. And another, and again, even more slowly...'

Anne's attacks had stopped by the time she was Young Alice's age and Tobias had never had one as bad as this before. I caught sight of Samuel who now had an arm round his daughter, his normally florid face ashen, and even Charles was looking distinctly worried. It crossed my mind that assuming responsibility for the farm was something that had never entered his head. It was uncharitable of me, I know.

At last, I felt it beneath my hand on his belly; that indefinable something which I've learned to recognise. Relaxing a little, I steadied my own breathing, knowing that the real danger was now behind us. Standing, I nodded to Anne to swap places so I could move behind her son and lay both hands flat on his chest under his shirt. I closed my eyes and concentrated. 'Keep that breathing steady now, just like that. Think of standing on the shore and breathing in the sea air.' I turned to his sister. 'Put the kettle on to boil, Alice, and go and get Mary. I need her to make some herbal tea, quickly now.'

Tobias squeezed Anne's hand, bravely trying to reassure her he was coping, and even managed a weak smile when a dishevelled Mary stumbled down the stairs, nightcap askew, bleary-eyed and astonished to see everyone in the kitchen.

'A tea, Mary, please. Ginger, Lungwort, Aaron's rod – anything like that – quick as you can.' She scurried away to the scullery and I heard her drag out the stool so she could reach the topmost shelves.

I closed my eyes again and concentrated on the heat under my hands. His breathing was still a little ragged but as the minutes ticked by I felt the change; the muscles started to relax, the breathing steadied and I saw the tension lift from Anne's face.

She turned to her family. 'He'll be fine now, no need to worry. Alice, up to bed now please.'

'But...'

'No arguments, Alice, Tobias needs to rest. You, too Charles.' Anne never shouted but the uncharacteristic edge to her voice suggested it would be wise to obey.

Samuel crossed the floor and laid a hand on his son's shoulder. 'You gave us a bit of a fright, Tobias.' Anne smiled up at her husband but her eyes swivelled to the door and Samuel took the hint, planting a kiss on her head before leaving. 'I'll see you in the morning, son.'

I was beginning to wilt. The healing takes it out of me much more now than it used to, but I didn't want to leave until I was sure. 'Bring me a chair, Anne, would you?'

Mary brought the infusion from the scullery. 'I'd leave it to steep a bit longer if you can, Mistress, it's still a bit hot'

Anne gave her a grateful smile. 'We will, Mary, and thank you for your help. Take an extra hour or so in bed tomorrow, I'll clear it with Cook.'

Finally, the three of us were alone, sitting in a tight triangle, Tobias taking tentative sips of the tea.

'I thought I was going to die. I've never been so scared, Mother. I don't ever want to feel like that again.' It was still a bit of an effort to get the words out but he was clearly feeling much better as he wiped away the sweat and tears. It was time to leave. I rose, kissed them both and left them to it.

Too tired to climb the back stairs, I decided on the wide front staircase but could see Young Alice waiting on the landing even before I reached the top.

'Tante, has he said anything?'

'What do you mean?'

'About what happened, because something must have upset him just before we left. He was perfectly happy until then.'

'No, child, he hasn't. Now go back to bed before your mother catches you. Goodnight.'

I was so weary sleep should have come quickly but, of course, it didn't.

~ 9 ~
July 1671

Elisabeth knew to trust her instincts. She set out early to see how her fox family was getting on but she was in no doubt that this was the day she'd meet Melina.

The three cubs now treated her as part of the woodland scenery, sometimes grubbing for earthworms and insects near her feet, though the vixen always kept a little distance with a slight dip of her head. The clearing though was unusually empty.

Strolling round its perimeter, she checked the badgers' sett for evidence of any neighbourhood skirmishes, fearing any fox would be the loser, but there was nothing obvious. Back at the tree trunk seat, and still casting around for anything suspicious, she bent to investigate a clump of pale flowers freshly sprouted near a cluster of puffball fungi. Quite lovely, their delicate drooping heads, each with pale cream fingers and a pale pink turned-up lip, hung from a tall, thin stem completely devoid of leaves. She'd never seen the like before but knew what they were – ghost orchids. With no trace of green anywhere, they were aptly named and their rarity only made them more mysterious. Lowering her face to the flowers for a few seconds she closed her eyes but there was nothing there and she pulled back, relieved that she wouldn't be tempted to use them. Something so exquisitely beautiful was surely designed to be medicine for the soul and should be left alone. Elisabeth studied them a little longer until the scent of fox made her whip round expecting to see her family. Instead it was him. Startled, her hand flew involuntarily to her chest. Majestic, standing tall and strong with bright, intelligent eyes, he was much closer than on the first occasion and she found herself holding her breath again. He blinked twice then turned his head to look across to the far side of the clearing where a woman had her back against an old hornbeam. Turning back, the dog fox blinked once more and she found herself nodding.

As he loped silently away, Melina crossed the clearing.

'Madame Tournier.' It wasn't a question. They both knew why they were there, but her perfect French accent took Elisabeth by surprise although it shouldn't have done; her mother was French after all. Not much older than Elisabeth, Melina was a taller, more elegant version of her daughter, but thankfully without the wide-eyed uncomfortable stare.

'And you must be Melina, your daughter is very much like you.' She smiled and nodded. 'Please though, call me Elisabeth, at least while it's just the two of us here in the woods?'

'As you wish, Madame.' She laughed. 'I'll try harder…'

There was a distinctly uncomfortable silence as they settled down on the tree trunk, side by side. Feeling it too soon to ask all the questions running through her mind, Elisabeth cast around for something else. 'I'm a bit concerned for the little foxes. They're usually here playing but I've seen neither hide nor hair of them today.'

'They're with their mother over yonder.' Melina tilted her head across the clearing. 'Learning how to fend for themselves. You won't see them much now.'

A pause again, but this time Elisabeth didn't hesitate. 'Lucille told me they're special. That they know what we are?' I turned to face her. 'Is that right, Melina?'

She didn't answer directly, but looked into the distance and described how her mother, Rozann, had fallen, in more ways than one, for the dashing English officer, Nicholas Crayford. 'My mother didn't have the gift herself but nearly all the other women in her family did and the witch hunters were crawling all over France at the time. Scared for any daughter she might have, she was only too pleased to escape with my father to England. Little did she know the situation wasn't much better here at that time.'

'And in the end, she had three daughters. Nan told me about your sisters, I'm so sorry.'

'Yes, I'm the lucky one.'

This time the silence was companionable. Elisabeth waited for her to continue.

'My mother had a bird. Well, not her bird exactly, but a bird that used to visit our garden. She grew the herb fennel because it reminded her of her mother's garden in France, and this little bird, a warbler she called it, used to come and sit in amongst the ferns and sing away. It was always the same bird because it had one white feather in its yellow bib. It came back year after year and my mother used to say 'Bonjour Maman' and fill up the bird bath. So, in answer to your question, yes I do believe some animals are special.'

Elisabeth knew she was right. As she'd known to follow the fox, years ago a ginger tortoiseshell cat had led her to discover the story of her grandmother. It was a cat she knew well from the nick in her ear and missing claw – but one which couldn't possibly have been a week's journey from where she'd last seen her.

It was going to take courage to ask the next question but, in the end, she didn't need to.

'My sisters and I were all born with the caul. It's supposed to be a sign, isn't it? Was that the same with you?'

'I don't know and there's no one who could tell me now.'

'I'm sorry. Did your mother have the gift also?'

'Oh no, most definitely not. But I did find out that the women on my father's side were all gifted in the same way.'

'I've never heard that before.'

'What?'

'The gift coming through the male line. How powerful that must be. No wonder the vixen is so odd in your presence.'

So many questions now, Elisabeth's mind was in a whirl. Is that true? Do I have powerful gifts? Are Melina and Lucille merely talented herbalists and peasant midwives or can they do what I'm able to do? Are Lucille's visions a glimpse into the future or just dreams? There was no aura here to guide her, but some force had brought them together here and perhaps that was all she needed to know.

'Melina, Nan told me that Lucille knew I was coming here. That she has visions. Can you tell me about them?'

'I should let her tell you or she'll be cross with me. I can tell you though that she's had the visions for as long as I can remember – probably since she's been able to talk. I never gave them much mind for many young girls dream of magical princesses and the like, and Lucille is a simple soul as you might have gathered. But I was wrong. She knew the day you stepped from the carriage at the Grange.'

Any remaining doubts were receding fast. If her calculations were correct, then it was possible Lucille's visions started when Elisabeth left the Convent of Montmartre to start her new life.

'Melina, do you know whereabouts in France your mother came from?'

'No. She did say the name of the village but I can't remember it now.'

'Do you know which area she came from?'

'The north-west somewhere. My father had been sent over to help the Protestants, she said.'

Elisabeth knew where that was. French friends in London had told her all about English soldiers being roundly defeated at La Rochelle. To get back to England, they'd have had to travel through Brittany. Her father came from Brittany, and so too her grandmother who was burned as a witch.

'What was your mother's family name?' She had to ask but wasn't surprised at the reply. She was clutching at straws and knew it, and yet she definitely felt a connection.

'I must go now, Melina.' It wasn't true but she needed time to think about what she'd heard before revealing anything else. 'I can't come tomorrow, but perhaps the day after?' They both knew there was more to talk about.

Melina rose too. 'Yes, I can do that. If I'm not here it'll only be because I've been called to help someone. I won't bring Lucille.'

Not quite knowing how to take leave of each other, Elisabeth said, 'À bientôt, then,' and Melina laughed her tinkly little laugh.

'À bientôt – Elisabeth.'

* * *

Elisabeth was still nervous at their next meeting, in contrast to Melina who appeared completely serene. Guiding them through a part of the wood Elisabeth didn't know, she pointed out secret places where the rarer herbs and shrubs could be found and was keen to compare notes about their various uses. The conversation was light and easy but it was very clear that she had opened up as much as she was prepared to on their last meeting. Elisabeth knew the next step would have to be hers.

She took it whilst bending down to examine a small fern. 'Do you have a name for people like us?'

Melina selected a few fronds for her basket and asked without looking up. 'What did they call you in France?'

There was a hint of pride when she answered. 'The Apothecary.'

Melina stopped what she was doing and stared. 'You had your own place, openly?'

'No, nothing like that. Let's sit somewhere and I'll explain.'

Quickly covering the 10 years she'd spent at the convent in Paris, working in the garden and trawling through hedgerows, she explained how her talent for producing herbal medicines had started to show real results. How one old nun had presented her with a copy of Culpeper's Herbal which had confirmed much of what she already knew, but how others had warned that this 'hobby' could get her into trouble.

'Looking back, I realise just how fortunate I've been. When I left the convent at 15 years old, knowing little of the dangers outside the convent, I was taken in by a woman who ran a 'gentlemen's club' – in truth it was a high-class brothel – and I paid my way by administering to the girls.'

This was not what Melina expected to hear from a woman like Elisabeth; her amused expression made that very clear.

'As you can imagine, there was much scope for providing precautions and treatments which put me far outside of Church law, but by then I had many doubts about my religion. It was the girls who called me the Apothecary.'

'So, were there witch hunters in Paris then?'

'Yes, although I was never troubled while at the club.'

'Well here we're just called 'cunning folk' and everyone knows it really means 'healer'. It's true some cunning folk say they can also tell the future and some reckon they can use magic to protect against evil witchcraft, but who knows for sure?' If she thought Elisabeth might be able to answer this, she was mistaken.

'Have you been troubled by witch hunters?'

'No, things are definitely better than when my mother first came

here. Back then, witch hunters didn't understand, or didn't want
to understand, what ordinary folk know – that cunning folk are
good and useful, and witches are either bad or harmful. The two are
completely different.'

'And are there any witches round here?'

'I don't know. The only witches I know are the sad old women
who force people to buy their wares or give them food for fear of
having some hex laid on them. Scaring children is usually a good
way to get parents to pay up. They're not so common now though,
villagers were so keen to point the finger that the witch hunters
swept up a lot of them.'

Elisabeth grimaced a little. 'It's a terrible death for someone who
behaves like that through poverty and desperation.'

Melina raised her eyebrows. 'You're softer than I am, Elisabeth.
There are lots of poor people who don't behave like that.'

She had a point of course, but it was hard for Elisabeth to forget
the description of her grandmother's death.

Clearly, they were at the point where they were skirting round
the one thing they were both desperate to know, but were unsure how
to ask. What powers did they each have? With no guidance and no
knowledge of what to expect, both of them had managed to survive
being different by not revealing too much. It was for that reason that
Elisabeth tried an indirect approach.

'Melina, would you mind telling me about your older sister?'

'No. No, I'd like to. For too long no one wanted to talk about her.'

Elisabeth listened in silence as the sad story of Lyssa's life
unfolded through Melina's smiles and tears. It could have been her
own story if luck had not been on her side.

'I can't remember exactly when the trouble started but we
couldn't have been more than 6 or 7 years old. There was barely a
year between us so the age difference counted for nothing but we

were very different in temperament. We had a little sister by then and she slept in my parents' room downstairs but Lyssa and I shared a bed in the attic. Each night she thrashed about, mumbling in her sleep, and each morning woke confused and cross that I couldn't share the sights that had frightened her so. We'd always been close and this caused her great upset. Always timid and shy, she became even more withdrawn, which irritated Father more than anything, and I tried my best to protect her. Once he shook her so hard, I saw her eyes roll back in her head. She was terrified of him.

I can't say I noticed that Mother was concerned about Lyssa. Looking back, I think she probably hoped it would all go away if she ignored it, because I know she never told my father about the cunning women in her family, frightened he'd leave her I expect. The truth was that they both had secrets and that made for a bad marriage – not that they ever made it official. Mother first met him when he'd just arrived in France, but after the fighting when he came back to claim her, she could see he wasn't the same. Something had happened to make him the angry, miserable man he became and if he couldn't take out his fury on Mother, then Lyssa was always next in the firing line. I used to think it was because he considered her weak but now I wonder if it was something else.

When our baby sister died and it was just the two of us once more, Lyssa and I spent as much time as possible in these woods; anywhere but in the house. By now it was clear I also had the gift although our powers were developing in different ways. Like you, Elisabeth, I was born knowing about plants and folk medicine but Lyssa knew animals – all animals, not just special ones like the foxes – and they knew her. She understood them, could feel their pain and was heartbroken on the few occasions her healing hands couldn't help them.'

Melina paused there, swallowed hard, and then rushed on before

Elisabeth had chance to say anything.

'We were about 11 or 12 when Father finally pushed Lyssa so far that she answered back for the first time. Even I was surprised. She stood her ground and there was a lifetime of bitterness in her words as she shouted back, willing him to punish her. And he did, dragging her upstairs by her hair and locking her in our room. 'Don't you dare go up there', he yelled at me. Furious, he paced up and down, Mother collapsed into a chair and I waited on the stairs for the sound of sobbing which never came. Instead, it seemed all hell had broken loose. Father pushed past me up the stairs, unlocked the door and stood on the threshold with clenched fists, hardly believing his eyes. Lyssa was sitting cross-legged on the floor, eyes bright and challenging, perfectly calm amid the wreckage of the room. The few bits of furniture we had were all upside down, no piece of pottery was left intact, and everything else including linens and shoes was all tossed hither and thither. The whole thing was impossible and he knew it. If he hadn't been scared of her before, he was then. He said nothing, just walked out past Mother, sitting with head in hands at the kitchen table.

He never provoked her again and took to staying away for days at a time. When he did come home, more often than not he was drunk.'

Elisabeth reached into her purse and passed a handkerchief to Melina who was struggling now. There were no words which could comfort and Elisabeth didn't offer any.

'Lyssa told me later, when we were trying to right the room, that it had come as a surprise to her too. She'd been ablaze with such anger she'd wanted to throw something, but before she knew it she was in the midst of a whirlwind. She was sorry about the room, but I didn't care.

She was quite lovely, you know, Lyssa, with fiery red hair and perfect skin. She made me feel like a carthorse she was so fine, like a real lady, with the most beautiful hands and long, thin fingers. Looking at them you could easily believe they could do magic.

She was never happy though. The demons in her nightmares never left her and she was tired of it. And then when the local lads started to notice her, word got around that she was odd and she just wasn't strong enough to take it. I blame Mother, I do. She was more worried about losing Father than she was about a daughter who thought she was going mad. Just before she killed herself I knew I was losing her. She used to say, 'There is evil out there Melina – you must be very careful. I'll be no help to you.''

Melina stopped there and Elisabeth held her hands, words failing her. Eventually she spoke again. 'It suddenly seemed the right thing to do, to tell you all that. Was it right?'

'Oh, yes, it was very right. I know all about the whirlwind, Melina. When I was very young, my angry tantrums wreaked havoc in the nursery where I was locked in for much of the day, unable to see Mama. Fortunately, they were witnessed only by my nursemaid and Mama but the danger was that my father would find out and have the perfect excuse to get rid of me. I wasn't his child, you see. So Mama and I fled to France.'

Elisabeth couldn't bring herself to explain how, even so young, she'd already been able to see and hear events far away from her body. She knew it was hard to believe. Had Lyssa perhaps experienced the same but couldn't find the words to tell Melina? Maybe the evil she'd seen wasn't confined to nightmares.

'Is that when you went to the convent?'

'Yes, we both did. Mama was not well and the Sisters cared for her. And I never experienced anger like that again until I left the convent and was in the final throes of a first love affair. Perhaps you can remember what that's like?' Elisabeth gave her a sideways look and saw her roll her eyes in agreement. 'The astonishment on *his face as he saw every book on his shelves swept to the floor in a heap – whilst I stood immobile in front of him – gave me immense satisfaction. It was dangerous, but I was lucky. He had plenty of secrets of his own that he didn't want seeing the light of day.*

Years later, I told all my secrets and fears to a wonderful man, my husband, who suggested that with time perhaps I would learn to control these gifts or powers, whatever we call them, rather like we train our physical body to write beautifully or play an instrument. And he was right, I can now do that.'

Smiling, she felt relief that she'd got all that out of the way. 'Lyssa might have done that too, had she lived.'

Melina shook her head. 'She didn't have your strength.'

'Or my luck.'

As if to save us from becoming too maudlin, our fox family appeared across the clearing, the two larger cubs play-fighting before disappearing into the den. The smaller cub didn't follow and neither did the vixen. Instead, she picked up the runt and approached us with head and belly low to the ground, dropping the mewling cub at our feet, before backing off a way. Melina reached forward, lifting the cub.

'Here, take it, she wants you to.'

'Why?'

'Because she needs your help. And because she knows you can, even if you don't realise it. And because she knows I can't.'

Elisabeth took it and it made no fuss, a warm little body throbbing with life but far too thin. She held it close to her chest, closed her eyes and rocked as if cradling a child, tears finding their way from under her eyelids with the burden of expectation and no certainty of the outcome. She felt an arm creep round her shoulders.

'I'm not like Lyssa, Melina.'

'We'll see, shall we?'

It had been said before, both at the convent and at the club, that

Elisabeth had healing hands, but it was said in jest and she never thought it possible. She always believed it was the herbal recipes and massages which had done the trick. Nothing though could convince Melina otherwise, especially after the cub not only survived, but thrived.

It was time for Elisabeth to start believing.

* * *

The tragedy of Lyssa reminded Elisabeth of something she should have done before now. As she was now settled in England, it was time to send for her will from her French lawyer. More importantly, the note attached to the will.

The note had been added shortly after discovering her family history and the knowledge that the gift can skip generations. She wanted any descendant of hers to know their history.

Not just to protect them from others – but also from themselves.

~ 10 ~
Autumn 1717

As Tobias is now keen to take whatever medicines we produce, Mary and I were once again in the scullery, mashing garlic and honey to soothe his poor throat and preparing as much liquorice and linseed as we could lay our hands on. We're determined to get as much down him as we can before he slides back to his old ways, although Anne is convinced it may be some time before that happens. He's had quite a shock and has been resting for the last two days.

Young Alice is still talking about the party and we're all a little tired of hearing how she had to disappoint so many young gentlemen who were keen to mark her dance card. Apparently, she and Sophia were 'quite the equal of Frances'.

When I took him his linctus, Tobias scoffed at the suggestion saying he'd never seen Frances looking more radiant, and that he was definitely staying in his room until Alice had stopped boring everyone to death. It was the first flicker of a return to his old self but Anne felt it was still too soon to ask if he knew what triggered the attack.

'Right, Mary,' taking off my apron, 'I think I'll leave you to do the rest. Céleste and Sophia are visiting sometime this morning so I'd better get cleaned up.'

'You'd better be quick then, Madame. There's a carriage coming up the lane, it's probably them now.'

* * *

'Grandmama!' Sophia ran half-way up the front stairs to greet me.

'Darling, don't you look lovely.' I held her at arm's length to get a better look. 'I'm not surprised you and Young Alice were in such demand at Frances's.' I glanced over her head at my daughter whose weary expression and eye-rolling made me laugh. 'Alice is in her room, why don't you go on up and we'll talk later.'

'Oh, nicely done, Maman,' Céleste whispered. 'Are you as heartily sick as we are hearing about it?'

I nodded. 'Anne sends her apologies by the way, she's had to go out but says she'll see you next week. And Samuel's working in his study so we'd better not disturb him. And as all the children are in the house, shall we go into the garden? I could do with some fresh air now I'm up and about again.'

Céleste linked my arm. 'And how are you really? Assuming you're going to tell me the truth.'

I led her to the seat at the furthest edge of the kitchen garden. 'The truth is, my love, I have a little murmur in my heart. It's not unusual at my age and I'm treating it, which is why I'm feeling so much better. And I have enough to put up with Anne fussing over me, so don't you start.'

She gave me a long, slow look with raised eyebrows. 'That's it, nothing else?'

'Well, let me think now. There's the creaky left knee which gives me jip once in a while and a very annoying little toe that keeps...'

'You can be very trying, Maman. Be serious for once.'

'I am, darling. I'm not going anywhere just yet. Stop worrying about me.'

'You know you can always come and live with us.'

'I wouldn't dream of it, not until Anne throws me out. And I like Jonathon far too much to put our relationship in peril.'

She laughed. 'Well, what about poor Samuel?'

'That's different, he isn't my son-in-law and he has no say in this house anyway, you know that. And Anne needs me in a way that you don't.'

Céleste nodded. She is well aware of my attachment to this house and the promise I made to her Aunt Alice.

'Changing the subject, do you remember going to see Aphra just before she died? You were about 12 or 13 at the time.'

'Yes, she took one look at me and said something like – You're very much like your mother, but it remains to be seen if you'll be as elegant and beautiful as she is – She was never one to be over complimentary, I remember.'

'That's true. Incidentally, Tobias has recently taken an interest in your Aunt Alice and Aphra. I've lent him the Anthology.'

'From what I've heard, Maman, he doesn't need the education.'

'True, but he was fairly shocked all the same. Perhaps surprised rather than shocked.'

'That's more like it. It's a great shame you didn't get to see him at the party. Not only handsome but very self-assured; charming all and sundry, and even dancing with a few of the mothers. I think Sophia may be more than a little bit in love with him and she won't be the only one.'

'And how were the newly engaged couple?'

A little shrug. 'Frances has got what she wanted and I hope it'll make her happy. Is that what you mean?'

'I thought I was the cynical one, Céleste. What's he like, Hadleigh?'

'It's difficult to tell. He didn't seem particularly at ease and he's not a great dancer. That's all I managed to glean.'

'Did Tobias dance with Frances?'

'Yes, of course. They had a couple of dances, I think. Why?'

'He fell into a bad state in the carriage as they drove home, the worst attack we've seen and no one seems to know what brought it on. Was he upset about Frances, was it the drink, or something else?'

'Can't you just ask him?'

'No, not yet, Anne says not to. It was a bad one, Céleste, I thought we were going to lose him.'

She shook her head slowly from side to side. 'Well, he didn't seem at all troubled in any way to me. I saw him congratulating both Frances and Hadleigh just like everyone else. We left the party a little earlier than your lot but he was perfectly fine as we all said goodnight. Quite jolly in fact.'

'Well, never mind. He'll tell me sooner or later, I expect.'

At that point, Young Alice leaned out of my bedroom window. 'Sorry, Tante, I thought you were in here. Would you mind if I show Sophia your red travelling costume? I've told her all about it.'

'No, go ahead. She can take it for her dressing-up box if she likes.'

Céleste laid a hand on my arm. 'Maman, you can't give that away.'

'Why not? You're not going to wear it and I'm certainly not going to. There's no point in holding on to these things now, that's why I let the blue gown go. Young Alice already commented that Sophia is the only who can carry off that colour and no doubt she'll have some fun with it.'

* * *

'How's the throat?'

Tobias uncrossed his legs, swung them over the side of the bed, and took the linctus. 'Better, thanks.' He reached for his jacket. 'I'll come down with you now if Sophia's gone. I was going to come down earlier but all that chattering, shrieking and running up and down corridors drives me mad. Why are they so loud?'

I couldn't resist a smirk, remembering just how loud he and his brother were not so long ago. 'I think you're quite safe now.' It was stuffy in his room and I went to throw open the windows. 'They went a couple of minutes ago and your sister is in her room.'

'Excellent, and Charles?'

'He's with your father in the study, I think.'

'Even better. Can you manage a little walk?'

'I can if you can.'

We followed the same path as before, just as slowly, and ended up on the same bench far from the house.

'How does your chest feel now?'

'A little tight but not too bad, considering.'

I had to agree. I'd been listening carefully to his breathing and could detect nothing to worry about. Talking had been out of the question until we sat down and now there was an awkward silence. I don't like awkward silences.

'Do you want to talk about it?'

'Yes and no.' He gave me a sideways grin. 'It's finding the right words that'll make it difficult. I can't possibly tell my parents the truth so I've dreamt up a plausible explanation.' He turned to face me, his expression one of innocence. 'It must have been that my late-night stroll in the garden for a smoke was responsible – quite possibly the result of inhaling the pollen of some strange plant. What do you think, will that do?'

'Definitely plausible, but you need to work on the delivery. Perhaps it was the last straw after an evening of vigorous dancing, heavy drinking and so on. I think your mother would believe that.'

Silence again, longer this time.

'I did go out for a smoke after Sophia and the others had gone, just to be on my own for a while. I can't pretend the evening hadn't been hard work for me, Aunt, because it had.'

'Well, Céleste was fooled.'

'Good. Pride intact, then.' He looked down at his hands, nervously folding one over the other. 'I strolled across the lawn to the far side, just so that I could look back at the house; it really looked magnificent all lit up like that. I don't expect I'll visit there again very often. Anyway, my pipe went out and I was just about to go back when I heard some activity in the bushes. I should have left them to it, I know, but I was curious and it amused me to see who was with who, so I crept round the back to get a sneaky look. Only I stumbled a little and he spotted me – Hadleigh.'

'Ah, I see. And he wasn't with Frances.'

'He wasn't with a woman at all, Aunt.'

He rubbed his face with both hands and let out a huge sigh. It had obviously rattled him. 'What am I going to do? I've thought of nothing else for the last few days. How can I let her marry him?'

'You mustn't get involved, Tobias. It has nothing to do with you anymore and, anyway, any intervention on your part will be misconstrued, you know that. No one will thank you.'

'Frances will.'

'You don't know that. Have you thought that it might suit her purposes very well? That she may already know or suspect, and not care? She was very quick to recruit you as her lover, I remember.'

'You don't have a very good opinion of her, do you?'

'I don't dislike her, Tobias, but if you think she's naïve and impressionable, I think you're mistaken. My advice is to stay out of it, especially now Hadleigh knows you've seen him *in flagrante* with...who, his best friend?'

He turned sharply to look at me.

'A lucky guess.' I was thinking of my dear Uncle George and his lover, Hugh. 'Don't forget I lived in both Paris and London as a young woman, when all manner of activity between sexes was rife across all classes, despite buggery being against the law.'

'They weren't exactly...'

'I understand perfectly Tobias, no need to elaborate. And another thing, in case you don't already know, some men, and some women too, enjoy relations with both sexes.' It had come as a shock to a susceptible 15-year-old but I was wiser now. 'What happens in their marriage, if it goes ahead, is now their affair.'

Anne would be horrified to know I was discussing such things with her son but I had no option. He had to know that playing the white knight, whilst thoroughly commendable, may not be the wisest choice. It's up to him whether or not he takes my advice.

It was after supper that Anne explained to me what Tobias thought was the cause of his attack. I agreed that he was almost certainly right.

~ 11 ~

August 1671, Sussex and London

E lisabeth's visit to Oakwood Grange was coming to an end. Always a wrench to leave, it was especially so now that she'd met Melina, but she had business affairs to attend to in London that couldn't wait and Alice was busy again and firmly back in charge on the farm.

In one respect though it was a relief, for it still troubled her that she had not been entirely open with Alice, having made no mention of her meetings with Melina. A promise, though, was a promise, and Elisabeth had too much respect for Jennet's judgment to tell Alice about her relatives. Aside from that, Melina's family secrets were not Elisabeth's to tell.

By this time, she and Melina were very comfortable together; the circling around each other was over and their last meeting had been an opportunity for Elisabeth to lay a ghost.

'Have you ever cursed someone?' Sitting side by side on their log in the clearing, Elisabeth was drawing patterns in the dirt with a stick.

'Like calling them lobcock or scobberlotcher, d'you mean?'

'No, I'd quite like to know what those are though...'

Melina laughed. 'Well, if you come to our village, there's plenty of both hanging around there.'

'You know what I'm asking.' It wasn't enough just to have the comfort of Alice's conviction that she'd spoken out of anger and retaliation. She desperately needed to know that she hadn't killed her husband.

'Yes, I do, and the answer is no. Have you?'

'Yes – no. I don't know. I cursed William Harryman on the night he…do you know what he did to me?'

'Yes, of course.'

Elisabeth threw her stick away. 'Does everyone round here know?'

'A fair few. Impossible to keep something like that quiet in a place like this. But according to Chicken Nan, all the sympathy was with you and Miss Alice, there was never a question that Harryman had any reason to do what he did. He was so unpopular that everyone believed he'd gone mad and there was already gossip that the marriage was in trouble.'

'It was because Miss Alice had already had two miscarriages and then that still birth. He thought me responsible for all three tragedies.

'He was mad, then.'

That was always a possibility of course, but Elisabeth had always felt there was another, more plausible reason. If he'd succeeded that night, he would have eliminated the one person who knew he'd been enjoying himself with a young dairymaid and he couldn't risk her hanging around. Perhaps the fear she would tell Alice really did drive him mad.

'I can remember exactly what I said to him once I'd been rescued. Moments earlier his boot had been on my throat and he'd landed such a blow across my face that blood was streaming from my mouth and my voice was hoarse from screaming, but I was determined to look him straight in the eye to show him he hadn't broken me. I said, "If I were who you say I am, I would curse you now. I would swear that neither you, nor any of your blood, will ever live long enough to find peace in that house". I wanted to rattle him and it succeeded because he spent the next few years frightened I was coming for him. You should see the witches' marks he carved over the fireplace in his study. I think it really did send him mad and I'm truly sorry for Alice who had to cope with all that.'

'Why did you phrase it like that?'

'Because, in my heart, I knew he'd only married Alice to get his hands on that property. And because he was desperate for a child. They were the only two things he cared about.'

'Well, forget it, I can't believe you can curse someone as easily as all that, even if it's possible. Even with powers as strong as yours.'

Elisabeth still wasn't satisfied. After all, William didn't live long enough to find peace in that house, and neither did he have children. Not with Alice anyway.

There was one more thing she needed to know.

'I remember you saying that both you and Lyssa had been born with a caul and that it signified something. What exactly…?'

'You know what it is?'

'Yes, I've been delivering babies since I was fifteen and I've heard talk, but I've never seen one.'

'No, me neither, not in all these years. My mother said I was born with part of the sac sticking to my face like a veil but Lyssa's sac hadn't broken at all and it completely surrounded her like a ghostly parcel until it was pierced. It's so rare that midwives are known to smuggle the caul away then auction it off to the highest bidder.'

'Why?'

'Because sailors believe that carrying a caul with them at sea will protect them from drowning. Who knows whether that's true or not but they'll pay a pretty penny for one anyway.'

'But being born with the caul is a sign of something to do with the baby?

'Of course, yes, it's considered a good omen. People born with the caul are said to be able to see into the future and some have the gift of healing by laying on of hands.'

She paused slightly. 'And some say it's the sign of a good witch – someone who's born to fight evil.'

* * *

Elisabeth returned to her old rooms in Mrs. Potter's house just off the Strand, from where she'd witnessed the first signs of the Great Fire of '66 which had wreaked such devastation. With 13,000 homes destroyed and heaven knows how many dead, London would never be the same again, but now that the rebuilding was well under way most people thought that was probably a good thing. No longer were wood and thatched houses allowed to be built where the overhanging jetties were so close that folk upstairs could shake hands across narrow streets – and flames could leap across in a heartbeat.

A grand plan to remodel the whole city had to be abandoned as too much land was in private hands, but at least one new road was being built to connect with Guildhall, one of the few original buildings still standing. Poor St. Paul's was no more, the wooden scaffolding for repair works having accelerated its destruction, but there were plans to rebuild it with work to be started soon.

It had always been Elisabeth's intention to invest the money left to her by Bernard in property, and she'd been briefly tempted by a smart new prime property within the city walls, on the advice of Uncle George and Aphra and most others she'd cared to ask, but her heart wasn't in it. Living in idle luxury in such a place was never going to suit her, and although Aphra knew that only too well, she still thought she was mad not to do it. Alice was the only one to really understand that Elisabeth needed to make her money, Bernard's money, do something useful and it had been her support that had made Elisabeth's decision easier.

Before checking on her new investment, however, she was keen to make Aphra her first call. Recently moved into new premises in the City, the place was decked out in her very individual style with some of the exotic belongings they'd managed to hold on to during Aphra's troubles. It was good to see her back on her feet.

'It must be wonderful to be able to move around your rooms again now that all my paraphernalia has gone.' They kissed, wrapping each other in a tight embrace. Elisabeth noticed her friend was a little rounder than before and felt this was a good sign.

'I can, but it doesn't feel the same, and anyway I'll be moving on myself soon. Mrs. Potter, incidentally, sends her regards and says she misses you but not the legion of admirers calling at all hours.'

Wide-eyed, Aphra shrugged. 'Tsh, she exaggerates, I swear there was only ever one or two. Speaking of which…if nothing's changed in the last few months, both you and Alice may as well be nuns. You should know I have friends who'd fight each other for the chance of a night with you. And even Alice, with her sweet wholesomeness, could have her pick too.'

Elisabeth sighed, knowing it wouldn't be long before she started on this. Aphra had no intention of marrying again but always maintained that a woman without a man's attention was like a day without sunshine – although not essential it certainly brightened one's mood. Before she was much older she had cause to change her mind about that.

'We're both far too busy to think of anything else at the moment. Alice has the farm and I'm about to…'

'And I'm not, I suppose. Two plays staged, both published this last year along with my poetry, and…' she indicated her writing desk, 'an Anthology about to be staged.'

'Fine, you win. I know what you're saying but it's been so long, Aphra. I'm not sure I w…'

'Isn't that my point? Heavens, Elisabeth, what would Bernard say? You're a beautiful woman and he wanted you to have a full life, not half a life.' Having touched that nerve her tone softened. 'Anyway, I have something to liven you both up. This Anthology is being staged in a few months and I want you to persuade Alice to come to opening night so you can have a little bit of bawdy fun and frolics before you're thirty. I love you both, you know that.'

The last was such an out-of-character thing for her to say out loud, that she delivered it with an embarrassed little toss of her head whilst rearranging a few curls.

Elisabeth felt a great rush of affection. 'Well, I certainly won't need asking twice, and I'm sure Alice would love a trip to London. It'll give her an opportunity to show off her new costumes and she's long wanted to see a play of yours.'

'New costumes, eh? Don't tell me they're all black.'

'Just you wait and see…'

Returning to Aphra and London had made it easy for Elisabeth to concentrate on the normal side of her life again, rather than the other, but she was in no doubt the time would come when they'd collide once more. As yet, she didn't know how or when.

* * *

Travelling east out of the City through Bishops Gate, Elisabeth halted the carriage at New Churchyard to lay flowers and pay respects at the burial place of Nicholas Culpeper, a man who wasn't as celebrated as he should be. It was on just such a journey two years before that fate had intervened, as it so often does, and she'd seen the future opening up before her.

Quite close by was a tavern, formerly Red Lion House, the place where Culpeper lived and worked until his death, creating an extensive medicinal herb garden and providing mainly free treatments and advice in his pharmacy and clinic. He had, by then, *published his Complete Herbal in English, not Latin, as a guide to natural medicines for ordinary people who couldn't afford the high fees charged by doctors. This did not make him popular with the College of Physicians and he was forced to escape their jurisdiction by moving to this area of Spital Fields outside the city walls.*

As a naïve young girl in France Elisabeth had been excited to find his philosophy so in tune with her own, only to discover later that it was conveniently regarded as heretical by those who approve of blood-letting, the use of toxic remedies and protecting their own interests. It had served as an early warning to her.

Happily, Culpeper's book was still popular with working class families, but inevitably very little had changed with the professions.

Her next stop was a converted warehouse, still in Spital Fields. Always eager to visit here, this time she had the carriage door open even before the horses pulled up, not waiting to be handed down. The sound of women's voices raised in song was drifting through the warehouse windows and Elisabeth let herself in, acknowledging greetings as she threaded her way between the singers spinning silk. Forced to skirt round a group of children playing in the corner, she eventually made the stairs and was still singing the French folk song she knew as a child as she climbed up to the weavers' gallery.

'Bonjour Philippe, how's everything going?'

Small and thin with a large hook nose and a mass of brown curls forever escaping from his hat, the weaver still looked every bit as French as the day he'd first landed on English soil. Smiling broadly, he stopped the loom, pushed his soft felt hat a little further back on his head and gestured for her to inspect his work.

'Venez voir vous-même, Madame Tournier. My latest design. C'est bon, no?'

'C'est bon, yes.'

Like everything else he designed it was beautiful, but before she could inspect it properly he'd taken her by the elbow, keen to show her something at the opposite end of the gallery. Elisabeth thought him extraordinary; here was a man who showed extreme patience and attention to detail when it came to designing, but was so quick and excitable in every other regard. And despite now being fluent in English, he persisted in dipping out of both languages when he spoke to her, as if he couldn't quite decide where she fitted. Elisabeth found she quite liked it, and it amused them both.

'Les tissus pour Madame 'arryman, I 'ave them. Regardez.' Reaching to lift two bolts of cloth from the rack, he placed one on the cutting table and expertly rolled off a yard or two for inspection. 'Si vous aimez cela, I will send it off to her couturiers today.'

'She will love this, Philippe.' It was impossible not to feel the silk and Bernard's voice popped into her head saying –Go on, treat yourself, look how it catches the light – but she had more than enough lovely costumes to last her for years. 'Miss Alice wanted a true midnight blue and the weight is perfect for what we have in mind. That can definitely go.'

As could the second bolt, a very feminine summer silk in a pretty peach damask design; not something Alice would have been allowed to wear when she was married.

'So, Philippe, the green. Is there anything to see yet?'

A single arched eyebrow, a tap on the side of his nose, and he disappeared behind the rack of fabrics.

'Voila!' He placed it gently on the cutting table; waiting impatiently for the reaction he knew would come.

Elisabeth shook her head. In truth, it was the most exquisite fabric she'd seen since leaving France and words temporarily failed her.

Philippe held up one finger. 'Vraiment, I did not make this for Madame 'arryman. It is for quelqu'un de haut, you understand I cannot tell you who, mais…I have this left over, et…' He grinned and gave a Gallic shrug, 'What ees to be done with it?'

Footsteps on the stairs, accompanied by much puffing and panting, made Elisabeth turn and cross the floor. 'Mr. Stokes, what a lovely surprise, I didn't expect to see you today. Who's managing the farm?'

Jerome Stokes, still nominally the owner and fully paid-up member of the Guild of Weavers, had recently retired to a place in the country. It didn't suit him as well as it did the other members of his large family.

'Oh, you know, sons, sons-in-law...' He gave a little crooked smile, '... it's still not as exciting as seeing what this chap is doing every day. It's hard to keep away.'

Now at the cutting table, he placed a hand on Philippe's shoulder. 'Just look at that silk Madame Tournier; I've been in this trade all my life and I still can't fathom how he does it. God must surely have been looking down on me the day your carriage was passing by.'

All three had cause to remember that day; it had been the making of each one.

When fate had intervened two years ago, Elisabeth was on her way back to the City from Spital Fields when she noticed a commotion outside the warehouse. A small, excitable man gesticulating wildly and loudly in French, was pleading with a round, balding English weaver who had no idea what the other was saying and wasn't in the mind to listen. Pointing to a woman with three young children clinging to her skirt and standing off to one side, the man was also desperately trying to unwrap a parcel she'd handed to him. The weaver was having none of it and was making his way back inside when Elisabeth stopped her carriage.

Fully aware of the plight of Huguenots, Protestant refugees fleeing Catholic France, Elisabeth listened to the man, took one look at the samples of his work, and marched into the weaver's shop to plead his case.

To be fair to Stokes, once he'd seen the samples he didn't need much persuasion. He engaged Philippe and his wife on the spot, quickly stole a march on other weavers by expanding his workforce with more talented French refugees and within six months his business had more orders than he knew what to do with. Eventually, he brought silk spinning and dyeing also under his control and the cream of London society had access to fabrics to rival those from France and Italy for the first time – but cheaper and more immediate.

For Elisabeth, everything had fallen into place on her journey back to the City that day. Spital Fields was where her money was to be invested. The area and the industry excited her, and there was a real opportunity to do some good in a community that needed her help.

~ 12 ~
Early Spring 1718

I woke in the early hours with a feeling I recognised but haven't felt for some time; a hollowed-out sensation in the very core of my being, accompanied by overwhelming sorrow.

It could only be Jean-Michel.

Céleste tells me he's been ill for months and that Claudette's letters have been increasingly pessimistic. It has never bothered me that he found someone else to share his life; I even remember suggesting he should do exactly that once he announced he was returning to France for good. He knew I wouldn't go with him and I suspect he was secretly relieved.

His letters to me dried up fairly early on, but he was always a loving father who wrote often to Céleste until it was necessary for Claudette to take over. I shall write to her expressing my condolences and my heartfelt thanks, but only once I get confirmation that my husband has died, for now that I'm old and a little forgetful, I need to be extra careful. A lifetime of pretending to be normal can't be undone now, not even to my daughter; she may discover the truth when I die.

Thank goodness Lucille is still around, otherwise it would feel very lonely indeed.

I have seen a lot of death in my time, the curse of being old, and I think the only gift we can give in the end is to be in physical contact with those we love as they pass peacefully on. I'm happy that Jean-Michel would have had that.

If only that had been the case when Aphra died. Although closer than we'd been for some time, she'd tried to keep much of her illness from me; out of pride, possibly? I'll never know, but it meant I arrived too late.

It's the death of François though that still haunts me, even close to 50 years on. I have loved other men, and both husbands, but never one so passionately as I loved François. Paralysed and determined to put an end to his suffering and spare his family, he died alone and this awful sensation hit me so hard and laid me so low, I cried for hours.

Alice's passing, like my first husband's, was as it should be. Lying next to her, she squeezed my hand every time I stopped reminiscing until she no longer had the strength to do even that. I carried on until her last breath, despite the tears.

Enough of death. This feeling will pass and I don't have that much time to waste being self-indulgent.

I need to concentrate on things closer to home, like Tobias. Although dearly loved by both his parents, Alice realised early on that he was the odd one out, not often understood. Because it was always Samuel with Charles, Anne and Young Alice, she made me promise to watch out for him after she was gone. It was unnecessary, of course, but I'm convinced Alice was giving me licence to do whatever it would take to keep both him and this house safe. And I shall.

Tobias, though, would be horrified to know that I've seen him in his room, little frown lines on his forehead like Anne's, and biting his nails, clearly fretting over something. I doubt it's to do with the farm. Taking over the accounts after his attack is something he continues to manage easily, much to Anne's relief, and he's now working full time with Gabe, learning every aspect of farming. The visions, though, arrive uninvited and always serve as some sort of warning.

I suspect it has to do with Frances.

* * *

Young Alice, busy demolishing some left-over pudding at the kitchen table, grinned when she saw me. 'Just for once, I'm getting in first before the men.' She waved her spoon in the direction of the larder. 'Cook took pity on me.'

'Well it's good to see you have a healthy appetite, Alice.'

'There's a little left if you want some, Tante.'

'No, thank you, darling, mid-morning is a little early for me.' I gave her shoulder a squeeze as I made my way to the back door where Mary was hovering, clearly trying to attract my attention.

'What is it, Mary?'

She took my arm and led me away from the kitchen. 'Lucille's been looking for you, Madam. She's at Gabe's till lunchtime if you want to catch her.'

'Did she say what it's about?'

Mary shook her head. 'She's not long on words, Lucille.'

'No. Right, thanks, Mary. I'll go there straight away.'

'Do you want the trap, Madam, I could get it for you?'

'No, really I'm fine. I was going for a walk anyway.'

Rather than go by the lane, I took a short cut across a couple of fields to get to Gabe's cottage, partly so I could pet the plough horses on the way. Strong, soft-hearted beasts, they towered over me, nudging and snuffling into my pockets for the treats that were always there. Of all the animals on the farm, these are the ones that make me the happiest.

Lucille was tidying up and laying the table for Gabe's lunch when I got there. I could smell rabbit stew and freshly baked bread; a hearty meal to keep him going all through the afternoon.

'Goodness, that smells wonderful. You spoil that man, Lucille. From what I remember, his wife wasn't much of a cook.'

Lucille untied her apron and hung it on a hook. 'I enjoy it. I've had no one to cook for since Mother died and it's no fun cooking for yourself.'

It was true, she did enjoy it; I could see the change in her. Suggesting to Anne that Gabe needed someone to keep house and cook for him after his wife died was one of my better ideas, and there was no one more suitable, or willing, than Lucille.

'Mary says you were looking for me.'

'Yes. He'll be back soon. Shall we walk?'

We took the cart track to the point where our ways diverged. 'Is it Gabe you're worried about?'

'Not really, but it's better if he doesn't see us together. I'm not sure he'd want you to know.'

'Know what?'

'He's asked me if I know something that'll stop babies.'

'Gabe? He's old enough to be a grandfather. Don't tell me he's chasing after young girls.'

'He says it's for a friend of his, someone at the tavern. I do believe him; he's not the sort, is he?'

'No, no he's not. When you say to stop babies, do you mean before or after the event?'

Lucille shook her head. 'I was so surprised, I didn't think to ask and I can't help him either way, anyway.'

'But your mother was always excellent at herbal preparations; she must have known of something.'

'Not that she told me.'

That made sense. The Melina I knew did everything she could to protect her unworldly daughter, and that included keeping her single.

'But you think I might know?'

'I'm sure you do, Madame,' addressing me the French way, like her mother used to. And it wasn't flattery; she said it as fact.

'Let me think about this for a while, Lucille. I'll come and find you in a day or two.'

We parted company and I wandered back slowly, old memories stirring.

I was only fifteen when I first discovered the seeds. I had a vague idea about how they could be used, but once I knew that Culpeper suggested the same thing, I felt confident enough to offer them to a desperate prostitute. Delphine had two children already and had fallen pregnant again; but this time there'd be no avoiding the workhouse for her family. She was delighted with the result but even after all these years, and having questioned my religion along the way, I'm still not comfortable with the idea of abortion. I've long argued with myself about the rights and wrongs, about whose life is more important, and I still don't have the answers.

Thankfully, the seeds also work as a preventative or I might have ended up in dire straits myself. I blush now to recall how reckless I was with a charming priest who should have been more concerned about my welfare, so I'm well aware that we are not always sensible and not always fully in charge of our own bodies.

What I do know is this; I shall need full knowledge of the circumstances before I do anything.

Clever Gabe for knowing exactly what he was doing. It seems the same can't be said for Tobias.

~ 13 ~
1673, London

T he two newly-built properties in Spital Fields were drawing a fair bit of attention; partly because of the design but mainly because of the quality. It appeared that the neighbourhood was on the up. Speculation about the owner remained just that; the builders had taken all their orders from an architect and the agent handling the project was tight-lipped about 'a foreign investor'.

Elisabeth had been resident in one of the houses for several months, taking huge delight in furnishing what was her first real home. An elegant suite of rooms on the ground and first floors provided her with more than enough accommodation, and although she already had plenty of ideas of her own for the other floors, it was circumstances that would dictate how she would use them. The influx of French workers showed no sign of abating and, with little or no English, the women in particular were finding life difficult given that many locals were not always welcoming or helpful. It wasn't surprising then that the first person they turned to for help was someone fluent in French, living on their doorstep, who was more than happy to listen to their problems. Before long, Elisabeth had the beginnings of a language class meeting regularly in one of the ground floor rooms, but it was the women and children's health problems that precipitated the establishment of her clinic; as if by *design, not far from where Nicolas Culpeper had set up shop.*

A message from the agent announced that the final touches to the second property had been completed and he was now ready to proceed if Madame Tournier would care to make an appointment. She most certainly did.

The agent had been in the business for many years and had never come across a woman of any age, far less one so young, with complete control over her own money. It had crossed his mind to offer advice at first but soon realised it was unnecessary. This woman knew exactly what she wanted and it was highly unlikely that anyone would succeed in taking advantage of her. All in all, it was probably true to say that he was rather in awe of her, and more than a little charmed.

Beaming at her over his desk, he presented her with a list. 'We've had so many enquiries from weaver families, Madame Tournier, it's going to take you a while to go through their details. They're delighted with the accommodation of course, but it's the set-up on the top floor that all the weavers mention; that amount of light is something they're not used to. I can guarantee other builders will be following the design given how trade is booming.'

Elisabeth accepted the list with a little shake of her head. 'Thank you, that's kind of you, Mr. Paget, but I really can't take credit for the design; that's down to a friend of mine.' It was listening to Philippe moan about the light in the warehouse that had given her the idea of the extra-large canted windows on the top floor. 'I shall take the list and give you my decision when I've had time to go through it all properly. My feeling at present is that it should be leased to two families, no more, and my preference is for one French and one English family.'

'An admirable choice, Madame, I understand entirely – community relations and all that…'

'Exactly. And I must stress, once again, Mr. Paget, and I'm sorry to labour the point, but my name must not appear on any of the documents. As far as anyone knows, I am renting my rooms like everyone else. Is that quite clear?'

'Absolutely, Madame Tournier.' Paget didn't understand it but then he'd never come across anyone like her before.

To Elisabeth, the reasons were obvious. No tenant wanted the owner breathing down their neck, no matter how good they were, and she too would be uncomfortable knowing others might treat her differently if they knew she owned the place. It felt slightly devious but she was soon to be thankful that she'd remained in the shadows, and not because the tenants were troublesome. Quite the opposite.

* * *

She stopped in her tracks when she first saw him standing there, with his back towards her, talking to Philippe. The height and figure, the long wavy brown hair, the mannerisms as he was explaining something in rapid French – how could it be possible? Of course it wasn't possible, and another glance told her François wouldn't have been seen dead in those clothes. But he is dead, she reminded herself, don't be ridiculous.

Ridiculous or not, she struggled to keep her heart from pounding as she crossed the warehouse floor.

'Madame Tournier, come, c'est Jean-Michel La Montagne, un vieil ami.' Philippe was all smiles.

The 'old friend' turned around. 'Enchanté, Madame, Philippe has told me all about you.'. It was not a trick of the light; the resemblance was indeed uncanny, or was it just the facial hair? She couldn't make up her mind but, whatever it was, with his eyes firmly fixed on hers, she was beginning to feel the stirrings of something she hadn't felt for a very long time, and looked away like some young ingénue. And, if she was completely honest with herself, even at 16 years old she *was never an ingénue. Aphra was right, she thought, I am definitely out of practice.*

Elisabeth lifted her chin, smiled at the two of them, so very different, and pulled herself together. 'I'm very pleased to meet you, M. La Montagne, are you a weaver also?'

As it had been with François, the attraction was mutual and immediate, but this time the roles were reversed. Jean-Michel was an artisan and the younger by several years whilst Elisabeth had status and wealth. Had she bought the new prime property in the City and continued to spend all her time with Aphra and her uncle, their paths would never have crossed. She had no regrets. This life she had chosen was fulfilling and joyous – and she felt it was about to become even more so.

Jean-Michel was indeed a weaver, perhaps not to the same standard as Philippe, but a class above English weavers, and ambitious. He took the two top floors above Elisabeth's with a small down payment and an old loom to get him started, courtesy of Mr. Stokes and Philippe. Surprisingly, the rent was less than he had expected.

* * *

When the three women swept into the theatre, fashionably late just minutes before curtain up, all eyes were on them.

'You will note I reserved the best seats in the house, ladies, not just to see but, more importantly, to be seen.' Aphra smiled and nodded to acquaintances before whispering in Elisabeth's ear. 'They're all nudging each other and asking who you both are. There'll be fun and games after the show, mark my words.'

Meanwhile, Alice was oblivious to the attention. This trip had marked so many 'firsts' for her she was having trouble taking everything in, but determined to enjoy every single moment.

She'd arrived in London a few days before and, as Elisabeth had predicted, her appearance had had the desired effect.

'Alice Harryman, what have you done to yourself?' Aphra, hands on hips, had stared at the young woman standing before her in a costume of the most becoming midnight blue. No longer just 'pretty in a wholesome way', she was now radiant, polished and showing a degree of confidence previously completely absent. 'I want to give you the biggest embrace but I'm frightened of spoiling the effect – you look wonderful.'

Laughing, Alice had thrown down her purse and wrapped her friend in a tight hug. 'Oh, Aphra, it is so good to see you. I can't tell you how much I've been looking forward to this trip.' Having released her, she'd executed a little twirl. 'And this, of course, is all Elisabeth's doing. Apparently, it's time I started acting like a grown woman of independent means; every so often, at any rate.'

'Quite right, my darling, better late than never.'

Billed as a 'drolery', the show was a series of mainly salacious prologues and epilogues drawn from other productions as well as verses by Aphra whose style of poetry was now well-known. The audience, therefore, had come expecting to be titillated by same-sex liaisons, cross-dressing and other explicit goings-on –and they were not disappointed. For Alice, though, it was an eye-opener.

Elisabeth, sitting in the middle, leaned towards Aphra. 'Did you think to warn her?'

'I did not. She's not a child, Elisabeth.'

'No, but...'

'Tsh, stop talking now.'

The final offering on stage was one of Aphra's more innocent poems depicting young lovers in a country setting and, as the curtain came down, she stood to acknowledge the applause. Alice was also on her feet, clapping loudly, apparently not as shocked as Elisabeth had feared.

The crowd congratulating Aphra had as much, if not more, to do with meeting her guests rather than anything else, and invitations flooded in. The next few days were hectic.

Having used the excuse of too much to do back in Spital Fields, Elisabeth declined several offers, but did attend one fashionable soirée which Alice was particularly looking forward to. 'Please say you'll come, Elisabeth. Aphra will be off chatting to all and sundry and I don't want to end up looking like a spare part.'

The very idea that Alice would be left on her own for long was laughable but Elisabeth understood completely. London society was a world away from sleepy Sussex.

The soirée, courtesy of Lord and Lady M, was in a grand townhouse and Alice had chosen to wear her new evening gown with its bodice and overskirt of green brocade. With her chestnut hair, soft brown eyes and a complexion shown off to perfection by her mother's emeralds, her natural beauty was in stark contrast to the over-whitened and rouged faces of some of the other women. Leaving her briefly in the company of a few young men, clearly under the impression she was nowhere near thirty, Elisabeth went to join Aphra.

'Talk about moths to the flame...'

'Well, after living with the awful Harryman, she deserves to have some attention.' Aphra took her by the arm and led her into another room. 'And, so do I... Come with me for a minute, I'm dying to introduce you to someone.'

Introductions made, Elisabeth found herself forcing a smile as she made small talk with John Hoyle, a lawyer, referred to as Jack by Aphra. A striking-looking man with hair and eyes as dark as Elisabeth's, the similarity ended there. The eyes were not kind. Feeling increasingly ill at ease, which had nothing to do with being left with someone who made no attempt to uphold his end of the conversation, Elisabeth excused herself and made for the terrace and some fresh air.

She felt sick with a terrible foreboding. Images were coming thick and fast into her head and in a few short minutes she knew everything she needed to know about Jack Hoyle; clever and arrogant for sure, bisexual certainly, though Aphra had the same tendency and wouldn't care. But cruel, violent and a killer – how would she feel about that?

'There you are, Elisabeth.' Aphra made her jump. 'Are you all right?'

'Fine, I just came over very hot suddenly and needed to cool off. I'm better now.'

'Excellent. So, what do you think, isn't he wonderful? I swear he is everything I am not; educated, self-possessed and quiet where I am talkative and demonstrative and, not only that, ridiculously handsome. And the best bit – he really likes me.'

'Of course he does, who doesn't?' Elisabeth pulled her into a loving embrace, squeezed her eyes tight shut and swallowed hard to bring herself back to reality. Aphra didn't seem to notice that she'd made no other comment.

They linked arms and went back inside to see what Alice was up to.

* * *

After four full days of engagements, Alice cancelled a shopping trip with Aphra to spend the whole day with Elisabeth in Spital Fields. Having made a quick detour to visit Culpeper's grave, they were on their way to see her properties.

'I swear I don't know how Aphra does it. I'm exhausted, and the amount of alcohol they all manage to put away is astonishing.'

'She's a force of nature, certainly. I've never been able to keep up with her, and I don't particularly want to anymore. I must be getting old.'

'That's not true, you're just sensible enough to dip in and out of it as it suits you.' Alice leaned a little closer and lowered her voice, unnecessary as there were only the two of them in the carriage. 'There's something I want to tell you.'

Elisabeth also leaned forward, expecting a nugget of gossip. 'Go on…'

'I've been seeing someone, ever since that evening at Lady M's. He's much younger than me, barely 20 years old, but we've had such fun together and things have been moving along– if you know what I mean.' She fixed wide eyes on Elisabeth. 'It nearly happened in his carriage the other day.' Elisabeth bit her lip which did nothing to hide the smirk. 'Don't laugh, I just about managed to keep my dignity. Anyway, he's taking me somewhere special tomorrow and then again just before I leave for home. It's going to happen and I certainly won't be doing anything to stop it. There's no future in it, of course, but I desperately need to know what it's like being with someone who wants to make love to me, in case it never happens again.'

Elisabeth reached for a hand and kissed it. 'I'm pleased for you, my darling, but I'm sure this won't be your last opportunity. However, you'll be the scandal of Sussex society if you return home unmarried and pregnant within a year of coming out of mourning. Luckily for you, I have something you can take.'

Alice grinned. 'I knew you would.'

After a brief visit to Philippe to thank him for Alice's beautiful fabrics, the two of them were settled in Elisabeth's elegant drawing room and the conversation turned to Aphra.

'Have you seen much of Jack Hoyle at Aphra's?

Alice wrinkled her nose. 'A fair bit. She's obviously obsessed with the man but I'm not convinced he makes her happy. It seems an odd relationship to me.'

'Mmm…'

'Mmm...what?'

'I had the strangest experience as I was talking to him; nothing like my normal visions that tell me something about the future. This was like a series of events from the past that just wormed its way into my head as I was talking to him. The sensation made me feel physically sick – and it frightened me. He stabbed someone Alice, and left him to die. I think he was young then, but I can see it in his eyes, he hasn't changed. He's going to make her life a misery and there's nothing we can do about it.'

They were both pondering the futility of any intervention when a loud knock on the door made Elisabeth spring to her feet and head for the hall. Alice caught only snatches of the rapid French but, amused by the change in Elisabeth's manner, she followed, curiosity getting the better of her.

'Ah, Alice, may I introduce you to M. La Montagne? He's my neighbour from the floors above me. He's a weaver.'

Perhaps overdoing the Gallic charm a fraction, Jean-Michel bowed, and expressed how delighted he was to meet yet another beautiful lady, before departing with apologies for interrupting. 'I see you tomorrow then, Madame Tournier?'

Listening for his footsteps on the stairs, she closed the door slowly before turning to face Alice.

'Well, you kept very quiet about him, Elisabeth. Are you sure you can spare those seeds you were telling me about?'

~ 14 ~
Spring 1718

This morning was the second time I'd woken very early and thought I might catch him alone at kitchen breakfast. It was also the second time he'd snatched up the remains of his meal on hearing my footsteps on the stairs and headed for the kitchen door.

'You're not avoiding me, are you, Tobias? Good morning, by the way.'

The pained look was meant to convey that it was unthinkable he'd do such a thing, but he didn't turn back. 'I'm sorry, Aunt. Good morning. I'd love to stay but we've got a lot on today so I'd better dash. See you later.' A quick smile and he was gone, without once really looking me in the eye. A bad sign.

Mary came over to clear the table and cocked her head towards the door. 'He's awful twitchy recently. I hope Gabe's not giving him too much to do.'

I doubted it. I'd caught him out telling bare-faced lies too many times when he was younger, and he was no better at it now. Anyway, I was fairly sure what was eating away at him.; Gabe must have told him by now that Lucille couldn't help him.

And if he wanted my help, he was going to have to talk to me.

* * *

'I hope you've left some for me.' We all looked up as Tobias burst into the dining room, kissed Anne, then went to inspect the remains of breakfast in the chafing dishes.

'This is a nice surprise, darling; we don't often get to see you at this hour. I'll ring for Mary if there isn't enough.'

'No, don't worry her, Mother, there's plenty here, unless Alice wants to fight me for the last few kidneys.' He gave her his silly grin and got a withering look in return. His sister had come in for much ribbing about her appetite of late, not that it showed in her figure.

'Well, at least I haven't had two breakfasts.'

'And neither have I. Gabe dragged me out of early breakfast to help with a lambing and I'm starving hungry.'

He sat down next to Alice who promptly stole a kidney, as he knew she would; the good-natured protests and arm-shoving a clear sign that whatever had been worrying Tobias had probably passed. Anne and I shared a glance and a smile, acknowledging the change in mood. I even felt her sigh of relief.

'So, who's doing the rounds this morning then, you or Gabe?' Anne dabbed at her mouth innocently with her napkin.

'That'll be me. Gabe's over by Home Wood checking something; not sure what.'

'Well then, Aunt Elisabeth is champing at the bit to get out in this lovely weather and I don't want her overdoing it, so how about you take the trap instead of riding? Then she could go with you.'

I studied him carefully before he replied.

'Yes, of course, I'll be glad of the company.' He flashed me a brilliant smile and I like to think he meant it, although it crossed my mind maybe he was just becoming a better liar.

Not long afterwards, we were driving briskly along the lane. 'I do appreciate this, you know. I'm sure it'll take you twice as long but I'm enjoying it too much to feel guilty.'

Tobias didn't deny it, but gave a little laugh as he urged the pony on even faster. I closed my eyes briefly, happy to feel once again the breeze on my face and catch the heady scent of blackthorn blossom in hedgerows alive with sparrows.

'I could tell you were desperate to get out.' He gave me a nudge and pointed with his whip. 'Look, up there.'

I shielded my eyes and followed the whip. High up above us, a male buzzard was performing his mating display, soaring and dipping dramatically over and over again. 'It's quite astonishing the lengths some birds will go to to attract a mate, don't you think? You men have it fairly easy by comparison.'

'Especially if a title is involved.' He said it without a trace of bitterness and winked as we exchanged a sideways glance. It made me wonder if I was worrying about Frances needlessly.

Turning off the lane and onto the cart track, the little pony went from a trot to walking pace making conversation that much easier, although I gained nothing from his small talk about the farm. I was about to lose patience when he pulled up at Gabe's cottage and jumped down.

'I'll only be a minute. Gabe wants me to pick up some tools for sharpening.' He was out again in no time with Lucille not far behind.

'Madame, nice to see you out for a ride on this lovely day. Are you well?'

'Very well, thank you, and even better now.'

Tobias climbed back onto the trap and missed the look that passed between us as he tucked the tools under his seat. He flicked the pony on and left her to pick her own way around the potholes that had got worse since the spring rains.

'Hang on to me, Aunt, until we get past this stretch. We don't want you sliding out of the side door.'

I did, although it wasn't necessary as I haven't yet lost my sense of balance. Still, the physical contact made broaching the next subject easier.

'Have you seen much of Frances since the wedding?'

A slight hesitation; he knew this was coming. 'I have, yes – but clarify what you mean by 'seen much' of Frances. If you mean does she remove...'

'Stop it, foolish boy.' We were both laughing now. 'You know what I mean.'

He was clearly making up his mind how much to reveal, so I waited.

'I ride over there about once a week and we meet in the parkland, as far from the house as possible to avoid any gossip. She's very unhappy.'

'Does she know about Hadleigh?'

'Yes, and you were right, she did have suspicions before, but imagined it would be an easy matter to turn things round. Perhaps he thought so too, who knows, but they were both wrong and if things don't change then the chances of Frances producing the child they both want are diminishing by the day.'

'He hasn't managed to consummate the marriage?'

'Not yet, and he's started blaming her.'

'Poor girl.' I meant it too, but I had only one concern. 'You are being careful aren't you, Tobias?

We'd just pulled up at a field gate and he turned in his seat to face me properly for the first time, taking one of my hands in his.

'There's no need to worry about me, Aunt. I'm all grown-up now.' And he was right, of course. Seeing someone every day, it's easy to miss those changes, but as Céleste had observed at the engagement party, he was a boy no longer. He gave me a quick peck on the cheek and jumped down. 'I won't be long, I'm just going to check these sheep. Do you want to stretch your legs a bit, or stay put?'

I got down. Wild carrot was growing in the verge, the frothy white flowers so pretty with their little red centre. I picked a small bunch and made a mental note of where I could find them again.

He was back before I could get very far, and we were soon on our way again.

'There's been another couple of births but they're all doing really well. None of the other sheep seem to be struggling, thank goodness, or I might have had to enlist you to roll up your sleeves and help.'

'Shame, I would have liked that. It can't be too different from human babies.'

'I see you've been stocking up on your herbs.'

This was going to be easier than I thought. 'No, not really, I just love the flowers and the smell. Medicinally, wild carrot's not much use until you can get the seeds in the autumn.'

'What do you use them for?'

'I'm not sure I should tell you.'

'Women's stuff, eh?'

'Yes – in that they can prevent a baby, if taken correctly.'

Silence. I was glad we were sitting side by side and not facing.

Eventually, the question I was expecting. 'So, how does that work then?'

'I'll tell you, if you tell me why you want to know.'

When the answer came it took me completely by surprise.

'Charles? Our Charles?'

'It may have escaped your notice, Aunt, but he's grown up too, and he's been seeing quite a lot of his Professor's daughter up at Oxford.'

'Clarify what you mean by 'seeing quite a lot of...''

'Touché. Yes, very quick, Aunt.' He gave a little laugh but we both knew this was no laughing matter. 'He's had no experience – none at all as far as I can tell – and I get the impression she's the one leading him on. She's older than him apparently, and I worry that she might be desperate. I've tried talking to him, you know, but he finds it hard taking brotherly advice from me.' As if reading my mind, he continued, 'Can you imagine the repercussions should the worst happen? He'd be chucked out of college, his reputation and future shot, and Mother and Father would be devastated.'

'He's going back next week?'

Tobias nodded.

'I'll see what I can do, but don't you dare tell him it has anything to do with me.'

* * *

After a few more visits to check on livestock and farm workers, we were heading for the furthest point of the estate and I could just glimpse Top Wood beyond the next fields.

'I don't suppose we can take the trap nearer to the wood?'

Tobias shook his head. 'There isn't a cart track and, to be honest, I can't even remember the last time I rode that way. I expect it's fairly overgrown by now. Why do you want to go up there?'

'It holds lots of memories for me. When your Grandmother Alice was first widowed, I came here for a few months to keep her company, and on the days she was busy, I used to walk up to that wood.'

'It's a heck of a walk, and all uphill. What was the attraction?'

'Difficult to explain.' Tempting as it was to tell him about the foxes, the danger was I would say too much. 'The first time I went there, it felt like discovering a forgotten world where I was the first person to set foot; mystical somehow. It's fanciful, I know, but there you are, you did ask.' I gave him a little nudge. 'And, as I was only in my twenties then, not much older than you, I don't remember finding it a difficult walk. You might, of course, given that you ride everywhere these days.'

'Ha, I expect you're right. Anyway, I'd be happy to take you up there by the Thatchling Road if you want. I think that's probably the only way to enter it now, short of hacking your way in.'

'No, I won't be doing that, but thanks all the same. I still have my memories.' Although I couldn't help wondering if descendants of my fox family were still finding a home there, if there was even a clearing at all now, and if ghost orchids and rare herbs were still growing apace. I hoped so.

Tobias leaned in to give me a quick hug and, stupid old woman that I am, my vision became decidedly blurry.

One more stop to check on villagers sowing crop seeds and then we were bowling rapidly downhill towards Home Wood. Slowing down as we reached the last bend we saw Gabe in the distance but he wasn't alone. A tall good-looking man, surrounded by a group of about a dozen young adults and children, appeared to be pursuing a conversation that Gabe had already opted out of. We saw him shake his head and turn back to enter the wood when the man grabbed his arm roughly and spun him round.

'Uh-oh, here comes trouble.' Tobias urged the little pony on and we drew up alongside the pair just as Gabe, face like thunder, was eyeball to eyeball with the man who was now, arms outstretched, taking a step backwards with an air of innocence.

'Master,' he doffed his cap to Tobias and I noted a few sniggers from his followers, 'I was just enquiring of your man here if you needed some excellent workers to help with the sowing?'

'As I'm sure you've already been told, we have enough workers at this time, but there are plenty of other estates round here where they might need help. Try the other side of Petworth.'

'Well, you see,' the man scratched his head, 'we've come from over that way and there's nothing doing. I thought, like, you'd be prepared to help us seeing as how my mother used to work here.'

I'd been studying the man's face during this exchange and I knew, without any shadow of doubt, whose son this was. It wasn't just the resemblance, his speech and the cocky way he had about him that made me sure, but rather the way my skin was prickling all over and the sound of her laughter that was blocking out everything else.

I saw Gabe turn to look at me and I think he knew too.

'Well I'm sorry, we don't need anyone else.' Tobias drove a little closer to make his point. 'It's a long time since we've used itinerant labour so I can't say I knew your mother.'

The man replaced his cap and motioned to the others to get going. 'If you say so, Master.' Then he looked straight at me. 'But there'll be others round here who knew her, that's for sure.'

I barely remember the drive back to the house or if Tobias and I talked about anything on the way. Alice was with me, sharing my fear that I might not have the strength if it was needed.

~ 15 ~
1673-1675, London

Had it been possible to design the perfect mate for Alice, the result might have looked very similar to Joseph Rawlinson. The third son of a wealthy landowner, he'd been lucky enough to avoid the duties and expectations of the heir and the spare, and had enjoyed a decade of mixing his political aspirations with an energetic life style in London. Now in his mid-thirties with his political ambitions finally realised, he'd become weary of city life, and had returned to Sussex determined to use his influence to work for the people who needed it most.

Outgoing, charming and good company, he'd never been short of female attention, but in the marriage stakes that counted for little without an estate, a title or a fortune. It had never bothered him overmuch; few young women held his attention for very long anyway, not when there were more interesting, eager, married ones grateful for a discreet lover.

Growing up in the same part of Sussex, Alice and Joseph's paths had crossed once or twice when they were very young at various parties, but they had no clear memory of each other. Back then, a seventeen-year-old boy wouldn't have noticed a shy, awkward twelve-year-old girl.

Eighteen years on, things were very different.

Alice had returned from her trip to London a changed woman. The realisation that she was considered attractive, even desirable, and that she could hold her own in conversations ranging from Art to Politics had given her a confidence she had only previously felt when discussing farm matters. From now on, she was going to accept any social invitations that came her way (she had the wardrobe; it would be a waste not to use it) and involve herself more in community affairs.

And so, it was inevitable that Alice and Joseph's paths would cross again – and this time they noticed each other immediately.

Meanwhile, back in London, Elisabeth had succumbed to the charms of Jean-Michel who had no idea that his new love was not only his landlady but also his patron, given that his rent was kept ridiculously low. She had no intention of letting him find out either, for fear their relationship would suffer.

But for Aphra, nothing seemed to be going right. Her latest play, The Dutch Lover, was a disaster and she was quickly running out of money. Proudly independent until now, gossip swirled around that she was being 'kept' by Jack Hoyle and her reputation dipped even further. Elisabeth, cross that she hadn't been asked for help, couldn't get through to her; she was completely in thrall to the man and desperately unhappy at the same time. Their relationship was a power struggle and it was one that Aphra was losing.

For well over a year, Elisabeth and Alice were both too busy to make the journey to see each other, but letters flew between them regularly as there was much to write about.

June 1674

Dearest Alice,

I have been remarkably fortunate. The two families I chose for the house next door are proving to be worth their weight in gold!

The men are both weavers, of course, and spend all their time in the attic, which seems to suit the wives very well indeed as they have their work cut out with childcare and keeping house to the standard laid down by the agent. Word has it that the owner is exceptionally fussy!

It gave me an idea, and now I have a crèche and a clinic in my basement in addition to the language class on the ground floor. Both next door wives are helping and because one is French and the other English, I'm thinking it won't be long before all the children are bilingual. It really does seem that we are forging a little community here. I even saw my maid, Julianne, who helps me with the herb garden, teaching the older children how to weed the other day. I always knew she was a smart girl.

The clinic is always busy but the scarcity of the 'magic' seeds is a bit of a problem for there are many occasions, as you can imagine, where I would love to give them away but am forced to ration them until I restock in the autumn. At least I don't have to worry about you now that you've finally learned the difference between wild carrot and cow parsley!

Other than that, I think all is going well. And yes, that includes Jean-Michel and me, but there is nothing more to add at present.

Please send your news. I'm sure there must be lots to tell now that you appear to be getting out and about in your new finery ...

With all my love, as always,

Your Elisabeth xx

July 1674

Darling Elisabeth,

Where on earth do you find the time to do all the things you do? I worry you're going to wear yourself out, especially as you're now helping Jean-Michel with his customers. Look after yourself, please, and remember; physician heal thyself.

So, where do I start? I think I've accepted so many invitations recently, I'm in danger of being labelled a social butterfly. Some, of course, are hard work, but I remind myself that you and I will be old and doddery one day and then will no doubt be grateful for a bit of lively company. I digress. What I really want to tell you is that I've met a wonderful man.

His name is Joseph Rawlinson. A little older than me by a handful of years, he's never been married but is as far from a curmudgeonly bachelor as it's possible to get. The first occasion I saw him was at a local meeting to discuss various county issues – he's a member of parliament – and he was so engaging, he had the audience in the palm of his hand. He caught my eye a couple of times and wasted no time cornering me afterwards to get my views. I may have dropped into the conversation that I'm a widow.

We've spent a fair amount of time together since then, but I'm not going to say any more just yet in case it all goes wrong. It's early days, but I can't wait for you to meet him.

Besides that, work on the farm is proving difficult, with this summer being so very cold and wet I fear the harvest will be late, again. Do you remember this time two years ago when you were here, it was glorious weather all summer and we were desperate for rain? I wonder if we'll ever see a summer like that again.

I'll write again soon but I must be off now because…well, you'll just have to wait and see in my next letter!

Love, as always,

Your Alice xx

PS. Any news on Aphra? I've written but no reply.
PPS. If you know any scandal about Joseph's time in London, now might be a good time to tell me.

'What is it?' Jean-Michel came up behind her and wrapped his arms around her waist.

She'd been standing at the window, not really looking out, too absorbed as she was in her own thoughts, but the kiss on her neck made her smile and turn around. If he knew just how that made her insides melt, she wouldn't get anything done. Kissing him back, she pushed him away slightly.

'I don't know whether to tell you this or not.' His face fell and she added quickly, 'It's my problem really but I suspect you and Philippe will want to get involved.'

'Go on…'

'A young girl and her mother came to see me today. The girl has missed her bleeding and fears she might be pregnant.'

'Young?' He shrugged in a manner suggesting it was nothing new.

'They said fifteen but she looked younger to me, and plainly terrified. Her father's one of the elders trying to establish a Huguenot church in Spital Fields. He's a clockmaker, highly regarded and very religious; I suspect Philippe will know who he is, although I didn't ask for names. If anything, the mother seemed even more scared of him than the daughter.'

'These things happen, Elisabeth. I don't see how we …'

'She was raped, repeatedly. I've seen the damage to her body, Jean-Michel, and it's a mess.'

110

'Oh, mon Dieu…'. He wiped a hand across his face and shook his head slowly.

'There were three of them apparently, but the ringleader urging them on was a relative of hers; some sort of cousin the mother said, and he works in the dyeing shed – for you and Philippe.'

Jean-Michel turned and paced up and down the room, looking grim. Like most Huguenots, he believed in family, hard work and living as decent a life as possible. Something like this in their community was as unusual as it was unwelcome and there'd have to be a reckoning. There'd be no keeping it from Philippe but the trouble would be stopping him from killing the boy; he had daughters himself.

'I can make things right for the girl – hopefully, if she follows my instructions – but I'm hoping I can leave the rest to you.'

'You know this boy's name?'

'I do.'

Jean-Michel left immediately and wasn't back till early evening. Clearly upset, he wanted nothing more than a hug. 'It's done, he won't be back, and we know the names of the others.'

'Don't tell me the details, I don't want to know. Just tell me the boy's still alive.'

'He'll be fine, given time. Quicker than the girl, I expect.'

* * *

Although Elisabeth was clearly thrilled with the way Anglo-French relations were going in their corner of Spital Fields, she was well aware that there were rumblings and unrest in the wider community.

English silk weavers had plied their trade in this part of London for many years but their products had only ever been suitable for linings and undergarments. Unable to match the skill of the Huguenot weavers, they now saw a substantial demand for silk they couldn't produce themselves and, although the upturn in the market saw an increase in demand for their own silks, resentment simmered, laced with xenophobia. New immigrants no longer needed to beg for a job with an English weaver, and they ended up taking home more pay.

Trouble was brewing, and she knew it.

'Does this bother you?' Jean-Michel propped himself up on one arm so he could better assess her answer.

She looked him straight in the eye and brushed a lock of damp hair away from his face. 'No, it doesn't bother me. It makes me very happy; I feel eighteen again.'

'But there is something; is it the girl?'

'No, that's all sorted now, I hope.' Elisabeth sat up and wrapped a shawl round her bare shoulders. 'It's just that some of the women and children have been having a hard time of late, name calling and such, petty stuff really, but still, it's a bit unsettling. I thought we'd got over all that some time ago.'

'It's jealousy, because we're doing so well. I wouldn't mind but it's not as if we're stealing their trade. Philippe's even put business their way. You can't please some people; stop worrying about it.'

Jean-Michel reached for his clothes. 'And talking of work, I must love you and leave you now. I'm away up to my attic.'

Elisabeth watched him dress, loving the way his back muscles flexed and relaxed as he pulled the shirt over his head and tucked it into his pantaloons. She waited, face upturned, for the goodbye kiss.

'And you, Madame Tournier, had better get up. I can't have you hanging round my room all day. Haven't you got work to do?' He flicked the sheet off her to expose her naked body and made swiftly for the door before she could grab something to throw. He was still laughing as she heard him taking the stairs two at a time up to his workroom.

Pulling the sheet back over, she fell back on the pillow and basked in the afterglow for a few more minutes before reaching for her clothes. It brought to mind Alice's experience with a younger man and it made her smile. How she was going to put it all in a letter she wasn't sure.

Delightful though this was, both Jean-Michel and Elisabeth were well aware of the risks, and neither wanted to commit too soon. Elisabeth had an impeccable reputation to uphold in a conservative community and Julianne, her maid, was far too observant for her own good. Not that she was suspected of disloyalty, but staff always liked to gossip about employers. To deny her the opportunity, strict formalities were observed outside of Jean-Michel's bedchamber.

By this time, Elisabeth was acting as unpaid coordinator for Jean-Michel. If he was to complete orders, it was clear that he didn't have time to spend with dressmakers dithering over patterns and couturiers quibbling over costs. Elisabeth, though, was made for the role, especially as she had commissioned gowns from most of them herself when she was a well-known woman about town, and she still had many aristocratic friends.

So far, the partnership was working better than they had both imagined.

* * *

Nothing much changed in the next few months; until Jerome Stokes was assaulted on a visit to see Philippe.

A weaver from another firm, either drunk because he'd been laid off, or the other way round, saw Stokes in his Sunday best and couldn't resist taking out all his frustration on him. The women spinners were the first to hear the shouting and swearing, 'You feckin' bastard, Stokes, this is all your fault', and then a crunch as fist met bone, followed by kicks and the unmistakeable thwack of a cane. A dozen women or more downed tools immediately and ran outside, some seeing to Stokes and the others setting about the man with nothing more than their hands. He was gone before the men arrived to see what was going on.

Stokes wasn't badly hurt but he was shaken, and so was Elisabeth when she heard about it.

It had been some time since she'd experienced visions, but they were back now and the warnings were clear. This incident wouldn't be the last and it most certainly wouldn't be the worst. How though to make others understand? And how to reassure Jean-Michel that her reluctance to spend time with him had nothing to do with a lack of feeling, for in truth it was the opposite. She knew that to see her awake but unresponsive in the grip of a vision was unsettling. So how then to explain?

In the end, things happened much quicker than even Elisabeth imagined. Just days later, close to midnight, she experienced something else entirely. She was there watching the plotting, smelling the grease and feeling the heat of the brazier – even though her body remained in her room.

She came out of it to find her water glass smashed on the floor. Ignoring it, she stumbled up the stairs in bare feet, shouting all the while, 'Jean-Michel, it's me, open up for God's sake,' and hammered on his door until he appeared in his nightshirt.'

Still sleepy, he ran a hand across his face. 'What's happened, are you alright? Come in…'

'No time to explain, put something on quick, you've got to go to Philippe's now. They're coming soon.'

'Who? You're making no sense, just calm down.' He attempted to hold her. 'And what have you done to your foot? Look, it's bleeding…'

She shook him off and took a deep breath. 'Men, vigilantes, they're coming to do damage tonight. Stokes's place will no doubt be the first but then they'll be coming here.' She raised a hand to stop him saying anything more and closed her eyes briefly. 'No, wait, I'm not *thinking straight…I'll go and get Philippe.'*

'You can't, not on your own at this time of night. And your foot…'

'Don't argue with me, Jean-Michel,' raising her voice for the first time, 'I know what I'm doing and I need you here to protect this place. Go and raise the men next door, and the women, you might need all the help you can get if I'm too late.'

Within a quarter of an hour, and breathless, she'd reached Philippe who was quicker than Jean-Michel to understand and rally fellow workers who lived close by. Together they ran to Stokes's works, Elisabeth refusing to return home, knowing what they didn't.

They wouldn't win this battle without her.

She saw them coming in the near distance, indeed it was hard to miss them. Fifteen or so men; the younger ones, brandishing cudgels and missiles, bent on a night of mayhem, the older ones holding their flaming torches aloft, clearly out for more than a bit of mindless violence.

Philippe and his men stood their ground outside Stokes's building and waited for the confrontation. Elisabeth slipped inside and saw from her vantage point on the first floor that their leader was the man who'd struck Jerome Stokes days before. It was likely he was still drunk and that was a worry.

'This is no way to solve your problem.' A small man but no coward, Philippe stepped forward until the two of them were a few yards apart.

'Well, Frenchie… we zink eet is.' Delighted with himself, he turned to grin at his rabble, one of whom threw a rock, narrowly missing Philippe's head and landing short of the building.

It was the start. More stones followed, this time finding their mark and shattering two front windows. The younger men were whooping and shouting, goading their leader to make the first move and he didn't hesitate. Smiling, he shoved Philippe hard, drew back his arm and looked up at his torch before aiming at one of the broken windows.

The next second, it was lying on the ground by his feet.

Clutching his dangling arm, the man's cry of pain was so loud it stopped the others in their tracks, but not for long. From nowhere, a colossal wind rushed along the street, the force more like a tidal wave, immediately snuffing out the torches and forcing bodies to scramble out of its path. It lasted as long as it took to disperse the rioters. Philippe and the others fled back to the building seeking safety, although they were in no danger.

Elisabeth's work was done and relief threatened to overwhelm her. As she so rarely used her powers there was always an element of doubt in her mind.

Slipping away unseen she made her way back to Jean-Michel, rehearsing how best to explain the 'dream' that had forewarned her.

Relieved to find everyone safe at home, it seemed that the few youngsters who'd been sent ahead to break as many windows as possible were unprepared to find a welcome party. After the first stone struck, they were given a taste of what would happen if they ever tried it again.

For once, not caring what anyone else might think, Elisabeth wrapped her arms around Jean-Michel's waist and laid her head on his chest, completely drained of all energy and feeling the pain in her foot for the first time. Carefully, he lifted her, nodded to the neighbours and carried her up the stairs, pausing outside her door.

'Carry on up, Jean-Michel.'

~ 16 ~
Spring 1719

'I was hoping never to have this conversation with you, Tobias.' I'd been leaning on the fence giving titbits to the horses when I saw him making a bee-line for me, and I knew then that something was up.

'It's not what you think, Aunt. It is most definitely not mine.'

Although surprised, I believed him. He wouldn't lie about something like that. 'So...as she wants rid of it, I'm assuming it can't possibly be Hadleigh's?'

'Correct. He's managed to do the business a couple of times, after a fashion I'm told, but he's been abroad with his friend for the last few months and, although he may not be the sharpest, I imagine even he can count.'

'So, if it's not yours or Hadleigh's...'

'I don't know, she didn't want to tell me. Frances has had several lovers, none of whom have been me.' He gave a rueful little grin and leaned towards me. 'This will astonish you, I know, but I took your advice 18 months ago and decided to protect myself, or my heart anyway. It's true we see each other regularly, but just as friends, and by God she needs someone she can talk to now. Hadleigh's back home soon.'

Hercules, the oldest plough horse, suddenly gave Tobias such a hefty nudge that we both laughed and scoured our pockets for any bits, delaying the moment when I would tell him what he already knew. 'Clearly, this is not your problem, Tobias.'

He gave Hercules a friendly slap, 'Go on now, off with you, there's no more,' and turned to face me. 'You're right, of course, and I know she's been foolish but, as an old friend who, truthfully, has no desire now to be anything more, I can't just abandon her. And I know you're going to say she had no such scruples when it came to me, but there's no one else. She turned up black and blue one night at her father's house, and he made it perfectly clear to her then that there was no getting out of the marriage.'

Tobias wasn't to know it but it was that last comment which made me think again. My equally young and reckless mother had been in a similar situation when she pleaded with my grandfather to take her back and his refusal was something he came to bitterly regret.

Much against my better judgement, I found myself asking, 'How many months is she?'

'I don't know and I doubt she does, but she doesn't look much bigger to me.'

'Well, I'll see her, Tobias, but you need to arrange somewhere neutral and I'm promising nothing.'

* * *

I did see the poor girl and yes, I did feel sorry for Frances. But she was too far gone for any help I could give and, at over 3 months pregnant, even if I could, I wouldn't have done it. I think she knew herself it was hopeless, and rued the weeks she'd spent in denial. Perhaps she also regretted trying so hard to make Tobias jealous.

I told her I hoped that Hadleigh would swallow his pride and accept that the child could solve all their problems.

She laughed at that.

* * *

I was in bed early; my head had been throbbing all day and I ached everywhere. It's difficult to know at my age if I'm sickening for something or whether it's just part of growing old.

I fell easily into sleep a couple of times but the same dream kept

118

waking me up. And I'm suspicious of my dreams – never knowing if they're the same as my daytime visions which invariably give a glimpse into the future – or just dreams. Even after all these years, it's hard to tell.

Then there are the others, where I leave my sleeping body behind to see, and often hear, what's actually going on elsewhere. But there's nothing dream-like about those.

Unless it persists, I'm thinking this is just a dream.

* * *

The door to Gabe's cottage was open and I could hear Lucille singing as she worked. I knocked and walked straight in. 'Madame,' she propped up the broom and wiped her hands on her pinafore, 'are you looking for Gabe?' She knew I wasn't or else I would have come at lunch time, but it wasn't in her nature to presume. I closed the door and she pulled out a couple of chairs from the table. 'Is it something I can help you with?'

'I hope so, Lucille.' I gave a wry smile. 'It's Tobias; it's always about Tobias, isn't it?' That wasn't strictly true, but she didn't know that last time it had really been about Charles. 'I'm going to need Gabe to keep an eye out for him, particularly in the tavern. I can't explain it, I just have a feeling someone's coming for him and if Gabe were there with him, I wouldn't worry so much.'

'The visions aren't yet clear?'

'They're not even visions, just slightly disturbing dreams where he's having a normal drink with his friends but I know it's all about to change very quickly – although how, I don't know.' I rested my chin on both hands and sighed. 'It's not much to go on, is it? I think my powers are deserting me.'

'So, what's he done?' That's Lucille; always quick on the uptake and to the point.

'Nothing, it's complicated, he's involved in someone else's mess, that's all. I just wonder if you could drop a few hints to Gabe that you've heard a rumour. He'd listen to you whether or not he believed you, he's long suspected you have the gift.'

'And not just me, either.'

I shrugged, too old to worry about that now. 'Possibly, but I can't run the risk of Tobias finding out that this request comes from me. He's happy to ask for my help on his terms, but he'd be furious if he caught me meddling in his affairs.'

'I'll do what I can, Madame. Let me know if anything changes.'

I covered her hand with mine and gave it a squeeze. 'I'd be lost if I didn't have you to confide in every now and again, Lucille.'

'And I, you, Madame, now Mother has gone.'

I got up to go, then hesitated. 'Has Gabe seen anything more of those itinerants who came here looking for work last year?'

Lucille pushed back her chair. 'No, but you know he'll be back, don't you?'

'Does Gabe suspect who he is?'

'He didn't say, but I know he had a bad feeling about them – and him, in particular.'

'I'm not surprised. If you'd seen him, Lucille, you'd have thought she'd spat him out of her mouth.'

'Gabe'll tell me if he sees them again. He tells me most things these days.' She couldn't quite disguise the note of pride in her voice.

'Well, be sure to let me know if he does. Heaven help us if all that trouble starts up again.'

'Do you think she's still alive, Madame?'

'No. I'm as sure as I can be that she died over a year ago and that he's come looking for some sort of revenge.'

'With the same powers?'

'Let's hope not, Lucille.'

~ 17 ~
Spring 1675

Aphra couldn't attend Alice's wedding, but sent her love along with an exotic vase from her own reduced collection. Staging a new production was keeping her in London and also far too busy to fret over the end of her affair with Jack Hoyle. As far as Elisabeth could tell, it wasn't working, but she hoped this truly was the end – unlike the time before, and the time before that.

On the day itself, there were no relatives joining Elisabeth in the front pew and it still troubled her that Alice knew nothing about her cousins living just in the next village, but having raised the subject again recently, she found Jennet still adamant that sleeping dogs should be left to lie.

Apart from Elisabeth, those representing the family were all staff who'd known Alice from birth; Jennet and her husband Edmund, the head groom, Henry Durling, the farm manager, and the cook, Mrs. Lynd. All sat proudly next to Elisabeth, safe in the knowledge that, this time, it would all work out just fine. Joseph Rawlinson couldn't be less like her first husband; a man they all loathed.

'Would you look at her. Nigh on 33 years old and I swear she could be 21 again.' Jennet whispered to Elisabeth. 'That's your doing that is, she never knew how to make the best of herself until you gave her a push.'

And Alice did look radiant, dressed in a gown of the softest moss green silk that was a wedding gift from Jean-Michel; a London couturier the present from Elisabeth.

'Well, right or not, I'm fairly sure she could have been in sackcloth when they met and Joseph Rawlinson wouldn't have noticed.'

Jennet gave a little laugh then bit her lip and blinked rapidly as it threatened to turn into something else. Clutching her handkerchief in one hand, she reached for Elisabeth's with the other and all the murmuring quietened down as the parson prepared to start the ceremony.

Elisabeth glanced behind to see their side of the church packed with estate workers and villagers, including Chicken Nan who'd been collected in the trap by Gabe and seated by the aisle for a good view. She was alone, dashing Elisabeth's hopes that perhaps Melina and Lucille might be there after all.

They nodded a greeting to each other.

On the other side of the church, Joseph's mother was present; a plain, large-boned woman who'd given her husband three strapping sons and two daughters. It was fortunate, thought Elisabeth, that she had only passed her physique on to the sons. Tightly corseted into a gown of dove grey, she sported a tall lace cap balanced on a wig of startlingly ginger curls, which appeared to have a life of their own as her head was constantly on the move. Joseph's father, unable to attend due to ill health, had sent his most sincere congratulations, delighted and surprised to be doing so as he'd long since given up hope that Joseph would settle for someone. Or perhaps the other way round.

The eldest brother, wife and children were perfectly pleasant but rather distant whilst the middle son was anything but. Dressed in military uniform, he had the handsome looks of the eldest brother combined with Joseph's charming nature and had clearly decided that Elisabeth should feel the full force of his personality after the ceremony. Avoiding his eye was becoming tricky.

Although the parson was ready, a glance down the aisle told him that young Gabe, as chief usher, had other ideas as half the villagers were now being urged to cross the aisle. All the shuffling around held things up for a good few minutes until silence resumed. Satisfied at last, having missed the tutting and raised eyebrows under the bobbing ginger curls, Gabe took his seat just as he caught the wink from the military gentleman.

The ceremony was short but full of joy and so relaxed that when Joseph kissed his new bride more enthusiastically than was the norm, the whole congregation, with a few exceptions, reacted with loud clapping and cheering.

It was safe to say that this was probably not the sort of wedding Joseph's mother was expecting.

Showered with good wishes along with the traditional wheat and rose petals, the newlyweds took their time to thank people before reaching the lychgate where Gabe was waiting for them with the carriage. He stepped forward with a little bow.

'Miss Alice, if I may still call you that one last time – pardon me, Master – this is for you.' He held out a tiny posy of clover bound with a white ribbon. 'Real ones this time. I'm sorry about the last one, and I hope, you know, it …'

Alice threw her arms around him and squeezed tightly before he could say anything more, sudden tears catching her by surprise. Feeling Joseph's hand on her waist she dashed them away quickly with a smile.

'Look, Joseph, four-leaved clover, we couldn't be more blessed.'

It was much later, when everyone was preparing for the evening festivities and they were lying in bed, that she told him how an 11-year-old Gabe had presented her with one before, only for her to discover later that it had been cobbled together from two common ones. 'I've still got it in a book somewhere; I was so touched.'

'Are you saying he was worried it had something to do with your first marriage?' Joseph kissed her shoulder and wound a chestnut curl round his finger.

'Possibly, country folk round here believe all sorts of strange things. And who's to say they're wrong?' Her tone was teasing but she wondered how he'd react if she told him half the things she knew about Elisabeth.

* * *

The evening's entertainment had been Joseph's idea, keen to give Alice the sort of memorable day she deserved. Coming from the sort of landed gentry where owners and workers inhabit different worlds, Oakwood Grange had opened his eyes to an alternative way of managing things where everyone was pulling together instead of apart. He lived in hope that his eldest brother, the current owner of the family estate, might learn a few things if he would only get down off his high horse, literally as well as figuratively.

In truth, it was impossible, even for Joseph's mother, not to enjoy the evening. The musicians had nearly everyone on their feet in the huge barn, the smell of roast hog was seeping in from outside and the refreshments were in plentiful supply. A loud cheer went up and the music stopped when the wedding party made their appearance; Elisabeth guiding the Rawlinson family to the top table whilst Joseph walked Alice to the centre of the barn.

Everyone fell back to give them the floor. Joseph made a pretty speech thanking them all for accepting him, which raised a laugh, and encouraged them all to eat and drink their fill as he had it on good authority that any lateness on the morrow would be overlooked. Another cheer.

If he thought that was it, he had another think coming. As the band struck up once more, Alice held him firmly by the hand, nodded to Jennet, and he found himself swept up into a dance made popular in Queen Elizabeth's time. Once it was over and the clapping had died down, he made a dash for the top table before he could be made to repeat it, dragging a laughing Alice behind him.

While the dancing continued without them, food and drink occupied the top table. Elisabeth was strategically placed between Joseph's mother and his eldest brother who were noticeably more friendly after a few drinks, or it could have been that they'd just discovered her aristocratic connections to both the English and French courts. (Alice didn't indulge in one-upmanship as a rule, but she'd made an exception in this case.). Whichever it was, the appointed hour for their departure came and went without either of them appearing to notice.

'Enough now, Mother,' Simon Rawlinson, he of the military uniform, leaned across the table, 'you're monopolising this lovely young woman and I can see she's itching to dance.' With the sort of smile born of supreme self-confidence, he made his way round to her side and offered his hand. 'May I have the pleasure?'

And it was a pleasure, although more because of the break rather than the dancing, but she had to admit that Simon, like most military men, was a very good dancer. It was possibly part of officer training, she thought, although the charm was definitely all his own. They managed to carry on a conversation between dance moves.

'My brother tells me you are about to be married shortly, Madame Tournier.'

'Yes, very soon, and please call me Elisabeth.'

He gripped her tightly round the waist and swept them both into a spin. 'Please tell me he's ugly and ancient, though wealthy, and that you'll be desperate for a little diversion every now and again.'

A change of partners meant it was a short while before they came together again, and she was still smiling.

'Not at all, sir, he's French, younger than me and works hard for any money he has.'

Simon briefly enjoyed what he thought was a joke, before catching her expression as they changed partners once again.

'Truly?'

'Truly, sir.'

A bow and a curtsey later and they were making their way back to the table. 'Well, I suppose I should say 'congratulations', but I hope you realise I'm now a broken man, Elisabeth.'

'I'm sure that's not true.' She was still laughing when Alice overheard them.

'What's not true?'

'Your brother-in -law was paying me compliments.'

'I bet he was. Why don't you find your own wife, Simon?'

'Because that's plan B when I leave the army. For now, I'm quite happy with plan A.' He grinned at Elisabeth. 'When it works, that is.'

Alice shook her head in mock despair. 'Well your flirting has come to an end for this evening as your Mama has sent for the carriage. She's feeling very tired.'

After the fond farewells when the party was still in full swing and Joseph was chatting to Henry Durling, Alice refilled Elisabeth's glass and they sat alone reliving the events of the day.

'Did you see his mother's face when she found half the village shuffling in behind them? Simon thought it hilarious and told her not to be so po-faced.' Alice leaned a little closer. 'Incidentally, you'll have to watch out for Simon when you get back to town; he's nothing if not persistent.'

No response. Alice immediately sensed the change, saw her staring off into the distance and grabbed hold of Elisabeth's hand. 'What is it?'

'Who's that woman?'

'Which woman?'

'Over by the far entrance, just walking in with …is that Ansell?'

Alice squinted through the smoky atmosphere. 'Oh heavens, yes, it is Ansell. I thought he'd have more sense than to bring her. He's taken up with this Zillah, and it's causing Henry Durling a bit of trouble. I've been meaning to tell you about it.'

She may have been a fair distance away, but Zillah's eyes had found Elisabeth's immediately and for a few seconds it was as if neither of them was aware of anyone else. Elisabeth blinked first, turned to Alice and said as calmly as she could, 'Tell me now.'

Alice shifted in her seat to face her. 'Well, it seems she arrived in the village a couple of months ago, no one knows from where, and fairly soon she was seen walking out with Ansell. Everyone was just dumbfounded. I mean…he's 40 years old, apparently never had a woman since his young wife died 20 years ago and, to be honest, he doesn't have much going for him. Whereas Zillah, on the other hand…'

'…is very different.'

'Quite.' Alice topped up her own wine glass. 'I've had too much to drink so I may be getting things out of proportion but Henry Durling certainly has a bad feeling about her. Only the other day, he mentioned how she has a look of you but added that that's where the similarity ends. He says she's taken to meeting Ansell on the farm at midday meal time which, naturally, causes a stir amongst the young labourers and Ansell, who used to be such a placid, contented man, is becoming bothersome.'

'He's jealous?'

'That, certainly, because she definitely enjoys the attention, but in other ways too. He told Henry that he expects a cottage on the estate, like other married workers, if he marries Zillah.'

'Is that settled, they're going to get married?'

Alice shrugged. 'Not if he has any sense, but that's debateable, isn't it? Anyone can see she has an ulterior motive, although heaven knows what it is. Why saddle yourself with someone like Ansell just for the sake of a cottage? Anyway, Henry replied honestly that, even if they marry, there isn't a spare cottage to be had so he'd have to wait until one becomes available.'

'Good, you don't want a troublemaker on the estate.'

'No, we don't but, very un-Ansell like, he wouldn't let it drop and was back the next day insisting he had the right to a cottage, being the longest serving farm worker, and that old Jonas and his wife didn't need one any longer as their children were away working and could afford to rent in the village.'

'How did Henry take that?'

'He was stunned, and furious; he knew where all this was coming from. There was an argument and I'm sure Henry told him exactly what he thought. He wasn't going to bother me with any of this before the wedding but Ansell threatened to raise the matter with me directly and so Henry felt he had to warn me.'

'Ansell hasn't spoken to you yet, though?'

'No, but he must know I'd back up Henry.'

Had it been any other day rather than Alice's wedding day, Elisabeth would have grabbed her by the shoulders and said – Alice, listen to me, this is very important. Under no circumstances let that woman anywhere near this estate – but now wasn't the time to worry her.

Instead, she tried to calm herself, but that was proving difficult now that everything was becoming clearer. Some age-old reflex that had dropped her body temperature and caused her skin to prickle all over, even before she'd locked eyes on Zillah, told her that this was no ordinary woman on the make.

And suddenly, all the unanswered questions in her life, the 'why me', the 'why here' and the 'what for', were beginning to make some sort of sense.

She needed to talk to Melina.

~ 18 ~
Summer 1719

This wasn't a dream.

Being present when something terrible is about to happen is a form of torture when there is nothing you can do to stop it. Thinking it was the dream I'd been having for some time, it soon became apparent I was witnessing the real thing, hovering invisibly above and around the inside of the tavern.

There was Tobias, seated at his usual table, playing 4-handed cribbage for modest stakes with friends; their rivalry more a matter of pride than avoiding settling the bill. It seemed that honours were even and the call for 'just one more hand' was trying the landlord's patience.

'Come on now, gentlemen, have a heart. I have a wife waiting for me in a nice warm bed, even if you don't. You've even outlasted Gabe, and that's saying something...'

It dawned on me that I'd placed Gabe in a difficult situation; with no reason to hang around when only the cards players were left, it would have looked odd had he stayed. If anything were to happen now though, he'd be wracked with guilt.

And the tightness in my chest told me that it wasn't 'if' something was about to happen.

There was a scraping of chairs as all four men rose and shook hands, Tobias conceding it was his turn to pay. I saw him wave off his three friends, place the tankards on the counter, then stack the cards before placing them tidily in their packets on the shelf with the cribbage board. Stupidly, it crossed my mind how pleased his mother would be if she'd seen that. His reward was a small tot of rum as he counted out the coins and apologised for keeping the landlord up so late. Everything was calmness and good-natured inside; but whilst Tobias was scratching the tavern dog's head and the landlord was kicking ash over the remaining embers, I was screaming that danger was lying in wait outside and he needed to shake off the drink-induced lethargy and have his wits about him.

I could feel my throat tight and hoarse with the effort, but nobody heard me, and even though I knew it didn't work that way, it didn't stop me hoping that, somehow, he might feel the warning. One final farewell and he was making his way to the door, my fear increasing with each step until I was gasping for breath and then...nothing.

When I came back to myself I was sitting up, with the bedclothes in disarray, wild hair and my skin slick with sweat. All was quiet and I guessed it was close to midnight. Gabe – I had to get to Gabe before it was too late, but my body was too old and slow. I made my way half way up the attic stairs.

'Mary, are you awake?'

I could hear nothing and managed another few steps; they're far too steep for me usually but it's surprising what can be achieved when a body has to.

'Mary...' Louder this time, just as I heard the creak of her door.

'Is that you, Madam? I thought I heard you having a disturbed night.'

It was pitch black but I could just make out her shape. 'Yes, there's no time to waste explaining. Do you think you could run to Gabe's and give him a message?'

Trusting enough not to ask too many questions, Mary stepped into her boots, wrapped a cloak over her nightclothes and ran off across the fields as if it was her life that depended on it. I sat on the attic steps after she'd gone, head in hands, feeling useless and praying that Gabe could get back there in time.

Restless and not knowing what else to do, I made my way slowly down the back stairs and out through the kitchen door. There was only the merest sliver of a moon making it impossible to see more than a few yards in front of me, never mind Gabe's cottage a few fields away, but I strained my eyes anyway. I reckoned Mary might be there by now and, after some useless pacing up and down in the kitchen garden, I set off slowly over the nearest field.

The night was so still, I heard her swishing through the long grass even before her figure appeared in the distance; her pace quickening when she saw me waving.

'Has he gone?'

'Yes, Madam.' She was out of breath. 'He pulled on his breeches, grabbed a stick and was away and off before I knew it. He didn't even wait to saddle his horse.'

I grabbed hold of her and felt her arms wrap around me, patting my back.

'Come, Madam, there's nothing you can do now. Let's get you back inside; your nightdress's sodden and you've got nothing on your feet, look. You're going to catch your death of cold.'

Lucille is the only one still alive who knows nearly everything about me, but Mary and Gabe were around during the Zillah episode, since when I've been fortunate enough to have their unquestioning loyalty. It's odd, I know, that there are folk here who know more about me than my own daughter and granddaughter, but that's the way I want it – for now. As neither of them have the gift, would telling them about their ancestors do more harm than good? I still don't know.

What I do know is that the gift can skip generations and, in that case, would the knowledge, if passed down, prevent another young girl from killing herself? Time's running out for me to make up my mind.

Turning to make our way back to the house, Mary paused. 'Did you hear that?'

I didn't, but then my hearing has faded like the rest of me. Soon though, we spotted a glow in the landing window at the head of the front stairs.

'Perhaps they're looking for you, Madam.'

'No, I don't think so, I'm sure no one heard me leave.'

Something was amiss though, and I had an awful feeling we were in for a long night.

The commotion was all at the front of the house, but we slipped in the way we had left, via the kitchen garden and through the back door. By the time we reached the hall, the front door was standing wide open and Samuel could be seen outside only just managing to cling on to the reins of a young mare. Steam was rising from its body as it wheeled every which way, snorting, its eyes wild, and it was hard to tell who was the more panicked.

Mary immediately went to help him; she has a knack with animals.

The rest of the household was clustered round a figure on the floor, Anne kneeling and fussing, Cook with a glass of water and the housemaid hovering on the stairs with a candelabra trying to throw some light on the scene.

'Aunt Elisabeth, thank goodness. It's Frances; the state of her, look. I don't know what to do. I'm sorry we had to wake you.'

Young Alice came up behind me, squeezed my hand and remained silent.

The sight of Frances made my heart lurch, and in the time it took for me to get down on my knees at her side, everything seemed to fall into place. The possibility that there might be more than one casualty tonight was suddenly very real.

'Let's get her upstairs, Anne, we can put her in Charles's room.' I sent Cook and the housemaid off to get more lamps, lots of them, warm water, a wash rag and some towels.

The three of us managed to get Frances on the bed; she hadn't passed out completely but she had little strength left, her breathing was ragged and she was in obvious pain. I started to loosen her clothing whilst Anne removed her shoes.

'She's not even dressed for riding, look. What on earth was she thinking?'

'Tell me what happened, Anne. Has Frances said anything?'

She shook her head. 'Not that made any sense. Samuel heard the horse in the drive and we knew it couldn't be Tobias, he never comes that way. And when he looked out of the window, he saw her practically fall off the horse and land on the front steps. It was dark and he couldn't make out w...'

'Anne, what did she....'

'Mother, for Heaven's sake...' Young Alice turned to look at me, the child she was only a few months ago evident no longer. 'I can't be sure but it sounded like –Is he here? – and then she fainted.' She got to work helping me tackle Frances's bodice and skirt. 'She must have meant Tobias, Tante, but he's not here.'

'Why would she?' Anne's voice rose higher. 'And where is he?' She flew out of the room, presumably to check for herself.

'Should I go and look for him, Tante? I'm not scared of riding in the dark.'

'No, darling, stay here, your Mama would have a fit. And, anyway, Gabe's already gone looking for him.'

'Is that where you were...?'. She stopped when Anne came back.

'He's not usually this late. I don't understand what's going on.'

Young Alice did though, even before we'd seen the state of Frances's body beneath her clothing. Anne took one look at Frances's face drenched in sweat, screwed up in pain and she too, began to understand.

'Oh, Goodness, I'd no idea.' Anne stared at the swollen belly released from its stays and then her eyes landed on the bruises and wheals. 'What on earth are we going to do, surely we must send for her mother?'

'No, don't, you mustn't...no one.'

The voice was weak and Anne was first with some water, desperate for answers.

Frances opened her eyes and grabbed Anne's hand, spilling the water. 'Is he here, Tobias? I've got to warn him.'

I jumped in before Anne could answer. 'No Frances, I think he's on his way back from the tavern with Gabe.' I avoided meeting Anne's eye. 'Tell us what's happened.'

'It's all such a mess...' Tears were rolling down her cheeks. 'He wouldn't listen to me... I pleaded with him...and when his henchmen saddled up, I just knew. I'm so sorry, so sorry... I came as quickly as I could.'

Another wave of pain overtook her and I drew Anne away from the bedside, leaving Alice to comfort her friend.

'Did you make that up, about Gabe being with him? Tell me the truth, Aunt, I'm not a child. And is all this what I think it is, that he deserves a beating?'

'It's not Tobias's baby, Anne. Frances will tell you that herself.'

'So, what's it got to do wi ...'

'Hadleigh knows it's not his either.'

Anne's mouth opened and closed without saying anything.

'So, like she says herself, it's all such a mess. I'm hoping Gabe's with him tonight and there's no better man to have in a crisis, Anne, you know that.'

'I know Tobias tells you things he wouldn't tell me ...'

'Not now, Anne, we've got other things to worry about. I suggest you send a couple of men out along the back lane to the tavern. The grooms are probably your best bet; they're young and handy from what I've heard. And tell them to go to Gabe's first in case they're there. Alice and I will stay here with Frances.'

In my mind I feared it was all too late, but at least it gave Anne something to do.

* * *

One of the grooms was back quicker than we expected. The good news being that both Gabe and Tobias were back at Gabe's cottage; the bad news that it probably wasn't wise to move Tobias tonight.

Regardless, the trap was prepared in double-quick time with Samuel and Anne about to be off as soon as they could lay hands on their cloaks and footwear. I imagine it was the first time in their adult lives that they'd ever been outside in their nightclothes. I knew Anne had a bottle of laudanum with her but, given the shock, Tobias's breathing difficulties and alcohol intake, I feared the combination could be dangerous.

'Remember Anne, only a little to take the edge off the pain. No matter how much he begs you, do not be tempted to give him more, and don't give him the bottle.' I kissed her cheek and wiped away the tears. 'He'll be fine, my love, just get him back here tonight if you can.'

Any other night I would have gone with them, but we both knew I'd be needed here tonight.

'I heard the boy say he's at Gabe's.' Young Alice was waiting for me at the head of the stairs. 'Is he badly hurt?'

'Nothing we can't fix, Alice, don't worry. Let's concentrate on Frances.'

Unconvinced, she nevertheless nodded, and we both stepped into the room.

There was more lamplight around now and it was clear that one of Frances's eyes was swollen and half-closed. If Richard Hadleigh had been in front of me now, I swear I would have horse-whipped him myself. Irrespective of Frances's behaviour – for which one might feel a crumb of sympathy given the farce of her marriage– there was never an excuse for battery on the scale I'd seen this evening. That she could then ignore her own pain to embark on a perilous journey in the dead of night to warn Tobias, was surely testament to her courage and there was no doubt I was changing my opinion of her.

I took her hand, waited for another wave of cramping to pass, and then gave a version of the truth.

'You can stop worrying about Tobias. He's quite close by at the farm manager's cottage and I dare say he'll be home very soon. And now, my dear, we really need to concentrate on you so, tell me, when did these cramps begin?'

'Is he unharmed? When can I see him?'

'I'm sure he'll come to see you as soon as he can. The cramps, Frances, when did they begin?'

She tossed her head from side to side on the pillow. 'Oh, I don't know, what does it matter?'

Céleste says there's a particular look on my face when it's obvious I'll not stand 'any messing' and that must be what Frances saw for she swallowed hard and carried on.

'It was shortly after I set off, I know that, but I've no idea how long it took to get here. I doubled over so much I was lying on my horse's neck until it passed and then...' She covered her mouth before carrying on. '...it happened another couple of times, and...'

'And what, Frances.'

'I'm a mess, down below. I don't know if I've soiled myself or it's the other...' She screwed her eyes shut, trying hard not to cry again.

I knew already what it was, the iron smell gave it away. 'Right, well I'm going to have a look and, don't worry, it'll be nothing I haven't seen before, many times. Just lie back while we get you out of all these clothes and then I'll sort you out. Alice, go and get one of the spare nightdresses for me would you please, and ask Mary to sort out an old blanket and towels.'

With Alice gone and Frances's eyes fixed on the ceiling, I was hoping she might find it easier to talk. 'Tell me how long he's been beating you.'

Any composure she had up to now disappeared, and her voice trembled as the answer came out in fits and starts. 'It started a week or so ago, as soon as he came back from abroad and the housekeeper told him there'd been no rags to boil for several months. He'd hit me before, but not like that, and afterwards, he pushed me onto my front on the floor and he... he pinned me down... and he...'

'It's alright, Frances, I can imagine what happened next, you don't need to spell it out. Just lift your bottom up for me a little, please. That's it, good.' I bundled away all the soiled garments and gently washed the blood from her body. I was fairly sure now that there was no saving the baby.

I moved to her bedside again and stroked the wet hair away from her face.

'I'm so sorry.'

'What sort of person does such a thing as punishment, Madame? What is so wrong with me if that's what it takes to...

I was saved from having to reply by Alice coming back.

'...and it's not Tobias's, truly. I want you both to know that he's been nothing more than a good friend to me. A very good friend...'

I looked at Alice and saw no surprise on her face. It seems brother and sister are closer than I thought.

'He kept it up for days; the yelling and screaming, the beatings, but I couldn't tell him it was his cousin. It was a stupid mistake, we were both miserable with our lives, we drank too much and it just happened. But he's a decent man, Madame, he has a wife and children and he doesn't know I'm pregnant. The scandal would ruin his life as well as mine. To be honest, I was so lonely it would have happened with someone else sooner or later, anyway, and I didn't care if Hadleigh thought I'd lain with some workman from the village, it was all the same to me.'

Neither Alice nor I could find anything to say.

'It was the gamekeeper who told him that Tobias had been seen in the grounds. And that was it, case proved as far as he was concerned. The more I denied it, the more certain he was.'

'He'd better not come after you here.' When Alice was cross, she looked just like her grandmother.

'He won't. He'll suppose I've gone to my parents' house.' She closed her eyes and gave a little shake of her head. 'As if I'd try that again...'

Despite the circumstances, I was unsure how Frances would feel about losing the baby. Experience has told me not to make assumptions.

'You've lost a fair amount of blood, Frances, and you probably know that these cramps are contractions. I fear the baby's well on its way.'

'Will it live?'

'Unlikely at this stage. I'm so sorry, but it's best to be prepared.'

Her little face crumpled and Alice, too, was close to tears.

'In my heart I know it's for the best all round, but...just lately, I've felt it move and even though I didn't really want it... I'd begun to think how wonderful it would be to have someone in my life that I could love.'

There was nothing anyone could say and words were going to be of little comfort in the hours to come. I tapped Young Alice on the arm and we moved away from the bed.

'These contractions may go on all night, if not longer, sometimes much longer. Can I leave you here with her? She shouldn't be on her own. There's something I need to do.'

'Yes, of course, I'll get some more blankets and make myself comfy in the chair. When do you think they'll be back with Tobias?'

'Soon hopefully. I'm going to prepare my room. We can't have him next door.'

Alice nodded. 'I hadn't thought about that...' just as Frances drew her knees up once more and let out a low moan. 'Is there anything I can give her for the pain?'

'Laudanum, when your Mama comes back with it, but I don't recommend it until the pain gets more severe. Crampbark tincture is better at this stage. How much do you have?'

'About half a bottle; I haven't had cramps for the last few bleedings.'

'Well that'll do for now. Go and get it and give her double the dose you'd normally take, and get Mary to give you some Valerian as well. With a bit of luck, that might be enough to send her off to sleep for a while.'

I was out on the landing when I heard the trap in the drive and went to tell Alice. She'd already heard it and met me at the bedroom door.

'Whatever you do, Alice, don't let Frances get up, lock her in if necessary, and stay here with her until we've got him settled. I promise someone'll come for you as soon as we've got him comfortable. Please, let me sort him out first.'

I waited as they brought him in, Gabe supporting, taking most of the weight as he and Samuel chair-lifted him up the stairs. It looked bad, but at least he was conscious.

'Take him to my room Anne, I've prepared it already.'

I went straight to the kitchen where Cook was boiling pans of water. 'I didn't know what else to do, Madam.'

'It's good, we'll probably need plenty of it, mark my words.'

Mary was in the scullery sorting bottles and jars. 'Miss Alice wanted crampbark, Madam, I've got more here and I'll make some Valerian tea. Is that Master Tobias back?'

'Yes, Gabe's putting him in my room. I'm afraid Lady Hadleigh isn't the only one needing help tonight. Mary, can you prepare some old sheet for strapping and bandaging, and we'll be needing something suitable for splints.'

I went back up the front stairs to report to Young Alice.

'A head wound and a broken arm, as far as I can see, but he'll be fine.' I hoped I sounded more convincing than I felt.

I reached my room just as Gabe was about to leave by the back stairs.

'Thank you for everything, Gabe. Did you see who did this?'

He shook his head. 'They were off as soon as they heard me coming – three of 'em, I think – he didn't stand a chance. I shouldn't have left him, I ...'

'Stop that now, if it weren't for you he'd probably be lying dead in a ditch.'

'Aye, they were definitely out to do him damage, but you knew that already.'

'How bad do you think it is?'

'Arm's most likely broken, and I reckon his head'll need stitching. He was lucky it was a glancing blow otherwise they'd have cracked his skull open.'

Mary came up the stairs behind him waving a large pair of boxwood butter-pats. 'Cook says what about these for splints? They're nice and smooth and about the right length.'

Gabe took them from her. 'Aye, they'll do. They need cutting down a bit, leave it to me.'

'Mary, give this man anything he wants tonight, we can't thank him enough.'

* * *

Tobias managed a very weak grin as I entered the room. Samuel was standing by the window, Anne sitting by the bedside holding his good hand.

'How's Frances?'

For fear of sparking an attack on top of everything else, I felt sure Anne wouldn't have told him everything.

'She is exhausted from the ride, naturally, and your sister is looking after her with something for her aches. She really needs to rest now; Mary's mixed a sleeping draught for her.'

'I don't think she should see you like this, son.' Samuel moved to stand behind Anne.

'No, you're right. I can't believe she rode all that way at night...' He closed his eyes and winced as he tried to change his position. 'Dear God, I don't know which hurts more, my head or my arm. Let me have some more of that laudanum, Mother.'

'No, not a good idea.' Anne stood, suddenly all business. 'Now Aunt Elisabeth's here we can take that sling off and have a good look at your arm. Samuel, we'll need your razor and then please go and get yourself a nightcap and leave us to it. I don't want to have to worry about you too.'

Gratefully, he left.

We decided to set the arm first, as the enormous bandage that Gabe had wrapped round Tobias's head, although bloody, was still doing a good job.

We worked as a team, cutting the clothes off him where necessary, and feeling mightily relieved once we saw the break still just about in alignment and not completely misplaced.

Gabe was watching, having delivered the strapping and splints. Satisfied we could manage and wouldn't need his strength to help pull the ends together, he dropped something by Tobias's good hand and gave him a manly pat on the shoulder by way of encouragement before leaving.

Had it not been for that leather 'biting strap', I reckon they'd have heard him out in the stables, for the manipulation was not easy.

He passed out briefly, giving us time to secure the splints and fashion a new sling, but the worry now was the head wound. All the straining had increased the blood flow.

Anne had found inner strength from somewhere, which was

just as well as I was beginning to flag.

Mary knocked and popped her head round the door. 'Here's Master's razor, and can I get you anything Mistress?'

Anne and I shared a glance. What we really needed was going to have to wait. 'One of your reviving teas will have to do for now, Mary, our night isn't over yet. We'll need some wadding and bandages and...what else, Aunt?'

'Another bowl of hot water and soap, some honey, vinegar and that ointment of Shepherd's Purse. And we'll need some really fine lawn, Anne.'

'A handkerchief?'

'Yes, that should do. Also, Mary, would you get some of that gut-rot the stable lads drink? We'll need that.'

'Good idea, Aunt...' Tobias was back with us.

'Not till we've seen to your head.'

Gabe was right. The wound was wide enough to need stitches but I've seen cases where they've mended the wound and then the patient has died later from mortification. Anne and I had already agreed to try something else.

Helping him off the bed and onto a stool was the first job. Then once Anne had shaved around the wound and Mary had delivered everything we'd asked for, we rolled up our sleeves, scrubbed our hands and set to work.

Blood was still pouring from his head as I stood behind him and laid my hands either side of the wound, gently pressing the edges together. I could feel him clenching his jaw and squeezing his eyes closed but he allowed me to continue without too much fuss. We'd done this many times before with childhood injuries and he knew to wait it out until whatever power was in my hands started to take effect. No one in the family had ever questioned it.

Eventually, the flow eased. His head felt heavy in my hands now and his only reaction to the vinegar and alcohol Anne was busy applying was barely more than a flinch.

'What do you think, is this big enough?' Anne held up a square of lawn fabric.

'Yes, I think so. Put some ointment all around the outside of the wound first, then a dollop of honey right on top. Press the fabric over it gently, then give me the wadding.'

She worked quickly, securing everything as tight as she could with strips of linen. Having helped him back onto the bed, we fell into a couple of chairs, too exhausted to finish our tea, but relieved.

'It hurts like a bas........ a lot, anyway.' He pointed to the flagon. 'Can I have some of that?'

'It's gut-rot.'

'I don't care, it won't be the first time.'

Anne held up the phial of laudanum. 'Take your pick. You can have one or the other.'

'Laudanum then. And perhaps just a little sip of the other...?' The grin made a brief appearance and he got his way.

'I must say this bed's very comfortable, Aunt, but I'm afraid I've rather messed up your linen.'

'No matter, you're staying here tonight, anyway. I'm going to sleep in your room for whatever's left of the night.'

I left Anne to help him undress and made my way back to Alice and Frances. I could have done with a tot of something myself but I needed my wits about me.

~ 19 ~

1675-1676, London and Sussex

These years were busy ones for Elisabeth, Alice and Aphra. Elisabeth's wedding was a simple, quiet affair. Held at the fledgling Huguenot Protestant church in Spital Fields, the congregants were neighbours and work colleagues with a few obvious exceptions.

Alice had been all for attending but wiser heads had forbidden any travel as her baby was due in a month or so. Elisabeth was adamant that no undue risks should be taken with this precious fourth pregnancy, even though she was certain there'd be no repeat of the earlier disasters.

Elisabeth's Uncle George was present with Lady Caroline, a constant companion for many years although the thought of marriage had never been entertained. As both parties only had interests in same-sex affairs, the idea had only ever arisen as a joke.

Despite Elisabeth's life-style now being far removed from that of her uncle, and their meetings inevitably less frequent, nevertheless they still retained the sort of closeness more associated with siblings rather than uncle and niece.

'He's an extraordinarily handsome young man, your Jean-Michel, I must say I envy you. I do understand the attraction, my darling girl, but is it absolutely necessary to work here like this when you *really don't need to. There are some lovely new homes in the city…'*

'Oh, do shut up, George.' Caroline frequently sounded more like his mother. 'It's obvious to a blind man that Jean-Michel lives for his work and Elisabeth is doing exactly what she wants to. She wasn't born to do nothing, like you.'

'She was, actually…'

'Well, born into privilege, maybe, but unlike us, her upbringing equipped her for so much more. Now leave the poor girl alone on her wedding day.'

Elisabeth watched the two of them with amusement; she'd heard all this before and knew that his real concern was for the family home in Kent. Built by her great-grandfather, it now belonged to George and was entailed to her, although he'd never accepted that she didn't want it. Despite living in London and rarely setting foot in Kent, he couldn't bring himself to sell the place but didn't have the sort of money needed to restore it – and there were no other heirs.

Elisabeth glanced around to make sure they couldn't be overheard and lowered her voice. 'I have news which may gladden your heart, Uncle. I am to have a child. It's very early days so, whatever you do, don't let Jean-Michel know that I've told you.'

Caroline kissed her, whispering 'Well done, my dear', and George's smile indicated he'd already worked out what she was really telling him.

'Yes indeed, congratulations. I thought you were getting on a bit for that but, well, that's very good news.'

'Yes, it is, and as you are still in your prime, a child coming of age in another twenty years or so may well be the answer to your prayers.'

'As long as it has a substantial inheritance.' He grinned and put an arm round her. 'So, I suggest you have just the one child, my dear, and remain here in this gloriously cheap enclave, spending very little so as to increase your already considerable wealth…'

Elisabeth laughed. 'There you are, that's cheered you up. Now forget I ever mentioned it.'

They glanced over to where Jean-Michel was chatting with Aphra, who'd thankfully arrived on her own, the affair with Jack Hoyle having finally died a death.

'Does she know?'

'Aphra? Not yet, but I know she'll be pleased, especially if it's a girl.'

Caroline gave a wry smile. 'I hear she's off men altogether.'

'Well, Jack Hoyle at any rate.'

'She hasn't told you then?'

'What?'

'It's common knowledge in my circle that she and a certain actress are practically inseparable at the moment.'

'Emily Price?'

'You do know then.'

'She's mentioned her…'

'I swear it's like trying to get blood out of a stone, Elisabeth. Don't you ever gossip?'

'Not about friends; you ought to be grateful. It appears you know it all anyway. Come on,' taking Caroline's arm, 'you can ask her for yourself.'

* * *

It was much later, when everyone else had gone home, that Elisabeth and Aphra sat up late talking over the day's events. Jean-Michel had kissed them both and tactfully excused himself under the pretext of something in the workroom that required his urgent attention.

'How are you feeling, really?' Aphra heeled off her shoes and stretched out her feet. 'I remember Alice always felt exhausted in the first few months, and it's been a long day for you.'

'A lovely day though, and I'm fine. Especially as I've had time to spend with you and George.'

'If you weren't always too busy to come to town, we could do this more often.'

'I recall you have very little spare time yourself, Aphra, at present. Tell me, how is 'Abdelazar' coming along?'

She gave a little smirk. 'Wonderfully! I had the perfect model for my protagonist; a lustful, villainous, unrepentant schemer of my recent acquaintance.'

'You won't be taking said model back again then?'

'Certainly not. Emily is much more conducive to a life without tension and I find myself happy most of the time.' She drained her glass and gave a not entirely convincing smile. 'With a bit of luck, the play will be finished soon and then, hopefully, it'll be staged at the 'Duke's'.'

'Do you think you'll have time to visit Alice? I'm going down to the Grange in the next few weeks to deliver the baby. I know she's looking forward to seeing you.'

'No, I can't. Perhaps next time.'

It was the way she swept invisible crumbs from her skirt that suggested to Elisabeth it was better not to press the issue. For although it was never the life Aphra wanted, seeing her two closest female friends happily settled, pregnant and comfortably off, was probably not a good idea at this time. As well as losing her financial security, Aphra had also lost much of her trademark 'spark' now that the thrill of sparring and competing with a man like Hoyle was no more. The only obvious benefit was no longer being regarded as a kept woman, although that had never bothered her too much. Elisabeth suspected Aphra's recent conversion to a quieter life would not last long.

'I'm wondering, Elisabeth, just how this place is going to manage while you're away.'

'Things are much more settled now. There's no need for the language class any longer and the mothers organise the crèche themselves; I just supply the premises. And you've met Julianne, she's perfectly capable of looking after the clinic while I'm away. She's going to be a very competent herbalist before she's much older, I reckon, and then I'll have to employ another maid.'

'I was thinking more about Jean-Michel.'

'Well, if you're offering, Aphra, I'm sure he'd be very grateful…?'

'Oh, very droll, Elisabeth. How long will you be gone?'

'Only a few weeks I expect, if our timing is right, and he's just taken on an apprentice – at long last. Also, most clients are well aware that it's a waste of time pestering him so they'll wait till I come back.'

Aphra looked at her friend fondly. 'He really does make you happy, doesn't he? I mean, not just because you have a weakness for Frenchmen and he looks like François?'

Elisabeth laughed. 'Yes, he really does, and not just because he's French and looks like François.' She rose to refresh their drinks and change the subject. 'Will you be needing anything from the clinic before you leave?'

'Something to make me feel young again, perhaps?'

'You're hardly old…'

'Well, I feel it, and my bleedings have more or less stopped. That must mean something, although I must say it's a relief.'

'What about the sweatings?'

'They're worse at night; all the tossing and turning keeps Emily awake.'

'I can find something that will help with that. Anything else?'

'No…I don't think so.' The skirt was getting her attention once more.

Elisabeth knew better than to try dragging it out of her.

* * *

'Are you worried about her?' Alice was lying on a day bed in the morning room of Oakwood Grange, her hands folded across her large belly, whilst Elisabeth massaged her swollen feet.

'Yes and no. Her mood is very low and it's not all about Hoyle. I think the fact that she's still short of money, despite her success at writing, is a constant worry, and she's desperate for this next play to be well received after the last one, which wasn't.'

'But she's taken up with this actress, you say. Has that not cheered her up?'

'I doubt it will last. The girl is very pleasant, possibly too pleasant for Aphra I feel, and nowhere near clever enough. There's no challenge there and she'll be bored in no time.'

'So, what else?'

'It's her health. She's beginning to move like an old woman with aches and pains in all her limbs and her back's troubling her also. When I mentioned it a little while ago, she assured me it was most likely gout from her time in Surinam where nearly everyone had it, but I'm not convinced. We both know these symptoms are just as likely to be something else and just as common in her circle of friends.'

'The pox.' It wasn't a question. 'Joseph tells me it's rife in the City. Can you cure it?'

'No, I don't think anyone can. I've heard that sailors from the East swear by a plant they call 'Stone-breaker' that grows out there and is used to help pain in the joints. It might help ease the symptoms if I can get hold of some. I'll get Jean-Michel to ask at the docks when I get back.'

'Joseph says people are using mercury. Does that work?'

'Only in that it stops you dying of the pox because the mercury poison gets you first.'

Seeing Alice's face begin to crumple, Elisabeth shook the foot she was holding. 'I'm sure it won't come to that. I'll have a serious word *with her, and remind her to stop drinking so much. She knows that doesn't help, she told me so herself. Perhaps I can get her to drink stinging nettle tea instead, that's good for joint pain.' She stood and put on a mock-stern look. 'And now, Mrs. Rawlinson, I'm going to go for a long walk so that you can get some sleep before supper.'*

A kiss on the forehead, and Elisabeth was gone.

* * *

The last time Melina and Elisabeth had met in the woods, it was four years before. Since then, they'd nodded to each other on one occasion when Elisabeth had been passing by Chicken Nan's in the trap, and on another shortly after Alice and Joseph's wedding when she saw Lucille and Melina chatting to young Gabe in the village.

This, then, was no pre-arranged meeting. In Elisabeth's head, it was a test, to see if the connection was still there.

It took longer than she remembered to reach the wood. The route had become rather overgrown, signalling that few, if any, came this way and that made her happy. Ducking under the fence, she could still make out the fox path and followed it as before until she reached the clearing.

The changes here were not so obvious. The banks were perhaps a little higher, the foliage somewhat fuller and the log seat had settled itself more comfortably into the earth, but apart from that, it looked much the same, if a little smaller. Standing in the middle, Elisabeth closed her eyes, flung her arms wide and breathed in the warm, fragrant essence of the wood until her head felt lighter, her hearing sharper and a contented smile spread across her face.

When she opened her eyes, she knew immediately that she wasn't alone. Like the very first time they saw each other, Melina was leaning against the same tree on the edge of the clearing. This time she was beaming.

'Madame, Elisabeth, I didn't want to disturb you.'

With no hesitation from either one, they embraced and examined each other for changes.

'You're with child.'

Elisabeth instinctively smoothed the front of her skirt. 'I'm hardly showing, Melina.'

'I see it in your eyes. I'm rarely wrong.'

'It's a bit late in the day for me, but I feel fine.'

'And you will be. How is Miss Alice, I can't yet think of her as Mrs Rawlinson…'

'She's huge, much bigger than with the other pregnancies. A good sign, I think. Anyway, enough about us, how are you, and Lucille?'

'We're well. It's the season for births so I'm busy and Lucille spends much of her time in the village looking after Chicken Nan who can't get out at all now. I don't think she'll last the year, which is how she wants it. She can't face another winter.'

Elisabeth nodded, knowing Nan would make it happen. 'I saw you and Lucille in the village shortly after the wedding, chatting to Gabe. She is quite the young woman now.'

Melina laughed. 'Yes, she is, but she's wasting her time with young Gabe. He has his sights set firmly elsewhere, I think.'

'Talking of relationships, I assume you've heard about the trouble the estate's been having with Ansell and this Zillah woman?

Melina gestured to the log. 'Oh, yes, I've heard. And all the village is talking about how cock-happy and cunny-whipped he is. I'm sorry but I don't know more refined words for it. Shall we sit?'

Elisabeth spoke quickly. 'Joseph has forbidden the farm manager from worrying Alice about it. He's told her that now Ansell's found a place in the village for them, the problem's gone away but, of course, it hasn't. That woman's going to cause more trouble, I know it but I can't say anything.'

Melina was quiet for what seemed like an age but when she finally spoke, she went straight to the point.

'I believe you need to prepare yourself, Elisabeth. I've felt the evil coming off her in waves – just passing her in the street – and she stares at me in such a way as to let me know I'm not up to the task. But you are. She'll be relishing the prospect of competing with you. And it's a fight you must win, not least because she won't stop at ruining Oakwood Grange.'

Elisabeth dropped her head into her hands, muffling her words. 'We saw each other at the wedding and, in truth, I knew then, and so did she. There's a reason we're together in this place, isn't there?'

Melina rubbed Elisabeth's back. 'She's powerful, there's no doubt about it. But you were born with a caul; I think there's no doubt about that now. This is your calling.'

'She knows I'm here, I suppose.'

'I'm sure she does, so be careful.'

* * *

Chicken Nan looked much more frail, if that was at all possible, although the gimlet eyes seemed as sharp as ever.

'I'm very pleased to see you again, my dear, and congratulation. I hear you're recently married, and to another Frenchman?'

'I am, and about to be a mother, like Miss Alice.'

'Your children will be like cousins then.'

'Yes, we're very fortunate, especially as neither one of us is in the first flush of womanhood.'

'Tsh – you both have the look of young girls to me. Have you seen our Lucille yet?'

'No, but Melina says she's quite grown-up now.'

'Aye, in some respects she is. She's a good girl though and fusses over me like a mother hen. I can't eat much now, y'know, no teeth you see.' She pulled back her lips to demonstrate, and gave a throaty *laugh. 'I don't have much appetite either but she won't give up trying to tempt me with all manner of things.' She pointed to Elisabeth's basket with a twinkle in her eye. 'But if that's Jennet Sandford's milk posset you've brought with you, I have no problem with that. The last lot she sent had such an amount of sack in it I slept like a baby.' She cackled so much, it turned into a coughing fit.*

'Just as well I brought some of this too.' Elisabeth reached into the basket for a bottle of linctus, uncorked it and helped the old woman take a drink.

The cough subsided eventually, and Nan slid back on her chair, suddenly serious as she wiped her eyes. 'I'm glad Miss Alice still has you to look out for her. What with her new husband and baby, I worry her attention will be elsewhere just when she needs to have her wits about her. Generations of good people have worked hard for Oakwood Grange and this village we all love; I don't want to leave this place until I know it's safe.'

It was an instruction and Elisabeth acknowledged it with a nod. She reached across and took both the old woman's hands in hers. 'Melina and I will do everything we can. I will know when I need to be back here.'

Nan's eyes were watering freely. 'Of course you will…'

* * *

The minute she stepped out of Chicken Nan's door, she knew. Just as Melina had described it, the air was different, foetid somehow, and that meant Zillah wasn't far away.

Things had changed since the weight of expectation had threatened to overwhelm her in the clearing, only a few days ago. The appearance of the grandmother she had seen only in visions, had visited again last night, silently reminding her of the courage of her ancestors; other women who'd used their powers for good. And she'd caught sight of her only that morning, her tortoiseshell coat glinting in the sunlight as she leapt onto the shed roof to avoid the yard dogs.

Elisabeth smiled to herself. As the woman who'd outwitted a rabble of vigilantes not too long ago, she wasn't going to slink away from meeting this Zillah. She went looking and found her by the fruit and vegetable stall, sampling the apples.

'What can I get you, Madam?' The stallholder was suddenly all smiles when he saw who it was.

'Half a dozen lemons, please, Mr. Hawkins.' Handing over her basket, Elisabeth glanced sideways and nodded at Zillah. 'Are they sweet, those apples?'

Caught off-guard, Zillah turned slowly, tilted her chin and tossed the half-eaten fruit over her shoulder. 'Not especially, I don't think I'll bother.' She walked away, glaring at Elisabeth as she brushed past her.

'You shouldn't let her get away with it, Mr. Hawkins.'

He pulled a face. 'Aye, well, it doesn't do to get on the wrong side o' that one.'

Zillah hadn't gone far. She sat by the well, unplaiting and re-plaiting her thick black hair, all the time watching Elisabeth until she was out of sight.

* * *

The was little time to relax once she entered the kitchen. Cook whipped the basket of produce from her the moment she crossed the threshold.

'Master's looking for you Miss Elisabeth; he's all of a doo-dah, bless him. Her waters have broken and Jennet's with her but she wants you…'

After reassuring Joseph that nothing was going to happen for a while, Elisabeth changed her clothes, checked that Jennet had everything to hand, then sent them both away to pace up and down elsewhere.

'Thank goodness, you'd think it was Jennet having this baby.' Alice, face bathed in sweat, reached for her friend's hand and pulled her onto the bed. 'I haven't been worried so far, but I am now. I can't help thinking about last time, that little body ...'

Elisabeth wiped away the sweat with a scented cloth. 'Trust me, this will be nothing like that. Just breathe through the pain like you've been doing and lean forward so I can massage your back.'

Last time, Alice had very nearly died giving birth to a baby girl with the cord round her neck, and it had left her with deep physical and emotional scars. It was no wonder she was scared. Seven years on though, everything was as it should be, damage to Alice was minimal and Elisabeth had little to do other than catch the baby.

'Would you just look at this little miracle...' Elisabeth handed over the clean, swaddled baby girl.

'What is it, Elisabeth? Is everything as it should be?'

'Yes, of course. Just look at your beautiful daughter, how could anything be wrong?'

'I thought I noticed something when you were wiping her. She has got everything, hasn't she? I daren't look.'

'She's perfect, just like her mother.' What Alice had noticed was a little frown as Elisabeth tried to make sense of a passing unease about the baby's airways, but it appeared to be nothing.

~ 20 ~
Summer 1719

There was no point trying to sleep now.

It was all quiet when I crept in expecting to see Young Alice asleep in the chair, but she was wide awake. She raised the candle to see who it was.

'Did Tobias hear her?' she whispered.

'No, I think he's well away now.' I held up the bottle of laudanum. 'Frances can have some of this next time the pain takes her.'

'Good, how much should I give her?'

'You won't be giving her anything because you're going to bed now. I'm taking over. How's she been?'

'Drowsy, in and out with the contractions. Perhaps everything will be all right, do you think?'

I shook my head. 'I fear the baby is already dead; our concern must be for Frances now.' I stroked some strands of hair away from her face. 'You've done very well tonight, Alice, but you should try to get some sleep now. Leave it to me.'

'Are you sure? I don't mind staying if you want company...'

'Quite sure.'

I knew sleep was beyond me but, also, I needed time on my own to think. Even though Frances is a married woman, Lady Hadleigh no less, and her wishes should be respected, not contacting relatives did not sit well with me. There was no question we were going to send her back to Hadleigh, but Anne was right, we had to send word to her parents.

It was a question of timing though. Any mother might become hysterical seeing her daughter in this state with no previous knowledge of her condition, and that's not going to help Frances. On the other hand, I have a bad feeling I cannot shake off, and leaving things too late would be something I'd find difficult to live with.

I was looking down on her as another contraction took hold, this one much stronger than before, and held her hand till it passed. A dose of laudanum settled her and I sat beside her, gently massaging the various places on the body that usually aid relaxation.

Hours later the door creaked open and Anne's head appeared, nightcap askew.

'Aunt, you've had no sleep. Let me take over, I've had a couple of hours and feel much better.'

'No, I'm fine. At my age, a body doesn't need much sleep. I'm glad you're here though.'

With little debate we decided that, come the morning, Samuel would go to tell her parents.

As dawn broke, everyone in the household was aware that the baby was on its way. It was left to Young Alice to explain things to her brother and physically restrain him from leaving the room.

The cursing and shouting became too much for Anne who marched down the corridor. 'This doesn't help Frances, Tobias. Things are difficult enough as it is without you adding to it. When there's news, we'll tell you, so stay here and be quiet!' Rarely has Anne been so forceful.

I was fifteen when I first helped to deliver a baby and I've lost count of how many I've delivered since. The happy births are all joyous in the same way but it's the others that stick in the mind; like the abused child, no more than thirteen years old, who chose drowning after giving birth to a healthy girl, or the shock of delivering a grossly malformed baby – or the tragedy of the ones that don't make it safely into the world.

The kind of powers I have are no help at all, and the feeling was growing that today's events would stay with me for the rest of my days.

Frances did exactly as she was told and, given what she had already been through, I felt her strength was remarkable. A final heave and she pushed out the baby who slithered onto my waiting hands. With my old legs feeling as if they were about to give way, I sat and marvelled at the tiny, lifeless body as I cut the cord and cleared away the birth matter.

Anne mopped Frances's face. 'It's all over now, you've been very brave.'

I suspect Young Alice had been listening at the door as I heard her creep in and stand behind me, looking over my shoulder.

'It's so tiny,' she whispered in my ear.

'Yes,' I whispered back, 'but everything in place already, see? He should have had another three months or so inside his mother and then he would have been fine. Fetch me a clean towel, Alice, I'm going to wash him.'

'Alice, you shouldn't be in here...'

'Oh Anne, where's the harm? Better this than being an ignorant young bride, don't you think?'

The argument was cut short. 'What is it? I want to see.' Frances's voice was hoarse with all the straining.

'A little boy, Frances.'

'He's dead?'

'I'm so sorry.' Anne's voice cracked.

'I want to see him.' She was crying and, in truth, I think we all were at that stage as Alice helped me clean and swaddle him and Anne presented the tiny bundle to his mother.

Frances kissed his head, then pulled back the linen to find one perfectly formed little foot, holding it delicately between two fingers. 'He has nothing wrong with him, look – apart from being dead.' She covered him up again, pulled him closer and lay back on the pillow, tears streaming from her closed eyes.

Young Alice left to sob outside.

* * *

Samuel had been gone well over an hour and it was to be hoped that Frances's parents would be here before long. If not, my faith in human nature would be well and truly lost.

At this point, there was no keeping Tobias away any longer but Anne sent him in with a warning.

'She still doesn't know those men caught up with you, so seeing you is going to be a shock. You're going to have to pretend it looks a lot worse than it is...'

I didn't stay to hear his response. Suddenly more tired than I ever thought possible, I went next door to Tobias's bedchamber and lay down.

* * *

'Aunt, please come.'

I felt a hand on my shoulder and, just for a moment, all I could see was white – until I realised it was Tobias's bandaged head. It took a little while for me to come to. 'Do you need some...?'

'Not me, it's Frances. There's something not right.'

He helped me off the bed and I made for the washstand, splashed cold water onto my face to sharpen my senses, then followed him next door. Still holding her baby, Frances was propped up on an extra pillow but her face was ashen and clammy.

'She was saying everything was a bit blurred and then just lost her train of thought; I couldn't understand what she was saying. I thought she was perhaps sleepy, but it's not that is it...?'

'No, go and call your mother to come at once.'

This was my worst fear. I've seen enough afterbirths in my time to know that what left Frances was not complete, and that can be a problem. I gently removed both pillows and laid her down flat on the bed, taking the little bundle from her without her making a sound.

Anne arrived panting, her worried expression mirroring mine as I shook my head.

'She's not still bleeding?'

I drew back the covers and showed her the evidence. 'It's soaked through the padding and it's still coming. There's too much, far too much...'

'But what's caused it? The birth looked straightforward to me.'

'I've seen it before when the afterbirth doesn't come away cleanly, or it could be that the damage was done beforehand, because of the beating or the...'

I stopped myself, realising just in time that Anne hadn't heard everything Hadleigh had done to his wife. 'I really don't know, but what I do know is that she can't go on losing blood at this rate. Her heart is racing wildly and her eyes are unfocussed. All these are signs that we may not get her back.'

'Is there nothing you can do?'

'I'm going to massage her womb; it sometimes helps but...'

I stopped as we both heard a carriage draw up in the drive. Anne's hand flew up to her chest and she took a deep breath.

'It's them, I'd better go down. Heavens, I'm not looking forward to this.'

* * *

Frances passed away an hour later.

Apparently, she rallied briefly to acknowledge her parents and made them promise to bury her with her baby boy in the family plot. Her last words were 'I'm so sorry...'

The mother's wails of anguish and grief were difficult to hear and the look on her father's face too awful to see as he left his wife alone and allowed himself to be led by Samuel to the study. Tobias joined them.

There was nothing more for me to do and I made myself scarce, taking the opportunity to wash and change out of my bloodstained clothes.

When Frances's mother eventually left the bedchamber, she collapsed on the landing and spent a long time with Anne before negotiating the stairs. In the hall, she held both my hands in silent thanks before turning to leave, refusing to look at her husband or take his arm when they made their way to the carriage.

After they'd gone, we all stood silent and motionless in the hall, not quite knowing what to do until Samuel coughed, and made for his study. Tobias, Young Alice and I went together to say our farewells to Frances, placing her child next to her once more and offering up a prayer to whoever was listening.

Much later, after we'd all come together to try to eat something, Samuel related what had happened that morning.

'I arrived just after Hadleigh had gone. As you can imagine, when he appeared at their place this morning, hammering for all he was worth on their door, they didn't have a clue what was going on. 'Is she here?' he kept saying, 'Bring her out.' Once he realised that she wasn't there, he got back on his horse and yelled words to the effect that he didn't want her back anyway and he was going to divorce her, whatever it cost him. His parting shot was this, and I'm repeating this so these aren't my words, 'Because your whore of a daughter is carrying Lyckfold's bastard.'

Tobias looked grim. 'They don't believe it now, thank goodness. Her mother was very kind to me before they left; she thanked me for being a good friend and was sorry I'd been caught up in the trouble.'

Anne reached for Tobias's good hand. 'She wanted to hear everything that Frances had told us and I couldn't deny her. If I were her, I would want to know it all, too. She also told me it wasn't her decision that Frances should marry Hadleigh. I fear she may never forgive her husband.'

Tobias hadn't eaten much but he'd had a fair amount to drink and even Anne felt it unwise at this point to admonish him. His jaw was set in a way we all recognised as struggling to keep his emotions in check.

'Well, he won't be needing that expensive divorce now, will he? That's a handsome reward for a coward who lacks the courage to face another man in a fair fight but manages to beat up a pregnant woman.'

There was silence around the table.

He stood quickly, pushing his chair back so hard it tipped over, and threw his napkin on the table. 'I swear I'll get that bastard if it's the last thing I do.'

He left the room without another word.

* * *

Frances and her baby were collected the very next day, but her presence lingered on and I wondered how long it would be before I could think of that room as Charles's once more.

Inevitably, all our attention was now back on Tobias and his injuries.

'Ow, you're pulling my hair.'

'It can't be helped. Do you want us to cut even more off?' Anne was definitely enjoying having a degree of control over her son once more.

'No, but just be careful...'

We held our breath as the last of the dressing came away and we had a good look at the head wound.

'Well, that's a lot better than I thought it would be. What do you think, Aunt?'

I looked, gave it a good sniff, and gently felt the area. 'How does it feel?'

'No worse.'

'Good, we'll put on a new dressing then and bandage you up again. This time we'll leave it for a couple of days, I think.'

It looked much neater this time. Anne left to have a word with Cook and I stayed to tidy everything away.

He watched me for a while and then asked the question that had been eating away at him. 'I saw her black eye, but just how badly beaten was she? Is that why she lost the baby? Mother won't tell me, of course.'

I shook my head. 'I'm not surprised. Giving you a bruise by bruise account isn't going to change how you feel. You knew he'd hit her before and this time I suspect it was worse. I can't tell you if that was the reason she lost the baby.'

He rubbed his face with his good hand. 'She must have known what she was in for. That's why she said she didn't want to see me for a while.'

A vision of Frances being brutally raped flashed into my mind and I was glad Tobias knew nothing of that. It was a difficult image to shift, and he had reasons enough to hate Hadleigh without adding to his misery.

~ 21 ~
Summer 1677

The early summer of 1677 saw Elisabeth back at Oakwood Grange, this time with her own baby, Céleste, and a somewhat reinvigorated Aphra.

In a favourite shady corner of the kitchen garden, the three of them were enjoying the first hot day of the year with Céleste asleep in a cradle at their feet.

Alice lazily swatted away an annoying fly with her fan. 'So…I want to hear all about 'The Rover' because it's unlikely I shall be able to visit London in time to see it.'

Aphra grinned. 'Well, the first thing to tell you is that a certain ex-lover was most definitely not the model for the main character, who is charming, witty, though not terribly bright, and interested only in relations with women.' She shrugged. 'What can I tell you? It's a light-hearted social comedy laced with much innuendo and the usual bed-hopping, but it has been so well received that I am now being paid properly for my efforts.'

'Bravo!' Alice and Elisabeth shared a secret smile. It was good to see the old Aphra back again; they'd missed her.

'Also, her name appears on the playbill for the first time, and the Duke of York, no less, sought her out to tell her how much he had enjoyed it.'

'Wonderful!' Alice beamed. 'With patronage like that, you should be set up.'

'I won't bank on it. It's well-known he's free with his praise but not so with his money.' She reached for Alice's fan and pushed her chair a little further under the trees. 'It's a little disappointing, but I think light comedy without the political and tragedy elements will have to be the way forward for me. It's proving to be very popular and I must take advantage whilst the going is good.'

Elisabeth pushed the cradle gently with one foot, hoping to keep her baby asleep a little longer. 'I thought the main actress was an inspired choice; by far the best comedienne I've seen, who held her own beautifully.'

'Yes, well that was a pleasant surprise. I've known her for years and she's never shone as an actress before, but I agree, she did very well.'

'That wasn't Emily?'

'Oh, no, it wasn't the right part for her.'

'You could have brought Emily, you know. Joseph wouldn't have minded one bit.'

'I know, darling, and you're very kind but to be truthful, it's a relief to be away from her for a while.'

'Well, also to be truthful, we're glad to have you all to ourselves, aren't we Alice?'

The moment was cut short by the appearance of a fat little toddler waddling down the path to fling herself at her mother's skirts. Jennet wasn't far behind, beads of sweat running down her face.

'Please excuse us. Anne just wanted to show you her daisy crown, Miss Alice, but I'm about to take her in now, it's far too hot for both of us. Do you want me to bring her to you before bedtime?'

Alice kissed her daughter's rosy little cheek and straightened the daisy chain on her head. 'Yes, please, Jennet, and would you ask one of the kitchen maids to bring some more cordial and another fan?'

As Jennet quickly swept up the child and made for the cool of the inside, Aphra observed archly, 'Heavens, they grow quickly, don't they? Just like weeds.'

'Well, that one has.' Elisabeth agreed. 'Most babies at that age are barely walking, never mind trotting. Luckily Céleste sleeps all the time and I'm enjoying it as long as it lasts.'

'You know Jennet's more than happy to look after her as well, while you're here.'

Elisabeth doubted that, but she smiled and said, 'I know, that's kind and I may ask her once or twice during the day but I'll keep her with me at night like I do at home.'

'So, tell me…' Aphra said, keen to move the subject on from babies, '…what's been the gossip here at The Grange?'

Elisabeth was wondering the same thing.

'Well…Gabe is now married and his new wife is working in the dairy, so he's a very happy man. Joseph and I have an eye on him as the next farm manager when Henry retires, although that's a long way off yet. Henry agrees with us; Gabe's hardworking and strong as an ox, honest as the day is long and was born on this estate. He's known nothing else and now he's married he'll be in line for the next cottage that comes free. I don't think he'll have long to wait.'

'Who's going?'

'Old Jonas, he can't look after his wife any longer, so they're going to live with their daughter once she's found a bigger place.'

'Isn't that the cottage Ansell had his eye on?'

'Yes, but thankfully that's not a problem anymore. His relationship with that woman didn't last long once she realised it wasn't going to get her a place here. He still moons around the place like a miserable old goat but she's long moved on.'

Elisabeth failed to keep the tension out of her voice. 'To whom?'

Aphra noticed and glanced from one to the other. 'Ah, I know *that type.'*

'Is she still in the village, Alice?' The question wasn't really necessary; any hope Elisabeth had that Zillah had left the area had been dashed as soon as she arrived here. She felt her presence everywhere.

'Yes, she was away for quite a while but now she's back and still makes a habit of walking in the estate and flaunting herself in front of the workers.'

Aphra gave a little snort. 'No wonder poor old whatshisname is miserable.'

'I thought Henry had warned her off.'

'He did, but he can't be everywhere and, of course, the men quite like it. Joseph thinks that as long as it doesn't stop them working, it's probably not worth making a big fuss about...'

Elisabeth's face told a different story. Soon she was going to have to share her fears.

* * *

Luckily, neither Alice nor Aphra was keen to go on a long walk the next day, and Jennet was happy to mind Céleste for a few hours. In truth, Elisabeth would have liked to ride as the way was overgrown, but then Aphra would have wanted to come too. By the time she arrived at the wood, she was hot, weary and thirsty.

Melina was waiting for her just a little way along the fox path. 'Come with me.'

'I had no idea this was here.' Elisabeth knelt, scooped the water up into cupped hands, then sat back on her heels, wiping the drips from her chin. 'The best taste in the world on a day like this, isn't it?'

'It's an ancient spring, like the one in the village, but it doesn't always run.' Melina sat down beside her. 'It's so good to see you again. I was hoping to see your baby but...'

'Another time, I promise, but it's just too hot today and I had

enough trouble getting here myself. I must be getting old.'

'Not you…but you heard that Chicken Nan passed away last year?'

'Yes, how was it?'

'It was good.' Melina smiled.

Elisabeth nodded. That was all she needed to know.

'Did you hear she left her cottage to Lucille?'

'No. I assumed it was owned by the estate.'

'It used to be, but apparently Miss Alice's grandfather gave it to Nan's mother. For something…'

'Ah, I see.'

Both women smiled and Elisabeth wondered how many other close connections there might be between the villagers and the Crayfords of previous generations.

'Lucille must be delighted. Are you going to move in too?'

'I don't think it's a good idea. Jennet Sandford may not be the only one who remembers my father. Miss Alice doesn't need to know all that now.'

'No, you're right.'

Melina unlaced her boots and dipped her feet in the stream with a contented sigh. She turned her head to look directly at Elisabeth. 'I expect you want to know what she's been up to.'

'Zillah?'

'Yes, of course, Zillah.'

'Alice says she's still in and around the estate.'

'She didn't mention Stephen?'

'Stephen?'

'Sandford, Jennet and Edmund's son.'

Elisabeth's stomach turned over. 'No…I don't really know him.'

'He's their eldest, born before they were married. That's how she came to be wet-nurse to Miss Alice, but he was looked after by her mother over the other side of Petworth. Anyway, he never really *came back and eventually got a steady job over there.'*

'But he's back now?'

Melina nodded.

Elisabeth's thoughts were racing ahead. 'And she's already singled him out?'

'Lucille hears things now she's in the village. People think she's a bit simple and they're less guarded around her.' Melina stretched her legs out to dry her feet in the sun. 'The talk is that Stephen lost his job from the only place he'd ever worked because he'd become lazy and argumentative over the last year. He went back to the Sandfords because he had nowhere else to go.'

'Do his parents know he's seeing Zillah?'

'Well if they don't, it won't be long before someone tells them. They've been seen walking together outside the village and there's rumours that they knew each other before he came back.'

Elisabeth shook her head. 'How come she's still here? Where's she living if not with Ansell?'

'You'll find this hard to believe, or perhaps not.' Melina reached for one of her boots. 'The Reverend needed someone to clean the church after his previous lady suddenly went down with a terrible case of gout. He fell for the story of a used and abandoned woman and now Zillah has a job and shelter in an outhouse behind the church.'

* * *

Elisabeth took her time walking back and was so lost in her thoughts, she didn't notice Alice coming to meet her until they were only a few yards apart.

'Hello, didn't you see me waving from the upstairs window?'

'No, I'm sorry, I was miles away.' Was this the right time to say what she'd been thinking about? It was tempting, but it was a topic that couldn't be easily explained to Aphra who was sensitive about

not being party to every discussion. No, on balance, Elisabeth decided it would have to wait for a couple of days until Aphra left for London.

'I wanted to walk the last bit with you.' Alice linked arms.

'So, what is it?'

Alice laughed. 'You read me like a book. It's Jennet, have you noticed anything different about her?'

'A little older and slower, perhaps. Aren't we all?'

'Well, yes, and she's not far off sixty, but it's not that. She's just not herself. I'm worried she might have something seriously wrong and she doesn't want me to know. I couldn't bear to lose her.'

'Do you want me to talk to her?'

'Yes, of course I do; she trusts you. I expect she'll tell you because she'll be wanting one of your remedies. Mind you, she'll swear you to secrecy.'

'Which you won't expect me to keep…'

'Don't look at me like that. You know it's for her own good.'

Elisabeth gave her a hug and planted a kiss on her cheek. 'I'm teasing. Leave it to me.'

Unlike Alice, she wasn't at all concerned about any potential illness, her sixth sense would have already alerted her to that. No, after what Melina had just told her, Elisabeth had a good idea about what ailed Jennet.

* * *

'Oh, Miss Elisabeth, you startled me. I didn't hear you open the door.' Jennet clasped a hand to her bosom and heaved herself out of the nursing chair.

'I didn't want to wake them.'

'Anne's still well away, I've never known such a good sleeper.' She went over to the crib. 'Your little one, on the other hand, woke a little while ago and seems happy to just chunter away to herself.'

Both women took a moment to listen before Elisabeth picked up her baby and sat on the floor with her. 'She's been a good girl, then?'

Jennet sank into the nursing chair once more. 'Really, no trouble at all.'

'What about your own grandchildren, Jennet, when do you get to see them?'

'Well, Martha's aren't babies anymore and they're living a way off. I see them every now and then but it's not the same.' She wrinkled her nose and gave a tight smile.

If Jennet knew the real reason Martha and her family had chosen to move away, she'd never said, and Alice had never let on that she knew her first husband had fathered Martha's eldest child.

'Do your boys have children too?'

'One of them does, lovely children they are. They all live on his wife's family farm and I see them quite a bit, but I was never needed, if you know what I mean.'

Elisabeth nodded. She understood completely and, not for the first time, cursed the man who'd made Alice's life a misery and robbed this woman of the sort of family life she deserved. She put Céleste face down on the floor with a rattle and a knitted ball, and waited.

'You knew I had another son then?'

'Yes.'

'He's a bit of a worry, that one.' She paused, then decided to carry on. 'Well, you most likely know he didn't grow up here like the others then. My mother looked after him.' She looked down at her hands, folding one over the other. 'But he's back now because he has nowhere else to go and…'. She broke off, her chin wobbling.

Elisabeth knelt down in front of her and reached for her hands. 'I'm listening Jennet, if you want to talk. Or I can go…'

'No,' she shook her head quickly, 'no, I've got to talk to someone and I don't want to worry Miss Alice.'

Although Elisabeth already knew the bare bones of the story, listening to it was still hard. It wasn't even a particularly unusual story, but witnessing the hurt and guilt that this woman had stored up for years was difficult to hear.

'The timing was bad, you see. We weren't yet married and I fell pregnant just as Edmund left to start his job here as a groom; it was all he ever wanted to do, work with horses. But, as luck would have it, just as my baby was being weaned, Edmund got me in here as wet nurse so we could be together, and so I left Stephen with my mother.'

Elisabeth said nothing; so far this was common practice.

Jennet carried on. 'I was young and it was stupid of me, but I was so desperate to be here that I lied and told Mrs Crayford that Stephen had died. I didn't think she'd want a strange baby around.'

'Did she ever find out?'

'Oh, I owned up eventually, once we were comfortable with each other, and they couldn't have been kinder, giving us the use of a tiny cottage in the village when we got wed so we could be a proper family. The trouble was it was too late then to change everything. My father was long gone and once I'd left home my mother was on her own and still not forty, so Stephen became the son she never had. They doted on each other, too much if I'm honest, and I became like a big sister. He visited often at first but he never wanted to stay and by the time Daniel and Martha came along, it was just once or twice a year.'

'Whatever you did, whether you took him or left him with your mother, you would have always worried you were doing the wrong thing.' Elisabeth picked up Céleste and rocked her.

'Yes, but it's that lie that stays with me.'

'And now he's back?'

'Aye, and he's changed, something's happened to turn his head since my mother died. The quiet, kind boy I knew has become a bitter, angry man, and I don't know why. Suddenly, everything's

my fault; I never wanted him, I abandoned him, I left him to care for my mother because I couldn't be bothered. It's also my fault he never married or had children apparently, and I expect it's my fault that he lost his job and my mother's home too, although I'm beggared if I know how. It's as if a malignant stranger has come to live with us. Edmund and I are trying to help him but there's no opening for him here and the way he is now, I can't see him getting one.'

Knowing only too well what, or who, had turned his head, Elisabeth was at a loss to offer words of comfort. 'I'm so sorry...'

Jennet stood up and shook her head as if to rid it of all the worries. 'I shouldn't go on about it. We'll sort something out, I dare say.'

'What does Edmund say about it?'

Jennet blew out a sigh and looked heavenwards. 'He says there's only so much you can do for a thirty-odd year-old man who blames others for his own failings.'

* * *

Questions, so many questions. Elisabeth turned them over in her mind as she went back to her own room to think.

There must be a reason Zillah was so intent on staying close to Oakwood Grange; did something happen generations back? If so, did that mean she wanted to ruin the estate or possess it? In the end, did any of that matter? Melina was firmly of the opinion that it didn't, and that this place was merely the battleground for a fight between Good and Evil.

That Zillah had great powers was not in question. Even if she'd wanted to, it would have been beyond Elisabeth to so infect men like Ansell and Stephen that they would become mere puppets to her cause, and she knew it wouldn't stop there. If ever Zillah were to become resident on the estate, Joseph would surely be next in her sights. And then what?

~ 22 ~
Spring 1720

'What's happened to your hand?'

He'd been trying to hide it, but given it was blue and so swollen he was having difficulty even holding a knife, far less using it, everyone had noticed.

Anne and I both saw Tobias shoot a warning glance at Young Alice who became more interested in the food on her plate.

'Tobias, I asked...'

'Yes, I heard you, Father, I'm sorry. It's nothing, really...'

'Well, accidents happen, but you ought to get it seen to, it looks sore. Surely there's no need for you to get so involved with the physical side of the farm now you've experienced it all, especially as your left arm is still not strong. We should have a word with Gabe, Anne, don't you think?'

There was silence around the table. Anne looked directly at Tobias who put down his knife and pushed his plate way.

'It wasn't an accident, Father.' He held out his hand so Samuel could see the damage. 'It was something I meant to do and it made me feel better than I've felt in months. I most certainly don't regret it.'

It was Samuel's turn to lay down his cutlery as realisation dawned.

'He had it coming, Father.' Young Alice quickly leapt to her brother's defence. 'If you'd seen how...'

'Enough from you, Alice.' He pointed at her without taking

his eyes off his son. 'Are you telling me you got into a fight with someone, Tobias?'

'Not anyone, Father. Hadleigh, and it wasn't exactly a fight because that would imply that he fought back. The truth is I punched him, several times actually.'

Samuel's face reddened alarmingly and he shook off Anne's hand on his arm. 'I'm assuming this happened whilst you were staying with Sophia?'

'Not at their house, obviously. We were at the fair.'

'When you were supposed to be escorting young ladies. Were they witness to this event or did you leave them alone whilst you sought fit to assault a peer of the realm? What on earth were you thinking? Are you trying to get yourself locked up?'

Samuel's napkin landed in his food. 'I want you in my study, now.'

Anne rose too.

'Just Tobias, Anne.'

* * *

There must have been a collective holding of breath because the three of us let out a huge sigh once the study door slammed shut.

'Tell us what happened at the fair, Alice.'

'Well, firstly, it was wrong of Father to say Tobias left us unchaperoned because he didn't. Sophia's friend, Rose, and her two brothers, Matthew and Gerald were with us.' She paused. 'I think Rose is very taken with Tobias...'

'Just get to the point, Alice.' Anne rarely lost her temper but all the signs were there now.

Alice closed her eyes briefly before bowing to the inevitable. 'We'd all had a lovely time and were just thinking of heading back to Aunt Céleste's for supper. Anyway, Sophia saw him first with his friend and it wasn't long before Tobias noticed them too. It all happened very quickly. He said to Matthew, 'Stay here, wait for me,' and then he was off, after Hadleigh.'

'So, it was two against one?'

'Not really. I swear, Mama, they were on their way to the paddock and, as soon as they saw Tobias, they made a run for their horses. Matthew couldn't resist following and saw what happened but Gerald did stay with us, I promise.'

Alice reached for her water glass before continuing. 'Hadleigh had the whip out because he was desperate to get away but the lad wouldn't let go of the reins until he had his penny. That's when Tobias dragged him off his horse and set about him. I don't know whether he'd ever punched anyone before but Matthew was quite impressed.'

It seems he wasn't the only one. And, I admit, I felt nothing but pride.

'Did Matthew join in?' I asked. I had visions of a free-for-all.

'No, I think he would have done if Hadleigh's friend had tried to help, but he didn't.'

I heard later from Céleste, whose information came from Matthew via Sophia, that Tobias had punched Hadleigh three times – once for Frances, once for the baby and once for himself. He'd called him a snivelling coward, yelling at him to stand up and fight but, luckily, Matthew dragged him off just in time. Tobias was in such a fury he might well have killed him.

'Was Hadleigh badly injured?' I asked only out of concern for Tobias and what might follow.

'I don't think so. He did manage to stand up but there was quite a bit of blood on his face.' Realising the mistake she'd made, she hurried on, 'I confess we did catch up with them, Mama, but only when it was all over.'

I'm not sure if either Anne or I believed her but it was immaterial now.

'So, that was it, nothing else you need to tell me?'

'Hadleigh was spluttering something and Tobias turned back. He didn't attack him again but he said something like 'The next time you send three men to do your dirty work, you'd better make sure you have your facts right.' And then he said Hadleigh would have done better looking closer to home for the father of Frances's baby.'

'Oh God.' Anne held her head in her hands.

Alice bit her lip.

I put an arm round Anne's shoulders. 'How many other witnesses were there, Alice, can you remember?'

'I can't recall seeing anyone other than the ostlers and the few lads paid to mind the horses. They were quite enjoying the spectacle, I think. We passed some folk on our way out of the paddock, but that was all.'

'Are you sure?' Anne looked up.

'Yes, Mama. May I leave now?'

Anne nodded. Lost in our own thoughts in the ensuing silence, I was the one who spoke first.

'I see the hand of my granddaughter in all this, I'm afraid.'

She pondered this for a moment. 'How?'

'I suspect the invitation to spend a few days with Sophia and attend the fair was made because she was well aware that Hadleigh usually attends. According to Céleste it's one of the high points of the social calendar for everyone over that way.'

'You think Sophia and Alice arranged this between them?'

'I wouldn't put it passed them. They were horrified by what happened to Frances and I think they both knew Tobias needed to find some outlet for his rage otherwise he'd go mad. I note he's much calmer now.'

'But Samuel will be furious. Tobias promised him that he wouldn't make things worse by going after Hadleigh.'

'Mmm...as far as I recall, Anne, all he promised was to stay away from Hadleigh's estate.'

Anne closed her eyes. She looked totally deflated.

* * *

As far as the house, farm and estate are concerned, Samuel has no role other than to listen to his wife and offer advice if it's asked for. When it comes to the law, however, Samuel is on very sure ground indeed, being extremely well regarded and not without influence.

We didn't see Tobias and Samuel again until the following evening by which time Samuel had taken complete charge of the situation and assured Anne that their son was not about to be clapped in irons never to be seen again.

In cases like this, Samuel's unthreatening, gentlemanly demeanour serves him well and belies the sharp, intelligent mind that relishes a challenge. Admittedly, it takes some time, but breaking a man down by sensible degrees with such quiet, reasonable argument is his forte. After commiserating with Hadleigh over the damage to his face, Samuel was at pains to agree that Tobias's behaviour was absolutely beyond the pale but felt duty bound to delicately point out that any retaliatory action on Hadleigh's part might not be in his interests. Who would want their private life aired in public?

'Indignant, completely unabashed, and with some spluttering due to the swellings, Hadleigh gave me the standard defence that whilst wife-beating and a husband's adultery were perfectly legal, a wife's adultery most certainly was not.' Samuel was enjoying repeating the encounter. 'Naturally, I conceded that this was generally the case and I absolutely understood how difficult it must have been.'

'How did you manage to stay so calm?'

'Practise, Alice. It does no good to let one's feelings override the law.' He smiled at her, this daughter of his, whose feelings would always be an open book. 'Anyway, it was at this point that he magnanimously informed me that he might accept a grovelling public apology if I could persuade Tobias that that was the best he could hope for.'

'I would have rather lost my right arm...'

'I know son, but this offer was to be expected. No doubt he'd been told that I would insist you accept but, with some apparent sadness, I explained that you were hot-headed and more than prepared to go to court. And I felt it was time to warn his Lordship that, quite possibly, there were things in his private life he may not want airing in public – like attempted murder, for example.'

Alice clapped her hands with glee. 'What did he say?'

'He just stared at me. I continued to explain that attempted murder of an innocent man, or even a guilty one for that matter, even by a peer of the realm, was an offence whether or not it was perpetrated by himself or by others at his instigation. I quoted the Act to add credence to what was, I admit, a somewhat moot point. He blustered and denied it, of course, but I assured him that there were reliable witnesses to both the offence and the orders to his servants.'

That was only partly true, I knew. Frances's loyal maid, who'd helped her escape and fled herself that night, was prepared to swear that she'd overheard Hadleigh's instructions to his men. Gabe, though, would have had trouble picking out the attackers.

'I also made it clear that if Tobias was forced to defend himself in court, then he would be obliged to protect his own reputation by naming the father of Frances's baby. And that was when I knew I had him. I'd seen that same defeated look on the face of others once they'd realised that it wasn't worth tossing the dice. The odds were against him. His grandfather wouldn't tolerate that sort of family scandal.' Samuel allowed himself a self-satisfied little smile.

'And you didn't even have to produce your ace card.'

Anne and Alice looked from Tobias to Samuel, puzzled.

Realising he shouldn't have mentioned it, Tobias looked to his father.

'I'm keeping that for later; it's something we may have to use if Hadleigh ever goes back on his word.' He refused to elaborate any further.

I knew he was right to hold off; offences against the Buggery Act of 1533 were notoriously difficult to prove, even though Jack Hoyle fell foul of it and was eventually jailed. It would have been worth mentioning though, just to see his face.

Surprisingly, this whole episode, which one might have expected to cause a rift between father and son, has proved to be quite the opposite. A mutual respect has now replaced the irritableness that was common in all their previous exchanges and the household is more comfortable for it. It has made Anne very happy, especially as it appears that Charles will be staying up at Oxford for the foreseeable future.

* * *

A few anxious weeks later, when nothing more was heard about the events at the fair, we all breathed a sigh of relief as things slowly returned to normal.

According to Céleste, local gossip has it that Hadleigh has been banished back to the continent for a prolonged stay, no doubt with instructions to find a more amenable bride. From his mansion in Kent, Hadleigh's grandfather, still very much the patriarch of the family, has apparently heard whispers about his grandson that he would prefer to keep quiet.

What happened to Frances will never leave Tobias, I know that, but he is definitely more at peace now and is devoting himself to farm work. He and Gabe are thicker than ever. Having practically worshipped the ground she walked on, Gabe's been telling him how his grandmother Alice was just about his age when she set about changing the old working practices, introducing different crops and improving the livestock.

'She knew what she was doing, your Grandma, always planning ahead.'

Tobias was relating this conversation whilst I was manipulating his mended arm; it was still weaker than it should be.

'I think old Gabe was more than a little bit in love with my grandmother, the way he talks about her.'

I laughed. 'He wouldn't have been the only one; the old manager, Henry Durling would have done anything for her as well.'

'I think he was trying to tell me…. woah, careful, that hurts.'

'Sorry. Tell you what?'

'I need to be thinking further ahead than I am.'

'Right.'

'Well, what do you think? You knew her better than anyone.'

'Tobias, I know nothing about farming. What does your mother have to say?'

'I don't think she has the same pioneering spirit Grandmother had. She's not a great one for change.'

'No, you're probably right, but perhaps Gabe was talking about himself. He's nearly seventy, Tobias, the man deserves a rest. Soon you'll need to employ an assistant who you can train up to manager.'

'Yes, I've been thinking about that. I'm going to have to get Mother to do the accounts again as well, it's too much for me at the moment.'

Once I'd finished with him, I sat for a while thinking how to help, knowing Anne would most certainly not want to play bookkeeper once more.

Lately, I'd been worried that Young Alice's education, which started so promisingly, has now been overtaken by balls, fashion and finding the perfect husband, in company with Sophia. It's natural, I know. Still, having tutored both girls for five years until they reached 15, I would hate for it all be wasted. They are both bright and teaching them was one of the most fulfilling and joyous times of my life. It also cemented what I hoped would be a lifelong friendship between my granddaughter and the granddaughter of my dearest friend.

Was it unthinkable that Young Alice might take over the accounts for Tobias? Clearly, it's not something Sophia would be allowed to do but then my daughter's family circumstances are completely different. I could see no good reason why Alice shouldn't help in the family business. Samuel wouldn't agree but, given that Anne had done the job herself until recently, he would need a very good reason to object.

Tobias was not hopeful and laughed as he wished me good luck. I broached the subject with his sister anyway.

'You're more than capable, Alice, and I see no reason why you shouldn't help your brother.'

She said nothing for a while. I think it came as something of a shock.

'Is it that you think it beneath you?' I prompted.

'Tante, that's not a very nice thing to say.'

I shrugged. 'It was a question, not a statement, and you haven't answered.'

'No, no, of course it isn't. It's just that I expect to be married soon and then I...

The gentle, loving part of me couldn't let her stammer on. '...and then you won't be here anymore, I understand. I'm not suggesting you become a spinster and devote yourself to the farm. Who's the lucky man, anyway?'

She gave me a sideways glance. 'No one in particular, at the moment.'

I smiled. 'Alice, you could do these accounts in your sleep, or at least in an odd hour or two. Were it not for my eyesight, I'd do it. It's nothing very arduous and think how useful it will be when you have an entire household to run. I guarantee it won't interfere too much with your social life and it would be a great help to your mother and brother. Tobias said you wouldn't want to do it, but think about it, that's all I ask.'

Naturally, the sibling challenge was too much to resist. And despite all the tutting at the state of the entries, the mess of bills and Tobias's handwriting, it soon became apparent that organisation and precision were Alice's great strengths, even though they threatened to make her insufferable at times.

With a little more time at his disposal, Tobias had a success of his own. Accompanied by Gabe, he took a trip to the fens in Norfolk where news of a plough imported from the Netherlands was rumoured to be far superior to the one currently in use. Pulled by just two horses instead of four, quicker and handled easily by one man, it was the talk of all the estate owners, but there were none to be had. Undeterred, and armed with his own detailed drawings and measurements, Tobias came back home brimming with enthusiasm and a determination to make his own version.

What eventually emerged from the blacksmith and carpenter's shop not only looked the part but worked even better than they'd hoped, due mainly to Tobias's draughtsmanship, a hitherto unrecognised talent. That one episode alone marked his passage from boy to man, and pupil to farmer.

She has been absent for a while now, but the next time I feel her presence, I shall tell his grandmother, unless she already knows.

~ 23 ~
Summer 1677

After two weeks away from London, Aphra was desperate to return to put the finishing touches to her adaptation of a play by Molière. Under normal circumstances, Elisabeth would have accompanied her – but these were not normal circumstances.

'Do you think Joseph would mind if Céleste and I stay a little longer?'

Surprised, Alice's face lit up. 'Mind? Of course not. I think he has to go up to town soon anyway. He could take Aphra in the carriage and you can keep me company for a little longer. It makes perfect sense.'

'What about Jean-Michel; would he mind?' Aphra raised an eyebrow.

The truth was that Jean-Michel probably would mind very much, and it would be difficult to explain why she needed to extend the visit. Aphra knew this as well as Elisabeth.

'I'll write to him, Aphra, if you wouldn't mind giving him the letter?'

Alice looked from one friend to the other. 'If it's going to cause an argument, Elisabeth, don't stay just for me…'

'No, it isn't. One more week isn't going to matter.'

Silently, Elisabeth prayed that one more week would be enough.

* * *

As Joseph hated to journey on his own and was keen to have Aphra's company, the trip was organised early for Aphra's convenience. Alice tackled Elisabeth even as the carriage was rolling down the drive.

'Are things not right between you and Jean-Michel?'

'We're fine, Alice.' Even as she said it, it occurred to her that it wasn't entirely true. He'd been a little distant since Céleste was born, or was it that she had been not quite herself? She wasn't unduly worried; a baby changed things.

As if reading her mind, Alice said, 'Joseph always says I spend far too much time with Anne, but then he didn't even recognise his own mother until he was about twelve.'

Elisabeth laughed. 'I'm sure that's not true.'

'Ask him yourself, although I grant you he might have exaggerated.' As their smiles faded, a slightly awkward pause remained.

It was time, but Elisabeth wasn't looking forward to this conversation.

She threaded an arm through Alice's as they walked back to the house. 'I have a good reason for asking to stay.' She took a deep breath. 'I'll start with Jennet who, you'll be relieved to hear, is not suffering from any ailment. What is worrying her though, is Stephen, and he should be worrying you, too.'

A little frown appeared on Alice's face.

'Stephen's seeing Zillah, although I'm fairly sure Jennet and Edmund don't know that yet.'

The frown deepened. 'Have you seen them?'

'No, don't ask me how I know, but I think he's been with her for some time, probably even before either of them came back here. Just think for a moment, Alice, how Ansell changed when he was with her. Everyone rolled their eyes at how coupling with a woman like Zillah had turned such a hard-working, patient man into the demanding, difficult person he became.'

'And you think she now has the same effect on Stephen?'

Elisabeth nodded. 'She's tried to keep it secret until he's absolutely under her control, which it seems he now is as he's making life a misery for poor Jennet and Edmund. There's no doubt she's chosen her victims well; despite both Ansell and Stephen being big, physically strong men, they're weak when it comes to other matters. But don't be fooled, it is not normal behaviour for decent men like them to behave the way they have, no matter how besotted they are with a woman.'

'When you say, 'not normal'…'

'She's like me, Alice, or rather the opposite of me; she has powerful gifts but doesn't use them for good. She's dangerous, but I don't know how dangerous yet.'

'You think Stephen's under some sort of spell, just to cause trouble for the sake of it?'

'Only she can tell us why she's doing it and I doubt she'll do that, but I'm sure her aim is to try to settle on this estate any way she can.'

'For what reason?'

Elisabeth shrugged.

'What are you not telling me?'

'I don't know whether she's determined to ruin this place or possess it, but my fear is it's one or the other. Or perhaps both, who knows?'

Alice was silent for the longest time, taking it all in, before turning to face Elisabeth, her eyes wide.

'Joseph sees no harm in her.'

It was Elisabeth's turn to remain silent but she fixed her eyes on Alice.

'Oh, God in Heaven, Elisabeth…'

'He may not be able to help you, Alice, but I'm here.'

'Do you think she knows about you?'

'Oh, she knows. The first time she clapped eyes on me at your wedding, she knew. And I knew her, too.'

'At the wedding? You didn't say anything…'

'Because it would have unsettled you at a time in your life when you didn't need to be unsettled. And because there was no point worrying you if it was to come to nothing.' Elisabeth put an arm around Alice and pulled her close. 'You are my dearest friend, and rest assured there will never be a time when you need me and I'm not here.'

* * *

When Alice heard first-hand the upset Stephen had caused, it affected her deeply; she and Jennet had always been close and she berated her for not saying something sooner. Edmund had tried talking sense to his son but Stephen's attitude had become so physically threatening, insisting he was 'owed' the right to settle in the Sandford's cottage, that they'd become frightened of him. He also felt he was entitled to take over as Head Groom once Edmund retired and expected Edmund to recommend him to Mr. Rawlinson.

It showed how little he knew about the workings of the estate if he thought Joseph ran everything, or perhaps it was Zillah's plan to outmanoeuvre Alice. As luck would have it though, Joseph was in London.

Alice was rarely called upon to engage, dismiss or discipline the workers directly; Henry Durling usually carried out her wishes which were, in any event, a joint decision. This meeting with Stephen, however, was not about to be delegated.

Sitting stiffly behind her office desk, with Durling standing close by, and dressed in a manner underlining exactly who was in charge, Alice listened to what Stephen had to say.

'I sympathise with your situation Stephen, but your father has *many more years in him and, when he does give up his post, that position has been promised to the head stable lad. That is the way we do things here. I'm sorry, but we currently don't need any workers. You will have to leave the cottage soon and look further afield for employment.'*

Having entered the study, slightly stooped with cap in hand, the very model of a supplicant with slicked down hair and clean clothes, his manner changed in a couple of seconds. Straightening up, he took a step forward, the softness in his face completely disappearing and it was then that Alice felt the underlying rage.

'Perhaps you forget my parents have given your family loyal service here for over thirty years, Mrs. Rawlinson, and there's plenty of room in that cottage.'

Henry couldn't help himself, 'Mind your manners now, Sandford', but was silenced by Alice's hand.

A tic had started up in Stephen's left eye. 'Weren't my brother and sister raised here?'

'Yes, that's true, and I certainly don't forget your parents' loyal service.' Alice was not to be thrown. 'But, other than retired workers, there are no other adults living on this estate who don't have a position here and I'm not prepared to make an exception. I'm sorry if you can't accept that but I'll not change my mind.'

Stephen narrowed his eyes and took another step forward, practically leaning over her desk, breathing heavily. Alice stood abruptly to face him, signalling the interview was over and motioned to a concerned Durling to stay where he was.

'I have nowhere else to go. Do you understand that?' He said it slowly to add emphasis. 'Give me a month or two and I'll show you and Mr. Rawlinson what I can do. I'm sure he could find something for me.'

Were it not for Elisabeth's dire warnings about Zillah, and Jennet's misery, the man looked so wretched that Alice knew she might have given in. Instead, she took a purse from a drawer and passed it across the desk. 'I'm truly sorry, Stephen. This should see you right for a month or so until you find somewhere else.'

Picking up the purse, he weighed it in his hand approvingly before stepping back, shifting his gaze from Alice to Durling and back again. With a little nod, he sniggered. 'Well…you are desperate to get rid of me.'

He replaced his cap and left without another word, leaving the door wide open.

In the brief silence that followed, Alice fell back in the chair with a loud sigh, feeling her beating heart even up in her throat. The atmosphere reminded her of what Jennet and Edmund must have been living with recently. Durling moved to stand next to her chair.

'You did the right thing, Miss Alice.' He was another of the old guard who could never get his head around calling her Madam or Mrs. Rawlinson.

'Thank you, Henry. Just make sure he's gone by tomorrow and tell Edmund what's just happened. I'll tell Jennet she's to stay here tonight.'

* * *

Two days after Stephen left the estate, Jennet and Edmund went down with a particularly itchy rash. It was inconvenient rather than anything else and nothing Elisabeth couldn't fix, but still, it was a reminder that Zillah was not at all happy to be thwarted a second time. She was watching carefully but instinctively felt that Zillah was too shrewd to wreak such vengeance on Alice and might very well have something more subtle in mind.

She didn't have long to wait.

At morning meal, the kitchen maid brought in the curd cakes and a large jug. She laid them both down next to Alice.

'I'm sorry, Mistress, but Cook says to tell you that there's a problem in the dairy and this is the last of the milk for the moment.'

Alice peered into the jug. 'Is there some for the babies, Prudence, or is this it?'

'That's all there is, Mistress.'

'Do you want oats, Elisabeth?'

'No, I'm quite content with bread and cheese, and those cakes.'

'Well, so am I, Prudence.' She lifted the heavy jug and handed it back. 'I suggest you keep that for the babies. What's the problem, do you know?'

'I don't, but I know Mrs. Sandford has gone over to see if she can help.' She bobbed and scurried back to the kitchen.

'There was enough milk there for them today, and anyway, Jennet will have sorted it out by tomorrow.' Alice took a curd cake and passed the plate over to Elisabeth. 'What are you planning to do today?'

'I'm not sure. What are you doing?'

'Henry and I are riding out to inspect the cottages for repairs; it's a while since we did it. Why don't you come with us? I bet you haven't ridden out for ages.'

'Thank you, but I don't want to leave Céleste again, especially as Jennet's needed in the dairy. If the trap's free, though…?'

'Yes, it should be. I'll tell Edmund to get it ready for you.'

* * *

Edmund made a great fuss of strapping Céleste's basket on to the passenger seat before allowing Elisabeth to set off. It would have taken an earthquake to shift it.

To him, Elisabeth was an enigma. Undoubtedly a woman of quality, with her education and fine manners, but someone who had so few airs and graces he often found himself being overfamiliar. Not that she seemed to notice.

Of course, Miss Alice had always driven the trap by herself around the estate but then how many women ran a place like this on their own, anyway? And now here was Miss Elisabeth, not only taking the trap into the village but minding her own baby at the same time.

He had to admire it, but he didn't understand it.

En route to the village, Elisabeth stopped off at old Jonas's cottage to see if their old milker had any problems.

'No, Madam. Ol' Betty don't give much these days but there's nowt wrong wi' it. Do you want some?' He hobbled to the fence for support, pipe clamped between his few remaining teeth.

'Thank you, Jonas, but we'll manage today and whatever is the problem will most likely be solved tomorrow.'

'Well, tell Miss Alice, just in case it isn't, eh? We don't want those bairns going short.' He removed the pipe and used it to wave goodbye.

'I will, and thank you.'

She drove on to the village, allowing the sure-footed little pony to set his own relaxed pace; the rhythmical sway soothing Céleste into a light sleep. Drawing to a halt a short distance from Chicken Nan's old cottage, Elisabeth stepped down and hitched the pony before carrying her daughter through the garden gate to the rear door.

'We knew you were coming today! Mother's never wrong.' Lucille clapped her hands excitedly before holding out her arms for the waking baby. Elisabeth handed her over with a laugh.

'Look, Mother, those eyes and the hair. Isn't she beautiful?'

Melina emerged from the back room, wiping her hands, and peered over her daughter's shoulder. 'Naturally, she looks like her mother.'

The cooing and baby chat didn't last long. Whilst Lucille played with the baby on a blanket in the back room, Melina and Elisabeth got down to more serious matters.

'If Lucille is right, Zillah is beside herself with fury, upsetting more folk than ever.'

Elisabeth nodded. 'I know, so furious in fact that Jennet and Edmund are only just getting over a nasty rash. If they connect it to her, they haven't said, but I have no doubts.'

'It seems even the Reverend may be having second thoughts about her. There hasn't been much work done apparently since Stephen left.'

'He has gone then? I wondered if perhaps he'd stayed around the village.'

'No, he's gone. Rumour has it that he came into a bit of money and, whether he was loth to share it or Zillah refused to go with him, no one knows. And it seems there was a bit of a to-do between him and Ansell before he left.

They paused for a minute, amused to listen to Lucille chatting to the baby, seemingly content with the odd gurgle in reply.

'Tell me, has Lucille bought any milk today?'

'I don't know, I'll ask her. Do you want some for the baby?'

'No, she doesn't really need any; I still have some.' A hand fluttered up to her breast.

'You're feeding her yourself?' Melina's eyes wide. 'I expect that causes a stir up at the Grange?'

'No, it doesn't, only Miss Alice and Jennet know. Anyway, it's only a night and morning comfort feed which, I must confess, I shall be sad to give up. I know Miss Alice is thinking of doing the same if she has another baby, although Mr. Rawlinson may have other ideas.' She pulled a face.

'Well, I'm sure it's the best thing for the babies, I wouldn't want to trust a wet nurse.' Melina stood and poked her head into the next room. 'Lucille, did you buy milk today?'

'No, I didn't need any, but the women there were grumbling the delivery was late.'

'That's because there's a problem in the dairy.'

'What sort of problem?'

'The milk's gone sour, and if there's none for the Grange and none for the village, it does look like the whole lot may be affected. Jennet's gone to see if she can help.

Melina didn't comment, but her expression made words unnecessary.

Elisabeth's face fell. 'I was hoping you'd put my mind at ease. It's her, isn't it?'

'Possibly, although we know so little about her and what she can do.'

Having pooled their knowledge, and with a promise from Melina to let her know if there was anything more to report, Elisabeth felt it unwise to stay any longer. I quick visit to Lucille to convey condolences for the loss of Chicken Nan would be understood by villagers, but anything else would be considered odd.

Zillah, though, didn't consider it odd. She waited until Elisabeth was nearing the trap, then crossed the lane and followed.

It seemed as if the little pony had no sooner clapped eyes on Elisabeth than he started fidgeting in the shafts and snorting, ears laid right back, eyes huge.

'Hey, Boy, what's the matter?'

Reaching for the bridle with her free hand, she tried to calm him and stop the trap from swaying. It didn't work, and by now all her senses were on alert. Holding Céleste tight, she turned, knowing what to expect.

'You look as if you could do with a helping hand, Madam.' Zillah held out her arms. 'Why don't I take your baby whilst you get up?'

The innocent request was belied by the mocking twitch at the corners of her mouth, enjoying every bit of Elisabeth's discomfort.

'I can manage.'

'It doesn't look like it.'

'Well, once you've move on, I won't have any trouble. It's clear the pony doesn't like you.'

'Is that so?' Zillah moved a step closer to the pony. Boy blew even louder. 'Perhaps you're right – and he's not the only one, is he?'

Laughing, she craned her neck trying unsuccessfully for a peek at Céleste, even as Elisabeth hugged her close and turned away. 'I'll leave you alone with your daughter then.'

She flounced off, but couldn't resist calling out over her shoulder, 'Pretty name, Céleste…'.

The victory didn't last long. As Elisabeth was tucking her baby into the basket on the trap, Zillah was face down in the mud, wondering how she got there.

Although it had been years since Elisabeth had reason to summon the force, it was gratifying to see she hadn't lost her touch.

* * *

'Did she threaten you?' Alice was pacing up and down, already worried about the herd. Jennet hadn't been able to find anything wrong with the cattle and there'd never been a problem with cleanliness in the dairy.

'No, she's far too subtle for that. It's all little inferences to let us know how clever she is, 'I know where you are, who you've been seeing, your baby is a girl and her name is Céleste', all designed to unsettle.'

'Well, it's unsettled me. And you think this milk thing is her doing?'

'Fairly sure, especially as old Jonas's milker hasn't suffered and nor has the blacksmith's cow. Whatever it is, it's only affecting the ones in your paddock.'

Alice looked the picture of misery.

'Don't worry, I've prodded the hornet's nest and it'll be over soon.' Hopefully, she added to herself.

~ 24 ~
Summer 1722

I have felt this last winter to be very long; not especially harsh, just long, and made longer by a miserable, wet Spring. I must admit it's taken its toll on me for the first time. Having been hitherto blessed with a robust constitution that belies my age, I've often wondered if this energy is connected to the other quirk in my make-up, which I still refuse to name. Predictably, family and friends teasingly accuse me of forgetting my true birth year, but I don't forget. I'm 79 years old.

It's clear, however, that time is catching up with me, or at least with my knees and hands which I can no longer rely upon as I was wont to do, even though my remedies somewhat soften the condition.

Still, summer is definitely here now, and the view from my bedroom window is glorious. The paddock grass is the sort of green only seen at this time of the year; so bright it almost seems unreal, and everything is coming to life at once as though nature has been holding its breath until the time was just right. Bird song is everywhere and I can even smell the soil. Leaning out to my left, there's the blue haze of bluebells over in Home Wood and my heart aches a little, knowing that I may never get another opportunity to visit what I still think of as Fox Wood, to smell the heady scents of wild garlic and woodbine on a summer's evening.

I need to give myself a good talking-to. Although a little melancholy may be acceptable, dwelling on infirmities is not when old age is not granted to everyone, and neither is a loving family and a life free from insecurity. I remind myself that no one wants to hear a privileged old woman's complaints and, as I may not see many more of them, I would do well to enjoy everything this summer has to offer.

Time has also led to changes on the farm this year with Gabe finally deciding that it no longer needs him. Happy that he's done his best by Tobias's grandmother, he's confident that it's now safe in the hands of a different generation. Tobias has grown in stature and earned the respect of everyone, not just Gabe, for he no longer views the estate as a job or an obligation but as a passion and a challenge. It helps that he has found Hendrick, or rather that Hendrick found him.

They first met over a year ago when he and Gabe took the trip to East Anglia to see the new plough in action, draining the boggy fields of the fens. Hendrick was one of the contractors who'd been brought over from the Netherlands. Of a similar age, they got on well from the outset and Tobias left him with an invitation to call should he find himself passing through the county. Barely a month later, Hendrick turned up, reluctant to return home and looking for work. He is now Tobias's assistant and will one day, no doubt, take over as manager. They make a strong team.

Happy to relinquish the manager's cottage, even though both Anne and Tobias insisted he could stay for as long as he wished, Gabe had made up his mind. He didn't want them to feel he was looking over their shoulders and, anyway, he had other plans. He was going to live with Lucille in her cottage; the cottage that used to be Chicken Nan's where she'd once taught a very young Gabe everything he needed to know about keeping poultry. That was nearly sixty years ago and it seems things have now come full circle with the ever-patient Lucille finally getting the only man she's ever wanted. Chicken Nan and Melina would be thrilled to see it, and perhaps they are, who knows?

'Come in.' The knock brought me back to the present, Young Alice's head appearing round my door.

'I've just come to see if you need any help, Tante, before I go to see if I can be useful in the kitchen.'

'No, darling, I'm fine. A little slow today, but I'll be down soon.'

'Well, I'll take that tray if you've finished with it. I don't want you trying to help by carrying it downstairs.' She planted a kiss on my cheek. 'I am so excited about today. It's going to be excellent fun, don't you think? If it's a success, then Tobias says we're going to do it every year. And, who would have thought it? Even Charles agrees it's a splendid idea.' She pulled a comical, surprised face and rolled her eyes.

'Oh, well then…it's guaranteed to be a success.' It was naughty of me to encourage her, but Charles, with his superior air and disdain for all things provincial, deserves no less sometimes. Still, his presence at the event is very welcome; it completes the family and delights his parents, which is all that matters.

'Is he going to play, do you think?'

'Only on the opposing team if Tobias has anything to do with it. My brother takes cricket far too seriously to carry someone like Charles. Even I can throw a ball further than he can.'

I suddenly felt a wave of sympathy for Charles.

'Who's on the opposing team?'

'Rose's charming brothers, Matthew and Gerald – I think you met them when they came over with Sophia once – and a host of villagers. The match is really just the Grange against the villagers and a few outsiders.' She picked up my tray. 'I really must go now, Tante, it's all hands on deck and Cook is in a panic to get everything ready.'

* * *

Tobias and Hendrick had organised the day well. There were so many wanting to play on each side, it was decided to have two wicket-gates, requiring two umpires and two scorers. With Gabe representing the Grange, and a volunteer from the village as umpires, that conveniently left an opening for another scorer in addition to Samuel. Charles was quick to step up, to the relief of all concerned. All he had to do was notch the scoring stick for each run.

For weeks the chosen field had been carefully prepared and the farmhands had put out as many chairs, benches and spare straw bales as they could find. It amused us all to see that their wives had also been involved; a string of colourful flags, made from old rags, was proudly adorning the entrance to the field. I didn't imagine that there would be many village spectators for a cricket match, but I was wrong; the seating was soon full with families, some minding babies rolling around on blankets, and scores of young children playing their own games. It reminded me of the time the villagers used to have an annual fair on the common, sadly never revived after the main organiser died.

Tobias made a little introductory speech, welcoming everyone and hoping they would enjoy the day. An announcement that free refreshments would be available at half time brought a cheer, quickly followed by the expected groan when it was made clear that ale would require a small charge. It was all very good-natured.

'Apart from this friendly event, which we hope to hold every year, our aim is to eventually fashion a team from the best players to represent the village of Upburton, and challenge the likes of the Arundel XI and the Duke of Richmond's XI.'

A huge cheer went up with a chorus of 'Hear, hear'.

'My assistant and I saw that match last year at Bury Hill, and I have to say that we weren't that impressed. So...play well my friends and the next stop might be Bury Hill!'

Another cheer, even louder than the last.

When play got under way, Anne, Céleste and I were mercifully seated in the shade with a splendid view. Young Alice, Sophia and Rose were a little closer to the pitch, their split loyalties ensuring that they cheered everything. The opposing team went in to bat first, which meant that Hendrick had taken up a fielding position close to us. I may be old, but I can still appreciate a handsome man and one would be hard-pressed to find fault with Hendrick. Tall, with broad shoulders and sleeves rolled up to display strong forearms, he moves with such athletic grace it's difficult to take one's eyes from him. Certainly, the girls thought so as he turned to retrieve the ball, flashing a brilliant smile in their direction whilst pushing back a lock of wavy, fair hair, before pitching the ball back to the bowler.

The silence was eventually broken by Sophia. 'My, my, Alice – you didn't tell us how the scenery has improved here of late.'

As my granddaughter had made no attempt to lower her voice, Céleste arched her eyebrows and leaned in to me. 'Really, Maman, I fear she must take after you…'. It was a standing joke, given how alike are mother and daughter.

The three of them made a charming sight, their heads so close together, laughing and clapping without a proper understanding of the rules; the dark hair of Sophia, Alice's chestnut curls and Rose with a thick golden braid. Hendrick was definitely playing to his audience and it made us three older women quite wistful.

At the break for refreshments, Tobias wandered over, wiping his face with a neckerchief.

'Ladies, I trust you're comfortable here. Do you need anything?'

Anne stood, the little frown on her forehead deepening. 'My goodness, Tobias, you're dripping wet. Are you all right?'

'Never better, Mama, don't worry. See…'. He breathed in and out as deeply as he could. 'Surprisingly, not even a tiny wheeze; I'm just not used to running around in the heat, that's all. What do you think of the match?'

Céleste answered quickly, never one to miss an opportunity to tease. 'It appears that their batting is considerably better than your fielding, with the odd exception, of course. Having said that…' and here she grinned, 'we're all enjoying it immensely.'

'Excellent, but we might surprise you yet in the next half. Now, how about something to drink?'

'We sent the girls to see to that and it looks like Mary's already on her way.'

Having relieved Mary of the heavy tray and set it down, Tobias made to go.

'Before you run off, are we going to be told the score?' I don't know much about cricket, but I felt this was probably a key feature.

He waggled a finger at me. 'Never fear, Aunt, Father and Charles are doing a tally as we speak and they'll be announcing it soon. Anyway, I'd better get back to mingling with the village players now...' He waved a hand over his shoulder as he ran off, laughing '...and make sure they've all got some free ale.'

'Well that's a clever ploy; intoxicating the opposition before they go out to field.'

'Oh, no, Céleste, I don't think he meant that.'

'I wasn't serious, Anne. Anyway, I have a suspicion they won't need any help. Hendrick may turn out to be their secret weapon.'

It was ever thus. Anne fell for it every time.

Their daughters, however, are altogether more alike. Now on the cusp of womanhood, they are increasingly forward, frequently opiniated and often a challenge to their fathers. Although I sense Rose is of a similar mind, she is outwardly more reserved and I suspect her upbringing has been rather more rigid.

I've been watching Rose and, as Young Alice once observed, I, too, think she is taken with Tobias. Her eyes rarely strayed from him the whole time he was fielding, apart from the brief Hendrick interlude.

The score was finally announced with no one the wiser about its merit. Céleste nudged me and pointed across the pitch to where a few men were obviously taking wagers.

'I wonder what the odds are, Maman. Who's your money on?'

'I have no idea, and I'm sure they don't either. Still, it adds to the fun, I expect.'

As the Grange team walked out to bat, our three girls were back, clapping every strike made by Tobias who spent so much time acknowledging the applause he was nearly run out. He made a fairly good score but, once out, was swiftly followed by several team-mates and it was looking like a rout until Hendrick stepped up and made hard work for the fielders.

In the end, the victory went to the Grange by the slimmest of margins and, as Tobias cheerfully admitted, 'It's clear the better side lost!' That, of course, went down very well and earned him a round of applause.

He went on. 'This event today has not really been about winners and losers, with apologies to those at the back there wanting to make a penny or two out of it. But what it has told me is that we definitely have the makings of an Upburton team! So, anyone wanting to sign up, who's prepared to practise, please give your name to our Captain over there, Hendrick de Groot.

Thank you, one and all, for making this a memorable event.'

There were three resounding cheers and I swear I've never seen Tobias looking happier, or his parents more proud.

It was then I felt her presence, his grandmother Alice, for the first time in years. My entire body welled up with emotion and I'm not sure if the tears were mine or hers.

* * *

During the game, I'd noticed Lucille sitting on the opposite side of the pitch, and when she rose to leave with the other villagers she made a point of looking at me and tilting her head to one side. I know her well enough to know a signal when I see it; she wants to see me about something.

As luck would have it, our party came across Gabe on our way back to the house and Anne stopped to ask how he was coping with so much leisure time.

'There's precious little of that, Madam. As soon as I've finished one chore, there's at least another two waiting to be done, and when she can't find anything in the cottage, Lucille has me out in the kitchen garden.'

We all laughed, knowing only too well that Gabe wouldn't know what to do if ever he did have an idle moment – and that that had nothing to do with Lucille.

'Speaking of which, Madam,' he turned to address me, 'we have some strange plants growing out there and we were wondering if any of them might be of use to you for your remedies?'

'Well, perhaps I could come over for a look sometime...'

'Yes, you should, Aunt Elisabeth.' Anne was instantly buoyed by what she thought was her own idea. 'Between you and me, Gabe, she doesn't get out nearly enough for her liking and we can't guarantee this weather's going to last. I'll make sure the trap's available for you whenever you want it, and perhaps you can take her for a ride out somewhere too, as long as Lucille gives you some time off.'

This is what old age feels like; little treats to pacify a child. I'm ungrateful, I know, for Anne is nothing but kindness and it's not her fault that old age makes me occasionally scratchy.

Gabe collected me the very next day. We were both a little awkward knowing that we'd conspired in a small deception, but it was only necessary to avoid curiosity about my friendship with Lucille.

Although a close, long-standing friendship, it never allowed her to call me by my name. 'Madame, I'm so pleased you're here.' With her mother, Melina, we would have embraced, but for Lucille it was enough to hold each other's hands. She rattled on before I could speak. 'Isn't it just the perfect day? I have a basket of sweetmeats and some cordial.'

There was no need for any of us to pretend there were herbs to inspect in the garden for Lucille knows as much as I do about plants, so I was still waiting for an explanation.

Gabe stepped in. 'Lucille knows you've been wanting to get back to Top Wood, Fox Wood I think you call it, so we thought today might be a good day.'

As treats go, this was beyond my wildest imaginings; something I'd given up any hope of experiencing again. But it was impossible.

'You are both so kind, and I'm truly grateful, but I'm not sure I'll be able to manage it. I understand it's very overgrown now.'

'Yes, you will, Madame, Gabe's cleared a path off the Thatchling road. It's a straight stroll now through to the clearing, a much shorter route than the one you used from the Grange, and I'll be with you.'

I looked over to Gabe, now knowing exactly how he's been spending his leisure time, and had to bite my lip to hide the emotion. It didn't work and I dashed away the tears before they fell, pulling Lucille into a tight hug which completely took her by surprise. Gabe shuffled his feet.

'I'll drive you to the opening, Madam, and collect you later on. You just take your time and enjoy yourselves, there's no hurry. I'll wait for as long as it takes.' He nodded to let me know it was settled.

I couldn't have refused, even if I'd wanted to, and I most certainly didn't want to. It was the most unexpected and thoughtful gift I've ever received. Immediately, I had a vision of Melina as I'd seen her on that very first day, over 50 years ago, standing on the edge of the clearing, and I knew this was my last chance to go back.

'I'm ready.'

~ 25 ~

Late Summer 1677

E lisabeth rose early, surprised to find no sign of Alice. 'Just a slice of ham and bread, please, Prudence, and a small ale. Have you seen the Mistress this morning?'

'Yes, Madam. I think she's in the dairy.'

Of course, she is, thought Elisabeth, but it won't do her any good.

Alice returned as the kitchen maid was serving Elisabeth.

'No, nothing for me, Prudence.'

She sat down heavily, tossed her bonnet to one side and gave a huge sigh.

'How long have you been up, Alice?'

'A while, I couldn't sleep. I was hoping the milk might have improved as they moved the cattle yesterday.'

Elisabeth said nothing but pushed her plate towards Alice.

'No, I can't, I'll be sick.' She pushed the plate back. 'There's something you're not telling me, Elisabeth, and I'm worried for you. You said yourself she's dangerous. Perhaps we should just leave well alone, and then she'll go away. I don't want things to get worse.'

'Well, I'm not worried.'

It was the truth. Just hours since Elisabeth had crossed paths with Zillah, she now felt stronger and more powerful than at any other time in her life. Where this confidence had come from, she didn't know, but she trusted it. There would be time enough later to tell Alice that there was more to her powers than she'd previously confessed.

Last night, prompted by unease, her sleep had been disturbed by another of those rare moments when her body was left behind to let her conscious mind roam free. In this case, it was to find Zillah standing in the paddock recently vacated by the cattle. Elisabeth saw her look around, hands on hips, then laugh before squeezing under the fence to go searching.

She didn't need to see what happened next, it was merely confirmation of what she already suspected.

'Things are not going to get worse, Alice. Soon you won't ever have to worry about Zillah setting foot on Grange land again.'

* * *

Elisabeth sat in her room, watching the moon rise. It wasn't full but there was going to be enough light. Fully dressed in outdoor clothes, she listened to the nightly sounds of the servants finishing their work for the day, then the calls of 'Goodnight, God Bless' before footfalls on the back stairs continued up to the attic. Alice would be asleep by now in her bedchamber at the front of the house, and soon those in the attic would be too, once the sounds of boots on floorboards and the squeaking of bedsprings stopped. A long working day usually resulted in sound sleep and Elisabeth smiled when the sound of Cook's snoring started up.

It was a very still night and a distant whinny suggested that Edmund was late with the nightly treat. Soon he would lock the stables and then be the last to turn in.

Leaning on the sill, she opened the window wide and caught the sound of a fox barking in Top Wood. It was subtly different from that of a dog and, anyway, dog barking usually came from the other direction, from the village. She strained to see if she could see top paddock, or hear any noise, but it was too far away and there was an inconvenient copse in the way.

A little shiver ran through her. The air was cooler than she thought and she picked up a thick, dark shawl to wrap around her body, crossing it over her front and tying it tightly behind her in the fashion of the village women to make sure both hands were free. A bonnet was out of the question; it would only hamper her senses and she needed every one of those this night. Instead, copying Melina and Lucille, she wrapped a long scarf around her head, knotting it in the nape and securing the ends in the plait draped over one shoulder. It was like donning a different character. As she caught sight of herself reflected in the glass, it crossed her mind that she might have that the wrong way round. Perhaps this was the person she always knew she was.

Earlier in the day she had wondered if she should leave notes for Alice and Jean-Michel, but as soon as the thought entered her head, she dismissed it. Nothing was going to happen to her. If Melina was right, then it was her duty to stand against evil – otherwise, what was the point of her gifts? And, surely, they didn't live in a world where evil triumphed?

It would be time soon. During the day when she was striding out, it took well over half an hour to reach the wood. This night it would take longer; having chosen a slightly more circuitous route, she would need to watch her step in the dark and move stealthily to avoid noise. With one last look at her room, she closed the door softly, crept down the back stairs and slipped into her boots before leaving by the kitchen door.

The moment the kitchen garden was behind her, Elisabeth knew she wasn't alone. If she had any remaining doubts about what she was doing, that's when they disappeared.

On any other occasion in the dead of night, nothing would have *escaped her notice; not the scurrying of nocturnal creatures, nor the starry patterns in the heavens, or the delicate scents that were obvious only at night. But on this night, her mind was so full of what lay ahead, she barely registered anything until the huge dark mass of Top Wood loomed closer. She entered the wood the way she had always done, along what she thought of as the fox path. Striking off to the right, she came across the spring and little stream where Melina had bathed her feet. Being unfamiliar with the way beyond, she cast around for a stout branch to use as a walking stick. Progress was somewhat slow, aware as she was just how loud one crack from a mis-step would sound, and soon she abandoned the wood to see exactly where she was.*

Surprised to find herself only yards from the field gate to top paddock, Elisabeth slipped back under cover of the wood. Everything appeared normal at the moment. The cows were lying down with their calves, huddled together at one end of the field; safety in numbers guarding against predators. Every so often, a shuffling around occurred, drawing the outlying animals into the centre with some gentle mooing.

Elisabeth thought this was happening again until it was clear that all the cattle were now standing. She moved to the edge of the wood to get a better view and saw them all backed up, pressing hard against the fence at their rear. Clearly frightened as they were, yet they made no sound.

Zillah had entered via the opposite field gate. Dressed entirely in the darkest green, she moved so stealthily it was only the whiteness of her face and the flash of moonlight on a metal clasp that gave her away. Now standing in the centre of the paddock, arms outstretched, she was softly chanting or singing – Elisabeth couldn't make it out. Whichever it was, it had wooed the cattle into silence.

Too far away to feel Zillah's distinctive presence, Elisabeth was hoping that she, too, had not yet been detected. Leaving the wood, she dipped down below the hedge line and circled around the paddock until she surfaced behind the cattle. Sensing her, one or two cows shifted, allowing Elisabeth to step through the fence and into the paddock to surprise the enemy.

Zillah immediately dropped her arms.

'Well, as I live and breathe, if it isn't Madame La Montagne.' She pronounced the name with heavy sarcasm. 'I hardly recognised you.'

She took a couple of steps forward, and Elisabeth matched them.

'I've been wondering how long it would take for you to show your true colours. And just look at the two of us now; dressed alike we could be sisters, don't you think? Your hair suits you like…'

'What do you want, Zillah? Is all this milk business just to get me here?'

'I want what everyone wants; something that you obviously have.' Her voice became hard. 'Somewhere like this.'

'Why here?'

Zillah laughed. 'Your Alice Rawlinson is a Crayford, and my kind have a long history with the Crayfords. No doubt that's why you're here. Not many of us are left now. There's that Melina woman, of course, and her simple daughter, but she seems content to have been cheated out of a piece of this estate. I, on the other hand, am not.'

'You know very well that Melina and I are not 'your kind'.

'Perhaps the difference is only in how we've been treated…'

'Or, more likely, how you treat others. Also, I know something of the Crayford's history and if they're guilty of anything it must have been generations ago, and no fault of Alice or her father.'

'Appealing to my better nature, Madame? You know better than that. I don't care how long ago it was, or who gets hurt, as long as I get what I want.' Zillah paused, then gave a little smirk. 'I didn't reckon on you coming back though, and I was hoping you were going

to leave with that other one. It would have made my life easier.' She gave a tiny shrug. 'On the other hand, it's a while since I've had to face a challenge.'

Through Elisabeth's eyes, what happened next was in slow motion, but in reality, was no more than a fraction of a second. As soon as Zillah prepared to thrust out her right arm in Elisabeth's direction, she cried out in pain, watching in disbelief as it fell and dangled uselessly at her side. The mocking smile, that had been present throughout their exchanges, now wiped from her face.

Without waiting, Elisabeth took a few steps closer and, for every step, Zillah was forced to take a step back, as though an invisible hand had prodded her in the chest. It happened again and again.

'You'll regret this. You don't know what you're playing at here.' Still forced to walk backwards, Zillah stumbled, slow to get up with only one working arm.

'Of course, I do. You're the reason I'm here, after all.'

Unwilling to reduce the distance between them, Elisabeth waited for Zillah to stand before resuming the force, gently, to push her further and further back. Perhaps she thought the humiliation of stumbling about in front of an adversary after her powers had so easily been overcome, was enough to make Zillah think again about what she was doing.

If so, she was mistaken.

After the next stumble, Zillah jumped up quickly. The arm appeared to have recovered fast, taking Elisabeth by surprise. Hardly missing a beat, Zillah threw her head back and yelled, 'ancumab snacan', pointing to the ground with fingers stretched wide, the whites of her eyes clearly visible.

Elisabeth had no idea what it meant, not until the grass began to move. The fear started in her stomach, but soon reached her chest where her breathing was coming ever faster. The air seemed to drop in temperature and her skin prickled as hairs stood on end. Run or stay? She couldn't think clearly and the hesitation cost her.

One each side of Zillah, the snakes moved slowly at first – and then they didn't. Leaving it too late to summon the force, Elisabeth sprang back, but not quickly enough. They were on her before she knew it. The first one she managed to kick away and the cat was on it before it had time to make a second attack. A flash of tortoiseshell, it had seemingly leapt from nowhere, clamping its jaws behind the snake's head and shaking it until the life left it. Meanwhile, the second snake was rearing up, determined to sink its fangs into Elisabeth's leg above the boot. The sight of her hopping around sent Zillah into a paroxysm of laughter.

She was still laughing as she was attacked from behind. Leaving her spread-eagled on the ground, an owl, on silent wings, continued on its way to deal with the second snake. Elisabeth felt only the draught from its wings, as its huge eyes and outstretched talons concentrated on seizing its prey. The owl swept upwards into the sky, the snake writhing uselessly from its beak, before circling the paddock and heading back to the wood.

Zillah pushed herself up onto her knees only to come face-to-face with the orange cat. As the dead snake dropped from its jaws and lay on the ground between them, the realisation dawned that she was beaten. Elisabeth was neither alone nor as powerless as she had supposed and she knew now there would be no simple retreat. She had played her best card and it had come to nothing. The animals Elisabeth had to help her were not the sort that Zillah had any power over – or anyone had, for that matter.

'You win; I'll stop.' As she'd taken full advantage of Elisabeth's fear of snakes, she anticipated what was in store for her. 'I'm begging you, do not do this.'

Elisabeth's leg was throbbing. She knew the snake had made

contact before the owl had pounced but had been hoping it would come to nothing. Furious that she hadn't been ruthless enough and may now have little time left before walking would become difficult, she shook her head and let go in a way she had never done before. Zillah found herself lifted clean off her feet and tumbled towards the gate she'd used earlier.

Elisabeth followed and the cat fell into step beside her. She knew it was the cat but, just for a moment out of the corner of her eye, she saw the shape of a woman. A woman dressed like herself but with flaming red hair; a woman she'd never met but nevertheless, was familiar with. A blink later and the cat was back.

Clutching the gate post, Zillah tried another attempt to save herself.

'Your leg, look, you're hurt. I can fix that and then let me go.'

'No, that's definitely not going to happen, Zillah.'

Both women turned to see Melina striding towards them from the wood. Elisabeth had never been more grateful to see anyone. With no words necessary, Melina looked down the field and back to Elisabeth, who nodded.

The dew pond was rippling gently, moonlight glistening on the surface, and it was waiting, just yards away.

When, with one final push, Zillah was ripped from the gatepost and rolled down into the pond, her terrified screams broke whatever spell was silencing the cattle. Their alarm calls filled the air.

Elisabeth sank to the ground. 'Don't let her escape, Melina.'

'But your leg…'

'I'll be fine.' She nodded to the cat who was already sniffing her leg. 'She knows what to do, I'll be with you shortly.'

The remedy was swift and painful, but with the venom no longer coursing through her body, Elisabeth was soon up and feeling the energy return with every step she took to the pond – where she found

Melina, skirt hitched round her waist, pushing Zillah under every time she came up for air.

'Are we going to do it?', she asked, water up to her thighs, straddling the struggling woman.

'No, we're not capable of that.'

'I think I might be…'

Elisabeth had never before seen her friend so worked up. 'You know you're not. Let's get her out.'

The cat had taken up a position on the nearest fence post and, if either woman had been looking, they'd have seen the white of the owl's breast in a tree at the edge of the wood. Elisabeth went closer to the pond.

'No, don't you come near here with that sore leg.' Melina hauled herself out of the pond and pulled Elisabeth away. 'Let her get out on her own.'

Zillah was a sorry sight. Clawing her way up the slippery clay bank with heavy, sodden clothing was slow going, all the while retching and bringing up lungfuls of filthy pond water. Melina stood by Elisabeth, unhitching her skirts, water running from her boots.

Once she was out on all fours and there was no more water to bring up, Zillah rolled on to her back gasping for air.

'So…are we just going to let her go, after she tried to kill you? You know she would have done it, don't you?'

'Perhaps, perhaps not. We'll never know, will we?' She laid a hand on Melina's arm. 'Stay here.'

She walked over to the woman still lying in the same position and still breathing heavily. 'As you can see, Zillah,' indicating her own leg, 'I didn't need you to 'fix' what you'd already started.'

Zillah's head rolled to make eye contact. 'I wouldn't have let you die. I just wanted to make sure you never came back. What are you going to do to me?'

'Nothing, or rather the same. You're free to go.' No longer fearful, Elisabeth went in closer, leaned over the prostrate woman and lowered her voice. 'However – know this, and don't forget it – from this hour forward, there's a curse hanging over you. Should you ever set foot on this estate again, or, indeed, any of your blood relatives, you or they will pay a terrible price. I don't do this lightly, Zillah. You have been warned.'

Elisabeth stepped back to stand by Melina. They kept their eyes on Zillah as long as it took for her to stand and make her way unsteadily out of the estate. It was noticeable that she never once touched the wood.

'What did you say to her?'

'I told her I'd cursed her, and her blood relatives. If ever they were to come back here, they'd pay for it.'

'With their lives?'

'That was the implication, obviously.' Elisabeth looked her squarely in the face. 'Anyway, it doesn't matter, does it? I distinctly remember you telling me that it can't be that easy to curse someone.'

'Right, well, let's hope she believes it then, like William Harryman did.'

The two women embraced, tears of relief falling unchecked. When they eventually pulled apart, Melina wiped her face and looked around for the cat.

'Where's she gone?'

'Who knows?' Elisabeth shook her head. 'All I know is that she's always around to point me in the right direction, or comfort and protect me, just like a grandmother.'

Melina nodded.

'And Lyssa? How long has she been with you?'

'I was never sure, you know, not until tonight when I saw her with that snake. And it makes sense; she loved this wood and the night-time. It's what she would have chosen.'

Having reluctantly taken their leave of each other, Melina squelched off into the wood and Elisabeth turned back to the paddock. A figure waiting by the field gate made her start.

'It's only me, Madam – Gabe. I heard the cattle making a row and thought I should check on 'em. You know, what with all the milk business and everything.'

Elisabeth stuttered. 'Of course, yes, me, too.'

He opened the gate to let her through, neither expressing surprise at finding her there, nor asking her anything else.

'How long have you been here, Gabe?'

'Long enough, Madam. Now you just lean on me, you're limping a bit. I think we should get back now.'

~ 26 ~
Summer 1722

There was still a clearing, of sorts.

It came as a surprise, and when I saw the newly-felled log, I realised that Gabe had been put to work here also. The poor man must have been working harder than when he was farm manager.

I sat down with a long, contented sigh. Even a short walk tires me out these days, but nothing could take away the joy of being here once more.

Lucille passed me a glass of elderflower cordial and, being thirsty, I took a long pull. It made me cough.

'If I'm not mistaken, there's a deal of spirit in this, Lucille. I shall be incapable of walking back if I have much more.'

'Just a little fortification, Madame, I know you're partial to a tot.' She grinned. 'Have one of these biscuits.'

I took two and held out my glass. 'If you're treating Gabe this well, he'll be double the size before too long.'

She smiled but didn't answer. We sat in companionable silence, eating, drinking and noting the sounds of the wood.

'Do you remember how you used to flit through the trees, secretly watching me when I first came to this wood? I used to call you my little dryad.'

'Of course. I knew you'd come one day, although Mother wasn't convinced until the foxes told her.'

That made me smile. For Melina, the foxes had always been family. It took a while and then, at last, everything fell into place.

I reached along the log and took Lucille's hand in mine.

'She's here, isn't she?'

Lucille gave the briefest of nods. 'I'll be back shortly, Madame...'. She took the basket. 'I need some more feverfew and shepherd's purse, I'll not be far away.'

I've become so sentimental in my old age, the anticipation was nearly too much for me. As soon as Lucille had slipped from sight, I fixed my eyes on the hornbeam where I'd first caught sight of Melina all those years ago. It looked nothing like it did then, but I knew that's where I'd see her.

With a lump in my throat, I watched her cross the clearing and, just like the first vixen I met in this place so many years ago, she came close and bowed her head. Back then I was too wary to touch. This time was different. I held out a hand and she came closer, then closer still, until she was leaning against my leg.

'Oh, how I've missed you.'

With her head on my knee, stroking the soft fur and staring into those intelligent eyes, I knew this was a privilege that wouldn't be repeated.

'I'll never forget.' I'm not sure I said it out loud for my throat was thick with unshed tears, but it didn't matter. She knew the way she'd always known; we were always able to communicate without words.

Leaving by the same route far too soon, she crossed paths with Lucille, exchanging a glance but nothing more.

'It was her dying wish to see you one more time.' Lucille took her place next to me on the log. 'It wasn't possible in this life as her end came so swiftly, but she was determined to make it happen.'

'I tried to get to her, Lucille, but...'

'Oh, I know Madame, the end surprised us all.'

* * *

Anne called out from her dressing room as I reached the top of the stairs. 'We're in here, Aunt, if you have a minute.'

I'd hardly set foot in the room when Young Alice, her face

reflected in the mirror, said, 'Honestly now, Tante, what do you think? I'm not sure it's grown-up enough.'

Anne, still wielding the hairbrush, raised her eyebrows behind her daughter's back. I went to stand behind the dressing stool, both of us now reflected in the glass.

'Not grown-up enough for what?'

'The ball I told you about, at Rose's, a week on Saturday.'

'Ah, yes, I remember now.'

As both Rose and Sophia each have their own accomplished lady's maid, I can well understand Alice's slight dip in confidence. Not that she has anything to be concerned about. Thanks to her new-found interest in the workings of the farm, she has grown up rather quickly in the last few months and so has her conversation. In terms of looks, it would be useless to point out that she can hold her own against them any day, because she wouldn't believe me.

'I can't say I'm up-to-date with the current fashion, Alice, but I think your Mama has done very well indeed. You're fortunate that your curls are so easily styled; the back here is quite lovely and it shows off your neck beautifully. You might want a little more height at the front but that's a simple thing to do next time you try, and you could use a few more tendrils on the forehead. Other than that, Anne, I think it's perfect for a young woman. Don't you?'

Anne breathed a sigh of relief. 'Thank you, Aunt.'

'Well, I don't know what I'm going to do about these.' Alice leaned forward to look more closely at her freckles.

'Your grandmother used to say the same thing. Her old servant told her to bathe them in May-dew gathered before sunrise and it would make them fade away.'

Wide-eyed. 'Really? Did it work?'

'Of course not.' I laughed. 'And, like you, she never could see just how attractive they are – especially to young men, I'm told.'

Alice pulled a face and spun round on the stool as I was about to leave. 'My new gown is coming tomorrow; can I show you?'

'I shall expect to see the whole ensemble...'

Anne stepped in smartly. 'That's enough now, Alice. You've

had a long day, Aunt, I expect you're tired, but tell me, how was the drive? Did you go far?'

'Oh, just a trip in and around the villages, you know, and a short walk with Lucille. It was a lovely day, Gabe is a true gentleman, and there's nothing quite like driving in the open air to brush away the cobwebs.' It wasn't much of a lie.

Wanting nothing more than to be alone in my room, reliving the events of the day, I did then plead tiredness and excuse myself.

Even at my great age, there is still so much I don't understand about those of us who are different. Seeing the vixen today, though, perhaps explains why I have never felt Melina's presence in the same way that I feel Alice's, Aphra's or Bernard's. They are dead and gone from this world, whereas that is not the case with Melina. Or my grandmother, for that matter.

After the Zillah affair, all those years ago, I quickly revised my intention to tell Alice everything about the events of that night. It couldn't be done without lying about Melina, the cat, and the power of Zillah, all of which was too difficult to explain. I'd already had to lie about the wound on my leg. I remember deciding it was far better for her to believe that having caught Zillah in the act of charming the cattle, I merely persuaded her that leaving the village was in her best interest. It was basically true, after all.

'So, she did use a spell to turn the milk?' She'd asked.

That was the one question I was able to answer truthfully and, to be fair, Alice had instinctively known not to dig any further. Like Aphra, I think she was content not to know everything on that occasion.

I do wish, though, I could have told her everything, because I never did. And I've never really got over the guilt of keeping from Alice her connection to Melina and Lucille, and my friendship with them. All this reminiscing has just reminded me that there is still no one who knows the whole truth about me, not even Lucille. How to explain the separation of the seeing mind from one's body?

Is it time to think again about leaving some sort of record? Even though my daughter and granddaughter do not have the gift, I worry I may not be the last.

~ 27 ~

Autumn 1677, London

As the carriage rattled through the city towards Bishops Gate, it struck Elisabeth once again just how quickly London had transformed itself in the eleven years since the Great Fire. Churches were the last to be tackled, and although most were now rebuilt, the wreck that was once St. Paul's still dominated the skyline with a new design far from settled and funding still a problem. A returning visitor would be hard-pressed to recognise the place.

For Elisabeth though, the thrill of being back in the bustle of London was the same as it ever was, and after a whole month away, she was longing to be with Jean-Michel again. Strangely, she also felt a slight nervousness. During the whole Zillah episode, all thoughts of Jean-Michel had been pushed firmly to the back of her mind, but now she acknowledged a vague, uneasy feeling she couldn't pin down. Their relationship had been a little strained when she left, and the extra week or two away wouldn't have helped. Perhaps that was all there was to it.

Catching her reflection in the carriage window, she tucked away a few stray hairs and pinched her cheeks; bouncing over the cobbles preventing any further refinements. Not that she was greatly concerned about her appearance. Courtesy of Alice's household, all her garments were now smelling lavender clean, having been washed or aired, and a little sachet of musky notes was nestling in a locket *on her chest. She'd concocted it for Alice, specifically for Joseph's return, but couldn't resist using some herself.*

Spital Fields seemed busier than ever. Streets were buzzing with vendors, and the silk business was clearly doing well if the number of carriages outside the workshops was anything to go by. Elisabeth hung out of the window, eager to catch first sight of home; not once had she regretted building in this area.

The carriage drew to a halt and Elisabeth let herself out without waiting for the coachman. Glancing first at the upstairs window to make sure Jean-Michel hadn't heard the carriage, she ran up the front steps and let herself in.

Hurried footsteps on the back stairs were followed by the maid, a little flustered at being caught unawares. She bobbed a welcome.

'Madam, I'm so sorry. I didn't hear the door or the carriage.'

'Not surprising, Julianne, it's noisy out there.' Lowering her voice, she pointed outside. 'Come and help me with Céleste, would you? She's awake in her crib.'

Julianne hopped up into the carriage and handed over the baby, going back to wrestle the basket through the narrow carriage door. Elisabeth ran back inside just in time to see Jean-Michel striding along the back corridor, his smile nearly as wide as his arms, which wrapped around them both.

'My two darling girls.' He was speaking in French, always a sign that emotion was getting the better of him.

Breaking away from the huddle with a mock frown, Elisabeth said, 'You spoiled our surprise, we were going to creep up on you upstairs.' Sensing the maid hovering nearby with the crib, she called over her shoulder, 'Would you take that downstairs, please, Julianne? We should give Monsieur a little time with his daughter and then I'll need you to mind her while I settle back in.'

Once the coachman and his lad had clattered out after carrying the trunks upstairs, peace descended, and Elisabeth flopped down into the nearest chair, always happy to watch Jean-Michel play with Céleste.

'She's grown, haven't you, mon petit-chou?' Holding her close with one arm, he tickled her tummy to produce a fit of giggles. 'What have you been feeding her on?'

Elisabeth laughed. 'Jennet may have given her a few too many treats; and not only Céleste either.' She pulled a face, slightly cross with herself. It was unlike her to fish for compliments.

Giving her the sideways look that always reminded her of François, he grinned. 'If she has, you'll not find me complaining about a bit of extra flesh. You look as beautiful as ever.'

'Oh, very convincing, Jean-Michel, well done. And you, too, look well cared for.' She paused. 'I thought Julianne looked a little fraught, though. You haven't been working her too hard, I hope?'

'Of course not.' Placing Céleste in her lap, he knelt beside her chair, inhaled her scent and kissed her, one hand firmly on the back of her neck. 'I have missed you so very much. Why don't you call her to take this little one now, so that you and I can go upstairs?' Again, the grin, this time with one cocked eyebrow. 'You'll be wanting to get out of those travelling clothes, I expect…'

As a welcome home, it was more than she'd expected. Lying in bed afterwards, it was easy to think she'd been imagining things. He'd brushed aside his disappointment over her extended stay, not even asking for an explanation. Everything seemed fine. So why had the feeling not gone away?

* * *

Guilt. It affects people in different ways. Whilst Jean-Michel was overcompensating, desperate as he was to atone for something, poor Julianne couldn't even look Elisabeth in the eye. It didn't take her long to put two and two together.

In her younger days, Elisabeth would have flown into a rage, recklessly letting loose the whirlwind. But age had tempered her and now she was chillingly composed.

'It's time to tell me what's been going on, Jean-Michel. Have you perhaps reached the point when being with an older woman has lost its novelty? Please don't deny it, I'm not a fool.'

As silent seconds ticked by, his face started to crumble and the words, when they came, were barely coherent. Eventually the story came out, in a messy, tearful, stammering fashion. He'd been out with Philippe one evening and returned late to the house, practically falling-down drunk, and making so much noise he'd woken Julianne. Finding him lying at the bottom of the stairs, she'd helped him to his room and into bed.

'Did you force yourself on her?'

'No, no… surely you don't think I'm capable of that, Elisabeth. I couldn't have done that.' He wiped his face with both hands.

'Not completely incapable though, if I've got that right.'

He shook his head and closed his eyes. 'It just happened. Truly, I didn't know what I was doing.'

'So, it was Julianne's fault, is that what you're saying?'

His head dropped into his hands, his voice muffled and weary. 'No, it could have been anybody. I was missing you so much.'

'But it wasn't just anyone, was it? It was a young girl who works for us. A young girl in our care. A young girl who probably didn't even know she had a choice – or nearly as bad, was infatuated.'

'She's not a young girl.'

'She's sixteen, Jean-Michel.'

He stood up abruptly. 'There is nothing more to beat me with, Elisabeth. I'm ashamed, but I'm no rapist. Whatever happened was a drunken mistake and meant nothing. If you can't accept that then you must do whatever you think fit. I'm going upstairs.'

* * *

Needing to get out of the house and feel fresh air on her face, Elisabeth found herself near Philippe's house and hesitated only slightly before turning that way. She caught his wife just about to leave.

'Do you have a minute to spare, Madeleine?'

Of course she did, Philippe's wife liked nothing more than a good gossip. Warming to the subject, she described in comic detail the state her husband had been in on the night he and Jean-Michel went drinking till the early hours.

'I don't know what they thought they were doing, it's not as though they're hardened drinkers, are they? I hear yours made it home alright…'

'Yes, yes, he did.'

'It was Philippe's fault, of course – I blame him. I think he thought getting him drunk was going to make him forget how miserable he was.'

Jean-Michel, you mean? Why was he miserable?'

'Oh, my word, Elisabeth, you must know.' She couldn't suppress a laugh. 'He's like a little boy lost when you're away.'

As an analogy it was unfortunate. Madeleine saw it, but it was too late.

'You must know I didn't mean anything by that, Elisabeth.'

'Take no notice of me, Madeleine.' She smiled and made a little dismissive gesture. 'I'm just a bit sensitive about that at the moment.'

Jean-Michel was not surprised when she retired to her old room that night. He'd taken supper alone at the local tavern, and he knew Elisabeth had arranged for a cold plate. Julianne was no doubt relieved not to see either of them.

* * *

It couldn't wait any longer. No one, apart from the baby, was going to get any sleep until it was settled.

Taking care to tread softly, Elisabeth descended the stairs to the kitchen where Julianne was minding Céleste. Crooning and cradling the baby, she rocked side to side as she stared through the window to the herb garden beyond, unaware she was no longer alone. Once she turned around, it was too late to dash away the tears and they fell even faster when Elisabeth smiled and held out her arms for Céleste.

'Sit down, Julianne. We need to talk.'

The girl shook her head firmly. 'No need, Madam. I know I have to leave.'

'Not until we've spoken about this.'

'I can't.' She fished a handkerchief out of her pocket. It was already sodden.

'I understand it's difficult. Perhaps it'll be easier if I tell you that I already know what happened?' Céleste had drifted off and Elisabeth put her down in the crib.

Julianne looked at her properly for the first time, unsure. 'If I could undo everything, Madam, I would. I'm so, so sorry. I love it here with you and the baby, the clinic, the garden...' By now, she was sobbing and couldn't go on.

'Monsieur knows he was wrong to put you in such a situation. That's not much use to you now, I know. Tell me, has he spoken to you since?'

Julianne nodded. 'Yes, Madam. He said he was very sorry and we should both try to forget it. He couldn't remember exactly what he'd done, on account of being so drunk, but he knew it shouldn't have happened. He was really upset.'

'Well, that's something, I suppose.'

There was a long pause, both looking anywhere but at each other. Julianne was the first to break the silence.

'He kept saying your name, Madam. He thought I was you.'

Elisabeth's hand flew to her mouth and she closed her eyes. 'I'm so sorry.'

'I've ruined everything, haven't I, Madam?'

'No, child. You're not the one to blame here.'

It was a while before Julianne spoke again. 'That's not exactly true, Madam. I can't have you think it was all his fault.' And this time she really couldn't look Elisabeth in the eye.

But Elisabeth could remember what it was like to be sixteen, and how easy it was to be seduced by a charismatic, older man in the heat of the moment. And at least Jean-Michel hadn't set out to seduce; she believed that now.

So reluctant was she to let Julianne go, Elisabeth's compromise was to allow her to take charge of the crèche and continue to work in the garden and clinic – work which didn't entail going above stairs. As Jean-Michel never had cause to go below stairs, this seemed to suit everyone. A new maid was recruited for the house.

* * *

The following weeks were busy; too busy. Jean-Michel was behind on several orders and was working as long as the light and his eyesight allowed. Elisabeth rarely saw Céleste, who was either with the new maid or with Julianne in the crèche. Thankfully, the arrangement seemed to be working well.

So, it was many weeks before Elisabeth had time to visit Aphra, who'd been on her mind for some time. She took with her several items from the clinic, stocks of which had been severely depleted over the last weeks; yet another job that needed seeing to. It was a world away from the sedate pace of her life at Oakwood Grange.

'I got your note. I do hope you weren't too hard on him, Elisabeth. It's not as if it was deliberate.' Aphra didn't rise from her desk chair, but held up her face for a kiss. 'And I imagine the work's been piling up while you've been away?'

'It has. This has been my first free afternoon since I got back. Anyway, how are you, and how is the writing going?'

Aphra batted away the questions. 'Later, first tell me why you stayed in Sussex and if there's anything I need to know about Alice.'

Elisabeth knew this was coming. Aphra had been keen to get back to London but, on the other hand, she hated to think she'd missed out on something.

'Alice is fine. I had a feeling that she might be pregnant again and wanted to make sure all was good before I left.' As it was the truth, it saved her from having to make something up.

'And is everything good?'

'So far. It's due early next year, we think.

'Good, I know she wants more children. What about you?'

'I can't be thinking about that now. I'm not sure I have time for another one.'

Aphra nodded to the side table. 'Well, there's a bottle of geneva over there. I think we should celebrate Alice's good news and your return home to your sadly neglected husband.'

As it was obvious Aphra was reluctant to rise, Elisabeth poured out two small glasses and they drank to Alice's health.

'How did Jean-Michel seem when you dropped off my note?'

Aphra drained the glass and held it out. 'Oh, that's good, pour me another one, please, Elisabeth. He was disappointed, as you would expect, and a little distracted. I think work was getting too much for him.'

'He works better when I'm there.'

'Clearly. Does he know yet that you're his landlady?'

'No.' A little wrongfooted at the change of direction, Elisabeth stood to return her glass to the side table. 'I've never found the right time.'

'Why not?'

She turned around with a sigh. 'I don't know. I expect I've just left it too long.'

'Quite. Have you thought how he'll feel now if he finds out from someone else? A careless remark from your Uncle George or Lady Caroline is not beyond the bounds of probability.'

'Since when have you acted as my conscience, Aphra? This isn't like you.'

Aphra threw back her head with laughter. 'Since I see my perfect friend making a big mistake. Despite his recent peccadillo, your Jean-Michel is a good man, and a proud man; don't let him feel like a fool.'

The conversation soon moved on to Aphra's welfare. Although her ailments appeared to have multiplied, her current good mood was firmly down to the recent success of her writings. Whilst not quite accepted at Court, she was now part of an intellectual group of well-known artists and writers –many of them aristocrats – and that suited her very well. She professed she had no time for a love life.

Elisabeth wondered if perhaps something had happened recently in Aphra's life that she wasn't prepared to discuss. It was unlike her to give unsolicited advice, especially when it was good advice.

~ 28 ~
Spring 1724

Marriage is the main topic of conversation at present, both here at the Grange and in my daughter's house, and it has stirred up memories from the past.

Predictably, Aphra never once entertained the idea of re-marriage after her husband died in the plague. Whilst I know that their short time together was happy, I'm doubtful it would have remained so. Still in her early twenties, and determined to make a living from writing in whatever form, nothing and no one would have been allowed to stand in her way.

And despite what she faced on a daily basis, for being an ambitious woman, relatively low-born and someone who made no bones about enjoying a libertine's way of life, she did achieve independence and considerable acclaim, if not financial security. Men, of course, loved her, and she was rarely without an admirer in tow even when most women were considered too old for such things.

Remembering one of her last flings makes me smile even now, nearly forty years later. It came after a fallow period for the theatre, when she was forced to take on copying and ghost-writing work to make ends meet. Suffering from poor health, she was at a particularly low ebb when I persuaded her to accompany me to Paris, on the basis that I wanted a companion and it would do her good. The trip was a particularly sad and nostalgic one for me as my old friend and mentor, Marie-Louise was close to death. Henri, her companion, had instructions to insist I attend her funeral, even if she had to be packed in ice until I arrived. She was used to being obeyed and imminent death wasn't going to change that, but the ice wasn't necessary, I was confident I'd know when I was needed. Arriving in good time for her to know I was there, I kissed her goodbye and was able to stay holding her hand until the final breath came in the early hours of the next morning. It was Henri then who needed the support; he'd aged considerably since I'd last seen him.

For Aphra, though, Paris was providing an unexpected degree of entertainment. It had come to the notice of a few intellectual women who held *salons*, that the fabled, female English playwright was in the city; invitations had rolled in, and Aphra was in her element. Looking back, I believe she was ready to grasp every opportunity fearing that none might come her way again. That included affairs of the heart, and an opportunity like George Granville didn't come along every day. A seventeen-year-old classics scholar with a love of the theatre, Granville had a romantic penchant for older women, whilst Aphra, well passed the first, and even second flush, could never resist a younger man – in this case, much younger.

Having just left Cambridge, if young Granville was in Paris to experience a different sort of education, I'm sure he succeeded for I recall that their affair did more for Aphra's health, mood and literary juices than any tonic I could have supplied. She was unstoppable for a time after our return to England, and published her first novel, an erotic fiction laid out in the form of love letters. It was probably wise not to put her name to it.

Every so often, I still hear her voice in my head, thankful that she lived when she did, for society now is a deal more censorious that it was in Charles II's reign.

* * *

Alice, on the other hand, having had such a disastrous start to married life with her first husband, had had no such qualms about marrying again once she'd found Joseph Rawlinson.

Having played the field in London for far too many years, Joseph had never met any woman, available or otherwise, who didn't eventually irritate him or try to change him. Not until he found Alice. One evening when she'd retired early and he was well on the way to being drunk, I'll never forget him confessing to me that, although initially attracted by her obvious physical attributes, it was something else that had made him realise what had been missing in all previous paramours; Alice required nothing of him other than the companionship of equals. The lack of womanly pursuits which had so enraged her first husband and caused some paternal concern, was seen as a distinct advantage to Joseph.

Together they embraced local politics; Joseph involved mainly with county matters to be raised in Parliament, whilst Alice concentrated on improving the lives and opportunities of villagers closer to home. They made a good team.

Determined to have as many children as possible, this was one area that didn't go according to plan. I delivered Alice of her second daughter, Astrea, two years after Anne, but the birth was difficult – both mother and baby lucky to be alive – and Joseph refused to allow her to try again. She frequently mentioned in later years that she considered it a failure that she couldn't give Joseph a son.

If it mattered that much to Joseph, he never showed it, but it was a joy to see him when his grandsons were born, although, sadly, he had precious few years with them. Anne proved to be every bit as down-to-earth and practical as her mother, accepting without question that she would eventually run the estate as her mother had done, before handing it on to Tobias.

Astrea, though, had much more of the young Joseph in her. As soon as she was allowed, she escaped the countryside and spent the summer months in London with her Rawlinson grandmother. This brought great rewards in the shape of Sir Henry Griffin, who made her his wife in short order and whisked her off to one of his homes on the continent. I liked Astrea; she had plenty of spark and wit, and we were all glad that she enjoyed what was to be a short life, for she died in childbirth not three years later.

* * *

I've been thinking, too, about Jean-Michel. Perhaps the years since his death have allowed me to be more objective, or more truthful. Was he the love of my life? The simple answer to that question may be 'no', and possibly, neither was François although it feels odd to admit that now. Which is not to say that I didn't love them both, I truly did, but if I'm to be completely honest with myself, it is my first husband, Bernard, who knew me best, whose voice I still hear and who pops into my mind at the oddest times. I suppose the easy explanation is that there are different types of love. The love I still feel for Alice and Aphra is, by its very nature, not the same as the physical, passionate love that consumed me with Jean-Michel and François. But where does that leave Bernard?

On the surface, of course, it sounds ridiculous that an old man in an unconsummated marriage of convenience to an eighteen-year-old girl could ever be a love match. But none of those things mattered to us. I've often thought it was because neither of us had any expectations of a good relationship that our love grew in such a natural way. From our very first meeting, when the strength of his shimmering yellow and blue aura rendered me speechless, I recognised it as a sign that here was a man I could trust implicitly. He became the father I'd never had but, possibly even more important than that, he was also my confidant who knew the part of me I kept from everyone else. For his part, I was the child he'd always wanted, and although he never criticised his first wife, it was clear they'd had few shared interests.

The depth of our love for each other took us both by surprise, and many were the hours we spent playing cards and chess, reading together and just talking well into the night. It didn't take long for the difference in age to become irrelevant. As I became a young woman, I saw more of the young man who just happened to inhabit an old body and that's how it remained. He counted the last years as the happiest of his life – and in return, his gifts to me were countless.

It's tempting to think that had we met when he was a young man we could have had a whole life together but, no, fate decreed

SUSAN GREENWOOD

that we should meet when we did, granting each of us something crucial that had been missing in our lives.

Dear Marie-Louise, I have you to thank for everything, for had you not browbeaten Bernard into meeting me, both our lives would have been the poorer. I know you never quite understood it – but it was more successful than you ever knew.

* * *

Enough of this reminiscing. It is Tobias's engagement to Rose that has the house all a-buzz.

I was right about Rose. Although the quietest of the three friends, I always felt she was a young woman with hidden depths who knew her own mind. And so it has proved.

Without the close friendship with my granddaughter, it is unlikely that Tobias and Alice would have ever been drawn into Rose's social circle. Her family has not been resident in the county for long and fraternises with similar folk in their large, newly-built properties, distinctly separate from the old established families who also tend to stick together. Both have their prejudices. That Tobias can trace his Crayford ancestry back several centuries on this estate, however, quite possibly helped Rose's parents to eventually approval of the match. And then, of course, there was Rose's threat that she would remain unmarried and be a life-long burden to them if they refused their permission. I'm sure her family would have preferred Tobias to come from the sort of landed gentry who never soil their hands and spend half their time in London, but it's clear that matters not at all to Rose. She is fortunate, also, in that she has two older brothers, which reduces the pressure for her to 'marry well' and improve the family's standing. My humble opinion is that she will have married very well indeed.

I doubt there will be the same reservations when Matthew, Rose's brother, gets around to asking for my granddaughter's hand. A delightful young man, he's been sensitive enough to wait until his sister's engagement has been announced and all congratulations made – but everyone knows it's coming. Céleste is delighted and I couldn't be more pleased; Matthew is strong enough to make sure Sophia doesn't get all her own way.

Perhaps there'll be a double wedding and I can only hope it's soon. To see both Sophia and Tobias settled is what keeps me going.

That's not to say that I'm not concerned about Young Alice, now that her two close friends and brother are to be married. I've long had the feeling that Young Alice will travel. It's a vague notion but I definitely see her on the continent somewhere rather than spending her days here at the Grange. I mentioned this to her some time ago and she laughed, accusing me of getting her confused with her Aunt Astrea – but that was before Hendrick arrived.

Despite all her original protestations that helping with the accounts would interfere with her social life, Young Alice has become a very competent bookkeeper and, inevitably, this has occasioned a certain amount of interaction with the new farm manager. Even Anne has remarked on her daughter's new-found interest in the estate. Hendrick, for his part, has been the model of propriety, never overstepping the mark, but some of us have noticed the way he looks at her.

I knew that Anne would mention it sooner or later.

'We know nothing about him, Aunt, and Samuel would consider a match between them totally unthinkable.'

I was thinking how to reply.

'Well?' Impatiently rearranging the cushions. 'What do you think?'

'Would it really be totally unthinkable?'

'Yes. Would my parents have allowed me to marry our old farm manager?'

I couldn't help laughing. 'That's ridiculous Anne. Henry Durling was an uneducated farm boy who'd worked his way up to manager and was decades older than you. He wasn't even handsome.'

'I don't think you're taking this seriously...'

'I am. I just think you can't compare two men merely because they have the same job title. Hendrick is educated, speaks several languages, is a talented engineer and obviously has farming in his blood. Frankly, I'm not sure why he's still here.'

'Because he and Tobias get on so well, I've always thought.'

'True, but there must be more to it than that, and now I suspect it's Alice who's keeping him here.'

And, of course, there was more to it. Tobias had been aware from the start that it was a family rift that meant Hendrick had no desire to return to the Netherlands, but that was all he knew. It was only when Hendrick became aware that Alice returned his interest that he knew he had no option but to explain himself.

This is what Tobias was told.

Hendrick's mother was a weak woman who'd been widowed young when he was a small boy. Clearly a shock to find herself the sole owner of substantial landholdings, it was no surprise when she quickly re-married and raised a second family. The trouble arose years later when Hendrick realised he was being groomed to marry the daughter of his stepfather's friend, expected to then leave the family home and work for his future father-in-law in commerce. Meanwhile, his young step-brother, who had no interest in farming, was in line to inherit Hendrick's father's estate.

With an appeal to his mother producing tears, hand-wringing and little else, the ensuing row resulted in a refusal to go along with his stepfather's plans; Hendrick walked out and has never been back. As he said to Tobias, 'I can't be bought to give up my birthright. If they're going to take it from me, so be it, I'll put it behind me and make my own way in the world.'

Anne and I both agreed it was a noble sentiment.

~ 29 ~
1678-83, London

'**I**'ve been paying rent to you all these years?' His face was one of astonishment.

'It was very reasonable, Jean-Michel, you must admit that.' Elisabeth shrugged and bit her lip. For some reason she was finding it funny and was struggling not to show it. 'And I haven't increased it once in five years...'

He opened his mouth to speak, closed it again and shook his head, trying to make sense of what he'd just heard.

'Am I the only idiot who doesn't know this?'

Aphra's words came back to haunt her and she leaned forward and took both his hands in hers. 'No, please, please don't think that. Truly, no one round here knows. You must understand it was a very sensible decision at first; I wanted to live here without people treating me differently.'

'But what about when we got married? Didn't it occur to you then that it was a good time to tell me everything?'

'It did, but I was scared that it would change things between us.' She could feel tears lurking and blinked them away. 'I only had good intentions, I swear.'

He released one hand and tucked a stray curl behind her ear. 'So, tell me truthfully Elisabeth, why own up now?'

She leaned back in her chair, took a deep breath and outlined her proposal.

He listened, nodding occasionally, not faulting her logic.

'But how would you feel about leaving the house – your house?'

'It will still be my house, and the extra rent we get from it will help to pay for the rent on the new place. We've outgrown it, Jean-Michel. Truth to tell, we outgrew it some time ago; your business is doing so well...'

'Our business is doing so well...'

She smiled. 'Yes, our business is doing so well that you're working your fingers to the bone trying to keep up. We need two more looms, at least one more experienced man and an apprentice, plus a proper office which serves as a reception for clients.' She suddenly realised that the picture in her mind was of Bernard's office.

He was silent for a while. As long as he had Elisabeth and the baby, plenty of work and enough food on the table, that was all he really needed, but competition was strong and even he was coming to realise that he would lose work if they couldn't improve their output.

'Are you sure we can afford to move to larger premises?'

'Yes, even on our current orders.' The fact that she could easily buy another property was not something she was about to admit. He wouldn't thank her for subsidising him again. 'This is not a risky move, Jean-Michel. I'm happy to use all that money you paid me in rent to buy two more looms, and if it doesn't work we can always go back to the old house.'

It was said to mollify him, of course. Elisabeth had already seen how successful Jean-Michel would become and how it would give him confidence and stature in their community. This was the best gift she could give him.

Nothing much was going to change in the old house; there would be no trouble finding new tenants for the upstairs rooms and Elisabeth was going to retain the basement and herb garden. This meant that the clinic and crèche could continue just as before, Julianne would stay on, and Elisabeth could keep her own work entirely separate from the business. Jean-Michel didn't know it yet, but Elisabeth was going to need an assistant; she couldn't be in two places at the same time.

It was in the middle of the big move, not too far away, still in Spital Fields, when Elisabeth received a message that Alice was about to deliver her baby. Jean-Michel was not happy, but there was no question in her mind that she couldn't be with her, and it was just as well. Unlike with Alice's first child, this turned out to be a long, difficult birth when things could easily have gone the other way and both could have been lost. She stayed an extra day to attend to Alice's body, reassure Joseph that all would be well, that the baby was a fighter and that Jennet was perfectly capable of looking after both of them, before hurrying back to London. There'd been no time to meet up with Melina.

* * *

Within a couple of years, there was no looking back for Jean-Michel, who'd finally grown into the role of employer and recently found time to indulge his creative flair. It was a busy, but happy and contented time for the family, with the only cloud on the horizon being the news coming out of France.

Spital Fields was seeing a fresh influx of French artisans; not just weavers, but clockmakers and silversmiths too, and the picture they were painting was worrying. King Louis XIV's tactic of paying Protestants to convert to Catholicism was having little to no effect and he'd finally resorted to ordering the destruction of Huguenot churches and schools in his determination to make France wholly Catholic. One rumour was particularly chilling if

SUSAN GREENWOOD

true – dragoons and infantrymen were being billeted in Protestant homes to intimidate and abuse the owners into either converting or emigrating.

Elisabeth remembered meeting the French king at her first husband's funeral. It bothered her that someone so charming, sympathetic and gracious, could be capable of such vindictiveness and cruelty as these reports suggested, and it reminded her that Bernard, himself no longer religious, had frequently urged her to pay lip-service to a religion that she no longer felt comfortable with. She blessed the day she decided to make her home in England.

Jean-Michel had had no news of his parents for nearly a year. 'Thankfully, they're far away from Paris and perhaps they're not affected by all this.'

Elisabeth nodded. 'Maybe, but you won't stop worrying until you know. You should go and visit them, we can manage here.'

'And leave you and Céleste alone?'

'I won't be alone.' She gestured with both arms. 'The place is full of people. Philippe and Madeleine are just around the corner and, if it makes you happier, you can always ask one of the men to stay over till you get back.'

It was settled. He went, but it was weeks before he returned, sad and frustrated that he wasn't able to persuade them to leave for England.

'My father refuses to leave his business and my mother refuses to leave her daughters and grandchildren.' He ran a hand over his face, still upset. 'If forced, they say they will convert and hide their true religion.'

Elisabeth nodded. She had an uneasy feeling that religion would cause problems in England too, before long.

235

~ 30 ~
Summer 1724

I haven't been myself lately. My head aches and my mind keeps wandering, try as I might to pin it down to just one train of thought. Hopefully, I'm just sickening for something, for I'd quite like my mind to be intact when the time comes for me to leave this world.

For weeks, the household has been busy with preparations for the wedding and, as there's nothing I can contribute, I find myself more often than not in the kitchen for company. Mary persists in dosing me up with remedies and I think it kinder to accept them with gratitude rather than tell her that nothing is going to help my poor body now.

Perhaps I'm unsettled because it is years since I've had the sort of visions that have plagued me for the last few days, and they've always left me feeling a little disorientated. I don't recognise the girl and I can't make any sense of them. She's possibly about 12 or 13, barefoot, and dressed like any other village child, but she's staring at me, as if willing me to understand what she's not saying. Then, a quick turn of her head and she's off, running away from me through the trees.

'Have you seen a strange peasant girl around here recently, Mary?'

'Strange how?'

'Not a local, I mean.' Although 'odd' applied just as well, I thought.

She slopped some rabbit entrails into a bucket and rinsed her hands. 'No, I don't think so. Why?' Now wiping her hands on her apron. 'Have you seen her on the estate?'

'I thought I saw her the other day. She'll be about 12 or 13, dark hair, probably just one of the village girls, I expect. They grow up so quickly these days and my eyesight isn't what it was.'

She gave me a sympathetic smile and laid a hand on my shoulder. 'Let me brew you a nice, herbal tea, Madame, you look cold. It's a bit chilly in here till that fire gets going properly.'

I was cold, she was right, and I inched my chair closer to the fire just as the kitchen door flew open letting in a surprisingly fierce gust of wind that sent smoke billowing round the kitchen.

Gabe shut it quickly and slapped two more rabbits on the chopping board. 'Good morning, Madam.' He smiled and pulled off his cap. 'Sorry about that, it's a strong wind today.' Leaning into the scullery, he raised his voice. 'These two should do for you, Mary, but let me know if you want any more.'

I smiled as he came closer to me.

'How are you both, Gabe? It's been a while.'

'We're well, Madam, thank you for asking. Lucille is still walking every day, you know, in the woods.'

I nodded. Of course, she was. I envied her.

A quick look behind and he leaned forward, whispering. 'She found a snare. I'm just on my way to tell Master Tobias.'

'Not in Fox Wood?' My heart gave a lurch.

'Aye...' He stepped away as Mary appeared behind him with my tea. 'I'd better be off then. Glad to see you looking so well, Madam.'

He nodded and replaced his cap.

'Remember me to Lucille.'

'Aye, Madam, I will.'

While Mary skinned, gutted and chopped, I nursed my tea and stared into the flames as I wondered who'd be stupid enough to lay snares in Fox Wood.

Tobias will be furious.

* * *

I've developed a summer chill, and I'm relieved now I know what it is. I'm also not the only one in the household to suffer it, but anyone would think I was in imminent danger of turning up my toes, the way everyone is fussing over me. Still, it's lovely to know they care, as long as they don't go worrying Céleste.

Young Alice has been keeping me company most evenings, even sharing supper in my room sometimes while she keeps me up-to-date with goings-on while I've been up here. That's mainly to do with Tobias and Rose and the upcoming wedding, of course, but Hendrick is a close second.

'I'm 22, Aunt. If Mother doesn't pluck up courage to have a proper talk with Father soon, then Hendrick and I are going to have to do it together. Either he's completely oblivious to what's happening under his nose, or he's just ignoring it and hoping it'll go away.'

'But it won't'

'No. The few chances we get to be together aren't enough and I resent having to creep around in secret when Tobias, Rose and even Sophie can...' A hand flew up to her mouth and she blinked hard. 'I'm sorry. I'm happy for them all, truly, I just...'

'I know, Alice, you don't have to explain. I see how difficult it is for you both but you're going to have to wait until after the wedding.'

She nodded. 'Well, thank goodness they've named the day now.'

I knew bringing up this next matter would embarrass her, but I felt I had to do it. I knew Anne wouldn't.

'Difficult though it is to believe, I can still remember being young, Alice, feeling exactly as you do now, and I know how easy it is to forget oneself. Is there anything you want to discuss?'

She dropped her gaze, the blush rose from her neck, and it was a while before she could find the words.

'If it were down to me, Aunt, I'd probably forget myself every time I see him.' She looked me straight in the eye and gave a grim, little smile. 'That's shocking, isn't it? Luckily, he's far too honourable for that.'

'I'm not shocked, Alice, you're a grown woman with normal feelings. And yes, he's a good man and I feel sure your Father will come to see that. Hendrick knows it wouldn't be the right thing to force his hand.' I paused to let that sink in. 'Having said that, if you do ever find yourself in trouble, you must come to me first, do you understand?'

There was nothing more to be said on the subject.

Alice rang for Mary to clear the supper things and placed the tray outside my door before coming back to kiss me goodnight.

'Oh, I forgot to tell you, I've been so caught up with myself. Tobias found out that someone's been setting traps in our top wood. Gabe found a gin and some snares.'

'A gin trap? I heard about the snare but I didn't know there was a gin too. Does he know who's done it?'

'No, but Tobias went to both the local inns last night, slammed the gin on the bar and challenged all the men to give up whoever is responsible. Hendrick went with him and said he'd never seen him so angry, reminding them all that the Grange has never stopped anyone in the village taking the odd game from our woods as long as it's done properly with a good kill. He said if he found they were protecting whoever had done it, then that would all change.'

'I'm assuming no one owned up then?'

'No, but one man stopped Hendrick in the village this morning and said he'd had to shoot a deer he'd found dying with one of its legs torn off.'

The foxes. Lucille. It didn't bear thinking about.

I don't believe any villager who works for Tobias would be stupid enough to use a gin trap. Everyone knows how he feels about that and they wouldn't risk losing their job. They might chance a snare, thinking no one bothers with Fox Wood these days – but surely not a gin.

All of this makes me think the culprit is an incomer. An incomer, perhaps, with a young girl who runs barefoot. Maybe a young girl who's keen to tell me something, but is too afraid.

Am I making connections that aren't there? Not for the first time, Bernard's voice is in my head, telling me to trust my instincts, and the more I think about it, the more I know I'm right. It must be four years since that man was here but I'm sure he's back now, my skin is cold and prickling at the very thought. Has he come to avenge his mother, now that he knows I'm too old to stand up to him? Or is he here to do what Zillah attempted all those years ago? If that's the case, I'm not sure how I can make Tobias understand the danger.

I need to see Lucille.

* * *

'The wind may have dropped, Aunt, but there's still a chill in the air and you are not yet recovered. Why don't you wait a few more days?'

'I'm quite well now, Anne, just bored with having to stay inside. I can't walk very far these days as you know, but a ride in the fresh air will do me a power of good. If it's inconvenient for me to use the trap tomorrow, just say so.'

It was so rare that I was short with Anne she knew not to argue. 'Of course it's convenient, I only offered the carriage because it's so much more comfortable for a trip out.'

'Yes, I know, Anne, and thank you, but I just need to be outside. If it's alright with you, Mary has offered to call on Gabe to see if he's free.'

'Good, well that's settled then.'

I knew she'd have a word with Gabe first, but still I was surprised to see the extra rugs, a stone foot-warmer and a flask of warm honeyed port already in the trap.

Gabe permitted himself a grin. 'I told Mrs. Lyckfold not to worry, that I'll take good care of you.'

I really don't deserve this, not after the way I spoke to Anne yesterday, and especially as I'll probably be spending most of the time with Lucille indoors. Nevertheless, they are all very welcome – especially the port.

I wasn't expecting to take a walk in the woods but Lucille persuaded me.

'From what you've described, Madame, it's the same girl.'

'You've spoken with her?'

'No, she stalks me when I go to the clearing but never comes close.'

I had to laugh. 'That's a perfect description of you, Lucille, when you weren't much older than her.'

'Yes, that's true. And, like me, I imagine she's always known about you. If she's going to talk to anyone, it'll be you. Gabe will take us as far as he can along the path and then it'll only be a short walk to the clearing if we need to go that far. There's no danger, Gabe found the traps deep in the wood.

I wasn't at all convinced she'd show, but Lucille was right. Although aware of her long before we reached the clearing, we continued there so we could sit.

'Perhaps I should leave you, Madame.'

'No, I want her to know she's safe with both of us.'

As silent as any woodland creature, the child approached us from the trees at our back and knelt behind us. We both half-turned to look at her. Large, expressive eyes in a heart-shaped face looked from one to the other. She touched my arm, then smiled and nodded to Lucille.

'Yes, this is Lucille, she brought me to meet you. What is your name?'

No answer.

I tried again, pointing to Lucille. 'Lucille' and then to myself, 'Elisabeth'.

She understood, pointing to herself. 'Vadoma.' Then a sentence which meant nothing to me, and 'Doma', repeating it twice.

I smiled. 'Doma, it is.'

'Do you speak her language, Madame?'

'No, it's nothing like French. I know bits of other languages, but it's nothing like those either.'

I searched around, found a stick and signalled for the child to sit next to me whilst I drew shapes in the dirt; first a child, then two adults, one larger than the other, with a circle around the three.

Quick to grasp what I was asking, she took the stick and rubbed out the adults.

'She's alone, no parents?'

'No parents, I'm sure, but I don't think she's alone.' I was racking my brains to think how to ask when Doma started scratching with the stick.

When she'd finished, Lucille and I both come to the same conclusion. It was a crude family tree – one large stick figure, two smaller pairs and three tiny figures grouped together with one small figure off to one side.

I pointed to the separate figure and she patted her chest.

Lucille traced a ring around all the other figures. Doma nodded.

Whether that meant the others were one family, or just that she considered herself separate from them, was hard to tell. But I had a good idea who the large figure represented.

Lucille pointed to the large stick figure and drew two faces; one with a smile and one with a frown. Doma took the stick from her and quickly drew a line from the figure to the frown. She jabbed it into the face over and over.

'What are we going to do, Madame?'

Before I could even think, Doma was tugging at my sleeve, repeating one phrase over and over, her little face crumpled with the effort of trying to make us understand. When that didn't work, she kept pointing to me as she stamped hard on the frowning face until her own was red and her little chest heaving.

The meaning was as clear as if we'd been speaking the same language.

~ 31 ~
1685-89, London

'Aren't you pleased, Elisabeth? I shall only be a short walk away; for you, that is. I'm not sure I'm brave enough to walk the streets of Spital Fields.'

Elisabeth raised an eyebrow and Aphra laughed. They both knew only too well the reason Aphra wouldn't be walking and it had nothing to do with the neighbourhood.

'Of course, yes, it's well-known that cut-throats and rapists prowl the area all the time. But I do believe New Street is right in Spital Fields, isn't it?'

'Oh, barely on the edge, Elisabeth, I really don't think it counts.' With a theatrical wave, the sardonic grin slowly turned into a rueful smile. 'Twenty years ago, weren't you and I running around with the cream of London society in the heart of the City? And now look where we are.'

'Two grown-up, independent women, Aphra. There are many who would envy us.'

'The difference being that you could still do that if you wanted to, whereas I ...'

Aphra patted the space next to her on the daybed and Elisabeth duly changed seats, linked arms and rested her head on her friend's shoulder.

'Seriously now, why didn't you tell me you were so short of money?'

'Oh, my love, do we have to go through all this again? I'm doing well, really. The novel is a success; so too are the comedies so beloved of the King, all of which have been staged in Court, but I can't hang on to money like you do, Elisabeth. If I have it, I spend it, and if I take from you I'd only waste it, so I thank you, but I'll not be accepting your generosity.'

Elisabeth turned to look her in the face. 'I'm well aware of your successes. They've been hard won and are richly deserved, but it's common knowledge that the King and his brother expect the honour of serving them to be sufficient. Wasn't it just the same twenty years ago when they sent you to Antwerp on a spying mission and left you there without the means to get home?'

Aphra shrugged. There was no point arguing against what they both knew to be the truth – that she wanted the fame and recognition more than she wanted the money. There was nothing more to be said on the subject.

'Tell me about your new accommodation. What's it like?'

'Small, but I don't need much and my maid is going to live out.'

Elisabeth was about to say something, but changed her mind when she saw the set of Aphra's mouth.

'Fine, well, I shall get Julianne to visit you every week with whatever you need from the clinic. I hope you can accept that?'

By way of answer, Aphra leaned forward and kissed her friend.

It was all Elisabeth could do to help, and if some extra little luxury items happened to be included with the pills and potions, then she was sure they wouldn't be refused.

* * *

Not long after Aphra moved into New Street, King Charles II died suddenly.

There was no denying it was a surprise to everyone. So much so that rumours soon circulated that the death may have been something other than natural. With no legitimate heir – although his illegitimate ones were legion – Charles II's brother, the Duke of York, became King James II. He was the first Catholic monarch of England for nearly 130 years and, despite his stated desire to give religious freedom to all, it did not sit well with the general public who saw 'Romanists swarming at Court'. Anyone wanting to further their ambitions and attain royal patronage soon converted. For Elisabeth, this confirmed something she'd foreseen, and for Jean-Michel, a confirmed Protestant, it felt like history was repeating itself.

Luckily, this didn't affect Aphra who had no particular religious leaning. She wrote and performed an elegy to King Charles, and penned a long public political ode to King James and his wife, Mary of Modena, playing up the close bond between the two brothers.

As Elisabeth knew very well, other, male poets had been well rewarded for such efforts, but nothing was forthcoming for Aphra. All her energies had yielded little in terms of anything tangible or, indeed, any improved status.

If it dampened her spirits, no one would have known. It failed to send her into a literary decline, and despite her poor health, more plays followed as she desperately needed the income, meagre though it was.

'Uncle George and Lady Caroline went to see 'The Lucky Chance', Aphra. They say it went down very well indeed, with nothing to alarm all the notable ladies of quality who lined the best seats and were quite vigorous in their applause. Of course, my uncle wants you to know that he regrets you feel the need to tone down your work, as he always enjoyed the more salacious parts the best.'

Aphra laughed. 'I thank him for that, but he may well be in the minority. And my bowing to the current mood hasn't stopped the usual suspects from the age-old criticism that I'm a 'bawdy female' playwright. Some men will never accept that what is fine for the gander, is also fine for the goose.'

'So, what's next? I saw a draft of 'Oroonoko' on your desk.'

Aphra picked another little sweetmeat from Elisabeth's latest delivery and savoured it before replying. 'I've been playing around with that tale for years, you know, and I've decided not to turn it into a play.'

'Oh, no, why? I remember the day you told us all about him. We were upstairs in the guest bedroom at Oakwood Grange and Alice and I hung on your every word.'

'You think people are ready to hear about an African prince ripped from his home and sold into slavery, then?'

'But it's so much more than that, Aphra. It's romance and death, treachery and tragedy and...'

Aphra was grinning. 'Well, it's just as well I'm going to write it as a story then, isn't it? It's true there's far too much going on for a play –and can you conceive of how it would be staged? The disembowelling scene might prove difficult.'

To make ends meet as she was writing the novel, Aphra took on some translation work; the only problem being that Latin was not her forté. Luckily, she knew someone who was willing to help.

'Are you sure?'

'Yes. We have an assistant in the office now, and Julianne rules the clinic so I have plenty of time to help you. To be honest, I'm looking forward to it. Latin was always my best subject, and something the nuns couldn't criticise me for.'

'I always forget you were raised as a Catholic, Elisabeth.'

'I'm not sure I was ever truly committed and, anyway, once I was out in the world I followed my own path. As you do.'

The ensuing weeks and months drew the two friends closer than *they had ever been, with Elisabeth faithfully translating Juvenal's poetry whilst Aphra moulded his words into heroic couplets for a modern public. It was a successful partnership which invigorated both of them in the intellectual sense, but it was the conversations and confidences exchanged between sessions that bound them in a deeper appreciation of each other.*

Two years later in 1688, 'Oroonoko' was published as a short novel, less than a year before Aphra died.

Elisabeth often wondered how Aphra would have reacted to the theatrical adaptation which took to the stage some 6 years after her death – a hugely successful play that ran and ran for many years in the following century. On the occasions when she heard her late friend's voice, Elisabeth was careful only to tell her of the continuing success of her novel.

~ 32 ~

Summer 1724

I wonder whether I've ever really come to terms with being absent when Aphra died. Having recently revived the closeness we'd known in our early years together, by 1689 we both knew the end was very near.

There was nothing more I could do for her. Not yet fifty, she moved like an old woman and even writing was proving difficult. Typically, she accepted her fate.

'You were right about the mercury, Elisabeth. It was gruesome and probably accelerated the whole process, but perhaps that's not such a bad thing, eh? I'm better off out of this world because nothing changes; a woman with 'the clap' is censured whilst the man who gave it to her is considered a cavalier.' She'd waved an arm over her desk. 'And, if I'm honest, I'm fairly happy with the body of work I'm leaving behind.'

On the day she died, Jean-Michel and I argued. It had been brewing for some time, I think, but it was a shock to realise just how resentful he'd been feeling. As I'd spent a long time training my personable and competent assistant to do everything the way Jean-Michel wanted, I'd chafed when he insisted I stay to welcome and parade new clients around the business – because I was sure that Aphra's time had come.

It all came out in rapid French, proof if ever I needed it that he was angry. The recent lapses in my behaviour had become too much for him, he said. An assistant should be just that, not someone to take over all my duties. He actually used the word 'duties' – to me, who'd made everything possible for him. In addition, I'd spent far too much time at the old house with Julianne and the clinic, teaching Céleste subjects she would never need when she married, and why had I recently taken on hours of translating work for Aphra? He never saw me. Was it really too much to ask that I give him, and our business, a few hours to impress new clients?

It was not the time to argue, but neither could I make him understand how I needed to be with Aphra on that particular morning. I performed my 'duties' for the requisite few hours and left as soon as the clients did.

Meeting Aphra's maid on her way to fetch me, we both hurried back to New Street but, as I feared, we were too late.

It was no comfort at the time to be told by Jean-Michel that the dying often choose the time of their passing for when they're alone. But all these years later, I wonder if he may have been right in Aphra's case.

Things were never the same between us after that. I couldn't have been prouder of the success he'd made of the business, or the way he'd become a prominent member of the Huguenot community, but there was no denying this had come at the expense of our relationship.

* * *

I remember 1689 as a busy year, and it reminds me that I've now lived under seven different monarchies. Having deposed James II, the new King and Queen, William and Mary, were given a splendid coronation and it seemed that England gave a collective sigh of relief that the throne was Protestant once more. It made Jean-Michel very happy indeed, although the situation in France for Protestants had worsened, with emigration for them now banned. That was the end of all hope that his parents or siblings might join him one day.

Aphra's funeral was held shortly after the coronation. She was buried in the East Cloister of Westminster Abbey, and Alice and I attended along with a host of artists and aristocrats keen to pay their final respects. The inscription on her tomb reads 'Here lies a Proof that Wit can never be defence enough against Mortality' and I heard her laugh as I read it. Alice and I both noted the position of the tomb – not in the main body, but off to the side. I know what she would have made of that.

Jean-Michel and I muddled along, as couples often do. I'm old enough now to look back and admit that, consciously or not, I was weaning Jean-Michel from his dependence on me. Motherhood and the clinic fulfilled me, I felt freer than I had for some time, and my body no longer ached for a man.

None of that was fair to Jean-Michel. He deserved a proper wife for life, I knew that, for he was a man who always needed a woman by his side.

Added to that was the pull from home. In his case, I'd foreseen that he'd return to France before too long; he now had money enough to care for his family and when the time came, he'd want to be buried in French soil.

And I always knew that I would end my life not in France, or even London, but here, at Oakwood Grange in the Sussex countryside.

* * *

Recalling Aphra's funeral brings to mind that my next trip back to the Grange that year was to be present at Jennet's. As wet-nurse to a little girl who had then lost her mother at fifteen years old, the relationship between Alice and Jennet was as strong as that of a natural mother and child. She had been a fixture around the place for so long that her passing left a huge hole, as witnessed by the packed church and very few dry eyes.

The following years saw many happy times at the Grange, mainly because Céleste loved being here. This was fortunate for me as Jean-Michel found it difficult to refuse his daughter anything – and what she wanted in the summer months was to be in the countryside, riding out with Alice's daughters, Anne and Astrea. She had a better social life here than she had in London, and I'm certain Julianne got to hear more about that than I did.

We did manage to get Jean-Michel to accompany us on a few occasions, notably to Anne's wedding and later, to Tobias and Charles's christenings. But I think it was in 1700 at Astrea's wedding that he finally made up his mind to return home to France. As Alice pointed out, one would have to be blind not to see that a certain young man from Petworth and Céleste appeared to have an understanding, and the chances were that Céleste would not be making her main home in London.

Barely a year later, all our lives changed.

Postponed because Alice's husband, Joseph, had recently died, when it finally went ahead, Céleste's wedding to Jonathon was a grand affair at Jonathon's family home. With so many people we didn't know, Jean-Michel and I, together with the Grange tribe, tended to stick together and it didn't go unnoticed that Jean-Michel was finding the occasion particularly emotional. Having recently sold the business, insisting on splitting the proceeds between us, this was going to be the last time he'd see his daughter for quite some time. Preparations were underway for his return to France.

Try as I might to blot out our final farewell, it's impossible. Even now, after all these years, it springs into my mind unbidden; I see his face, taste his kiss and feel his tears on my cheek in that last embrace. Knowing it was the right thing, didn't make it any easier for either of us.

I had no desire to go back to my old house, and the new business owners were more than happy for me to stay in our rooms, but I knew it wouldn't be for long. I'd been waiting for a message from Alice to tell me when Anne's third child was due, but when I received it there was another reason for me to make haste. Alice had been laid up with a broken leg.

I can picture her now after the birth, Alice in bed cradling her latest grandchild, a sister for Tobias and Charles.

'Anne and Samuel have just told me that this little mite is to be called Alice Elisabeth Lyckfold. What do you think of that?'

I remember feeling quite ridiculously pleased. Although both Anne and Astrea had Elisabeth as their middle names, for it to be passed to another generation somehow anchored me to this family. The proof came later when Anne insisted I move into the Grange permanently and I felt it came from the heart, and not just because Alice knew I wanted it.

Grandparents aren't supposed to have a favourite grandchild – I avoided that pitfall by having only Sophia – but it had been clear from the start that there was a special bond between Alice and Tobias. He adored her, and losing her when he was 10 years old left a void that Alice was determined I should fill.

In one of our last conversations, she said, 'I'm handing him over to you, Elisabeth, because I know you understand him the way I do. Please keep him safe for me. He has a big job ahead of him, looking after this estate and he may need your help.'

I promised.

'And do you think you might now tell me how you got rid of that Zillah woman?'

She'd waited nearly thirty years to ask that question and I wasn't about to lie.

'I told her to go and she did. That's the truth.'

'Yes, you told me that before. Is she dead?'

'I didn't kill her, Alice. If you want to know if she's still alive, I don't know for certain.'

'It was a quite a battle, wasn't it? I saw the state of you when you returned and that ugly wound on your leg was never caused by a fall. I didn't press you then because I could see you weren't willing to talk about it, but I'd like to know now – please. You can't deny a dying woman.'

So I told her nearly everything, only leaving out Melina and her role in it. It was too late in the day to explain Melina and Lucille, and I couldn't face her knowing I'd kept that from her. But I did own up to the curse.

'I was hoping she'd believe it, as William Harryman once did.'

Tears threatened as she grabbed my hand and pulled me close. 'You could have been killed, and it wasn't even your battle.'

'But someone needed to stand up to her. Who else had the

power to do that, Alice?

There's a reason this conversation is circulating in my head now. For my own piece of mind, I've long convinced myself that curses don't exist other than as a tool to scare. Melina agreed, although she may have been placating me. Whatever the truth, it seems the curse was enough to keep Zillah away from here, but what of her family? *'Should you ever set foot on this estate again, or, indeed, any of your blood relatives, you or they will pay a terrible price.'* I remember clearly what I said, so if they know about it, they clearly don't believe it. I'm sure the son is back, I have no idea of his capabilities, I'm old, it's years since I used my powers – and now I have a gypsy girl convinced I can save her. No wonder I'm unsettled.

* * *

'I think it's the same group of itinerants who tried to find work here a few years ago.' Tobias was leading Hendrick into the kitchen. 'If it is, the leader's an insolent chap. I remember he tried to pick a fight with Gabe back then and I'm a bit sorry I stopped him to tell you the truth.'

They clattered in in their boots. 'Ah, Aunt Elisabeth, sorry to disturb you, we've just come to see if Cook's left us some pie and ale. She said she would...'

I nodded a greeting to Hendrick. 'It'll be under the cover on the slab in the larder. You won't be in for midday meal then?'

'No, would you tell Mother for me? We're going to tour Top Wood with Gabe to see if we can find any of those traps.' He came out of the larder and handed the jug of ale to Hendrick. 'I think you were with me, Aunt, when we saw those itinerants a few years ago with Gabe. Do you remember, we were taking a ride in the trap?'

'I remember it well, and him in particular.' Wishing I could tell him about Doma, I settled for the next best thing. 'I had a bad feeling about that man then, Tobias. I think the three of you should stick together.'

He grinned. 'We'll be fine, don't worry. I think Gabe's looking forward to it.'

I'll bet he is, I thought. Especially if Lucille's told him about Doma.

I had a restless night. Tobias, Hendrick and Gabe had come back with another gin trap, evidence of a small fire, and nothing else. Doma came to me again last night, not pleading as before, but sitting slightly apart from the rest of the group, her hands in a bowl scrubbing dishes, the bruises on her arms already turning yellow. I knew exactly where they were camped.

I thought about sending a message to Gabe via Mary, but I'm too impatient.

'Tobias, I'm glad I caught you.' He was just finishing first breakfast in the kitchen.

'This is a bit early for you Aunt, couldn't you sleep?'

I shrugged. 'Nothing unusual at my age. I've been thinking though about where those itinerants might be.'

'They've gone, I think. We've looked all over the wood.'

'Yes, you said. But over by the north-west corner, on the very edge of the wood, the land falls away sharply into a dell – do you know where I mean?

'I don't think I've been that far and I'm not sure if we own that area just beyond the wood.'

'Well, it would be the perfect place to hide, that's what I'm thinking.'

His face broke into a grin. 'And what would you know about hidden dells where nobody could find you, eh? Did you perhaps have a secret liaison, Aunt, with a handsome travelling man back when you were first here?'

I treated him to one of my withering looks and he laughed out loud.

'I know about it because I used to walk over there regularly. I told you that ages ago, and it was a place where I found some rare herbs. Satisfied now?'

He was still grinning. 'Well, I'll mention it to Gabe. I dare say he'll know where you mean and we'll check it just to make sure. It would certainly be handy for laying traps into the wood.'

I sat alone after he left, thinking about his comment that the dell may not be Grange land.

~ 33 ~
Summer 1724

I won't be sleeping tonight.

Gabe confirmed that the travellers are in the dell, and he and Tobias are going to try and catch them in the wood after nightfall. All I can do is lie here and worry. Gabe is taking his blunderbuss and Tobias his flintlock, but they may be no match if Zillah's son has the sort of weapons his mother had.

I can't foresee what's going to happen and feel useless; so much for my promise to Alice.

The next time I blink, I'm in their camp in the dell. My redundant old body is left behind and my senses are wandering free. It's a little disorientating. I didn't imagine this was possible again but there's no time to indulge the feeling as it usually serves as a warning. I'm here for a reason.

I see Doma squatting outside a makeshift tent. It is nothing more than a few scraps of fabric stretched over some bent branches and I'm shocked to see an anklet and chain nearby. She is not chained at this moment and I watch as she sways to some inner music whilst she plaits her hair over one shoulder. Abruptly, she stops what she's doing, sits bolt upright with head cocked on one side, eyes darting to left and right, before settling back with a slight smile. She knows I'm here.

I leave her behind to hover near the others huddled in a circle around a dying fire.

Vano, for that is Zillah's son's name, I discover, is telling a tale that makes them all laugh. There are two other men and two young women, with looks that suggest they are Vano's daughters. Both are cradling sleeping babies and another small child lies asleep on the ground. As if it's some sort of signal, Vano knocks out his pipe and both women stand, gathering up the older child, but stop short of their tents when a sound echoes from the wood. All five look at each other.

Vano holds up a finger. 'That was a deer's cry if ever I heard one, lads. You'd better get up there quick, it'll need the both of you.' He stands and kicks over the last few embers. 'Go on now, girls, to bed with you all. We'll be busy tomorrow, if I'm right.'

'What about her?'

Vano looks over to Doma. 'I reckon she's learned her lesson.' He rattles something off in Doma's language. She replies and I see her kick away the anklet with a question mark in her eyes.

He shrugs and turns back to his daughter. 'Leave her. She knows there'll be good food tomorrow.'

As he turns away from her, I see another little smile creep over her face and I sense what she's going to do. She crawls into her tent and pulls down the flap.

Relieved that Vano is staying behind, I watch the two young men walk to where the overhang is not so steep and tread a well-worn path to the top of the bank. One carries a knife and a sack, the other a hammer, and neither appears to have a firearm. I wonder if Vano always leaves the others to do this work.

I'm hoping the cry I heard was Gabe and not some poor animal, for that might complicate matters. The plan, as Tobias explained it earlier today, is for Gabe to mimic the animal cry and draw the travellers to the wood to search all the traps, then watch whilst they remain in hiding. It was the best way of finding where they'd placed them all – as Gabe reckons there are more than he originally thought and no markers he could make out.

Their plan seems to be working well so far and I can't see that I'd be much use to them. Vano is the only one who troubles me but, even if he decides to follow his men, it's doubtful I could help.

I drift back to Doma's tent. Within seconds, I hear her humming a tune and assume that she knows I'm still here. I concentrate hard and fix an image of Lucille in my head. The humming stops and I hear one tap. I add Gabe to the image, standing next to Lucille, a broad smile wrinkling his eyes. Another tap; I try to hurry things along with an image of Gabe and Tobias in the wood. Nothing, she's confused. I try again with an image of myself and Tobias, smiling and holding hands.

I don't need to do more. As if excited, she taps a few times and I think she understands.

I see her twitch the flap of her tent. She'll know when the time is right and all I can do is stay to give her encouragement and companionship.

All is quiet from the women's tents. One baby woke earlier, but its cries were soon muffled by a milky breast and everyone settled down again fairly quickly. Vano has now taken out his tobacco pouch and lights another pipe from the dying embers. I was hoping he wouldn't stay up to wait for the men to return with their prize, but it's a vain hope. He is impatient, pacing up and down.

Twice, I see Doma think about making a move, but he never gives her enough time to reach cover. His twelve or thirteen paces forward and back are not enough. I begin to feel her desperation and try to calm her down.

Just when I think she's missed the opportunity, I see him loosen his belt, change direction and head for a stand of trees. There'll be no better chance. Doma seizes it, leaves the tent clutching a hessian bag to her chest, and runs to a small holly bush at the base of the steep bank. It's not the most comfortable of hiding places but it's the only cover available. I stay with her.

Looking behind her to assess the distance to the next safe point, she hesitates for a few crucial seconds. She might have made it, but now Vano is back, pipe clamped between his teeth whilst he fiddles with the fly buttons and his belt. I fancy I can hear her little heart thumping away.

She looks behind again. There is still the path to climb before she can reach the relative safety of the wood, and the full moon isn't helping. Her clothes are drab apart from a white scarf wrapped around her head and I concentrate hard on that until she rips it off and stuffs it into her bag.

Vano is still unsettled, although I'm thinking it's too early to expect the men back yet. He senses something, I'm sure of it; something different about this night, perhaps he even knows I'm close. He wanders over to the women's tent where the young child, a boy, pokes out his head and Vano waits with him while the lad relieves himself against a nearby tree.

Doma may not get another chance, and decides to go. Snatching up her bag, she panics slightly when the handle is caught on a holly branch and tugs it free. The rustling is loud in the stillness of the night, and she sits tight as Vano turns, eyes trying to focus. She has no choice now; she has to go and makes a dash for it just as he's kicking her empty tent and bellowing into the night.

By the time she's half-way up the path and within sight of cover, Vano gives chase, removing his belt as he goes. He's still shouting. Doma is fast and I'm still with her – the advantage of not having a body to drag around – but there must be something else I can do or what use am I?

She's reached the top of the bank by now, and plunges into the dark safety of the wood.

'Left, left,' I'm urging, hoping I can make her understand. Turning right would take her into much more open woodland and far away from where I know Gabe and Tobias are lying in wait. She sets off left and I stay behind. Vano has nearly reached the top, he's faster than I gave him credit for, but he's panting and still raging. I'm glad I don't understand the threats he's yelling, but the thick leather belt wrapped round one fist is enough to worry me when I think of the damage that could do to young flesh.

He hears her as soon as he reaches the top, looks left, but doesn't immediately follow. Instead, he cups his hands around his mouth and makes a call. I understand now; he's calling his men, but there's no response. He becomes agitated, running a hand through his thick hair and shaking his head as he steps one way and then the other. And I know why – it's decision time.

I hold my breath. If the curse has done its job and stopped Vano from entering Grange land, then Doma will be safe.

I watch him as his mouth sets into a grim line and the continual slapping of the leather against his breeches seems to make up his mind for him. He plunges into the undergrowth after Doma.

She's scared; she hears him crashing after her and doesn't know what to do for the best, for if the others join the hunt and it's three against one, she knows she doesn't stand a chance. I find her in a mossy hollow behind a large oak tree, visibly trembling. She's well hidden, but it's risky. Vano is no fool, large trees are an obvious choice and he's going to be aware of the faintest movement.

If I weren't so old I would be here in my body now, summoning the force and dispatching him in much the same way that did for Zillah. Vano may have a sixth sense, I feel sure he has, but I suspect that's the end to his talents and he'd be no match for me.

Oddly, as soon as this thought enters my head, I see Vano stop to wipe dust from his eyes. A little vortex of swirling leaves has appeared, kicking up debris from the woodland floor, and he has to skirt around it. It is nothing like a whirlwind, but it takes me by surprise as I'm in no doubt that I've caused it, and never before have I even attempted to summon the force whilst in this state.

It's a little late in the day to discover talents I never knew I had, but it couldn't be more timely.

Still blinking and rubbing his eyes, Vano blunders on, now only a short distance from Doma's hiding place to his left. I need to think quickly and lock on to a bush, yards away over to his right. It shakes and rustles as the force rushed by it and I'm mightily relieved to see I can do this at will. He's over there in a trice but finds nothing, and it won't be long before he figures out what's happening here. I've got to try something different.

As the strength of the force seems to be increasing with my confidence, my next move is a more ambitious piece of misdirection. I choose a high branch on a tall beech tree even further away, and hear a loud, satisfying snap and crash as it hits the woodland floor. Birds fly from their roosts; the air is suddenly alive with noise, and very soon I see the flaw in my plan.

Startled, Vano does not set off immediately to look for her in the tree, as I hoped, and Doma thinks all this commotion is the ideal time to find a better hide-out. Everything is happening too quickly and it's too late to warn her to stay put.

It's my mistake; he sees her and he's after her in a flash.

I catch up with Doma and see that he's gaining on her. She's fast but she can't keep up this pace and his long legs cover more ground than hers. Positioning myself between the two of them, I try to use the force to slow him down but he's moving too fast and it has no effect.

I scout ahead of them both to see what I can use, and what I see makes me terrified. There's no time to see if I can move it away completely and I'm forced to try something else.

There's a huge fallen tree trunk blocking the route; there's no way around it without getting tangled in brambles, and they're both going to have to jump it. I concentrate hard on my left hand; Doma seemed to understand this before and I hope she does now. Jump to the left, Doma – the left, the left.

Being small, she can't leap over the trunk, and wastes valuable seconds scrambling to stand on the top before jumping, mercifully to the left. She gets to her feet, looks back to see that Vano is nearly at the tree and starts to run, but she's flagging.

I don't follow her. I stay, half hoping I'm wrong, but knowing I must bear witness to what I'm now powerless to stop.

The sound of metal jaws snapping onto bone is a fearful sound, but it's those agonising screams that will stay with me for the rest of my life. There's nothing I can do to help him...

Doma, where are you? I can't see you... I can't see anything...

* * *

I'm dimly aware that there are people in my bedchamber. I can't think why. I could open my eyes and ask them but it's too much

260

effort at present. My head feels light and strangely disconnected from my body, full of thoughts and images I can't quite grasp, whilst my body feels heavy, like something's pressing down on my chest making it difficult to breathe.

I'm only catching snippets of whispered conversation until I hear Mary's voice.

'She had a very unsettled night, Mistress. My bed is right above here and I've heard her have the odd nightmare before. But I've never known her to be dead to the world like this so late in the morning.'

'I think it might have been more than a nightmare this time, Mary, but you weren't to know.'

It's Anne's voice, a little strained, and I only realise she's holding my hand when she starts to rub it between her own. 'And she's so cold. Fetch me a bedwarmer, will you Mary, and perhaps another coverlet.'

'Shouldn't we send for the doctor?'

'No, Samuel, not yet. She certainly won't thank you for that.'

'No... I won't.' I manage to get the words out just as my room swims into view, and I see Samuel on one side of my bed, and Anne on the other, both peering at me intently.

'Oh, thank goodness, Aunt, you had us all worried. How are you feeling?'

'I'm not sure.' I try to sit up, but Anne pushes me back, gently but firmly.

'Just lie still.' She squeezes out a cloth and wipes my brow with soothing warm water. It appears that Mary's been in already with my jug and bowl, but I didn't hear her.

'What time is it, Anne?'

'Around nine. I'll get Mary to bring you something to eat after she fetches your bedwarmer. If your feet are anything like your hands, they must be freezing.'

She's right, I wiggle my toes and can't feel them. 'Thank you, Anne, but I'm really not hungry. Some tea would be very welcome – and the bedwarmer – but then I think I'll just go back to sleep for a while. I must have been awake most of the night.'

It is Samuel who makes the first move, and pointedly waits for Anne at the door. Reluctantly, she folds the facecloth and places it back on the washstand.

'If you're sure.' She turns back at the door. 'You'll tell me, Aunt, if there's something amiss?'

'Yes, my love.' I smile to let her know all is well.

Except, of course, it isn't.

Physically, I have never felt worse. Is it my tired, old body, finally giving up, or the result of what I was doing last night? Perhaps it is a combination of the two; perhaps the older one is and the longer the mind and body are separated, the greater is the period of readjustment. Probably, but I'm hoping not to have to test that theory again.

By the time Mary has tucked the bedwarmer under the bedclothes, poured my tea and propped another pillow behind me, my head is feeling more normal and I can clearly recall the events of last night.

I suddenly feel quite sick.

* * *

The whispering has started again.

'She's looking a much better colour now, Tobias. Don't wake her, you can come back later.'

I call out just as they're leaving. Tobias pokes his head round the door and tries to give the silly grin that always makes my heart swell.

'I've been told to come back later.'

'Well, I'm telling you to come in now and talk to me; I've had enough sleep.'

He closes the door behind him. 'I hear you had a bad night, or is it something you're not telling us? Mother's in a bit of a panic.'

I pat the bed and move over so he can sit. 'I'm much better than I was earlier; so you can tell her not to worry. Anyway, Mary tells me I wasn't the only one to miss first meal.'

'Yes,' he pauses and looks down at his hands, 'it was a very eventful night. Gabe and I didn't get back until nearly dawn.'

Eventually, it all comes out.

Round about the time I was hovering near Doma's tent, Tobias and Gabe were encamped in the deepest part of the wood where the first gin trap had been found. Gabe had already let loose his deer distress call; so realistic, Tobias said, the woodland creatures were unsettled for a time. They'd chosen a spot where the moonlight couldn't penetrate, and lain down, their firearms at the ready.

At first, everything went according to plan.

The two men Vano had sent quickly checked the traps and snares, until it was obvious there was nothing more rewarding than a couple of rabbits.

'We were a little too far away to hear properly, but we both thought they said there was one more trap to check, and, as they set off in the opposite direction, that's when we had them.' I note there is nothing prideful or vainglorious in this statement. 'There was no point in them running, not with Gabe in front with his blunderbuss and me behind, so they did as they were told and collected all the snares and traps and left them in a heap.'

'Did you then go back to the camp with them?'

He gave little shake of his head, his mouth turned down. 'We were about to. I asked them where the older man was and they said he was 'down below', but before we'd made it halfway out of the wood, we heard this awful scream. I swear, Aunt, I've never heard anything like it. All four of us stopped and looked at each other, frozen to the spot for a second or two; we all knew it was no animal noise.'

Tobias told me what I already knew, that the trap was designed and placed to catch a large animal jumping over that tree trunk. The iron jaws were wide and the vicious teeth were now embedded, not in a deer, but in a man's thigh practically up to his groin.

'It was the older man from the camp and it looked as if he'd taken off his belt to strap round his leg as a tourniquet, but he hadn't managed it before he passed out. Gabe did it up as tight as he could, and the two others opened the clamp so we could drag him away.'

I reach for his hand. 'How awful, Tobias. Did he survive?'

He shook his head again. 'Even in the darkness, it was clear

there was no saving that leg, and the amount of blood was just...'
He ran a hand over his face as if to wipe the memory. 'One of the
men was trying to console the other who was crying 'No, Vano,
no...' over and over as he knelt by the man trying to rouse him, but
it was too late. Gabe had already checked for signs of life and there
were none. I swear it took no more than a few minutes for him to
bleed out, Aunt. We were all covered in it.' Without thinking, he
rubbed his hands over his thighs.

'I understand it can happen like that when a big vessel is
ruptured. There were many such cases in the Civil War battles.'
I've been waiting to hear if he mentions anything about a young
girl, but there's nothing.

'I suppose there were.'

'Did you manage to get him back to the camp?'

'Yes. Gabe stayed behind with one of the men, and I went to
the camp with the other one to fetch a sheet to carry him in. I can't
tell you how awful that was, too. The sound of the women's wailing
and crying followed us all the way back to the wood, then back to
the camp. I've never felt as wretched.'

'It wasn't your fault, Tobias. You didn't lay that trap or drive
him onto it. It could have been you or Gabe lying there dead.' Or
Doma, or Lucille, I couldn't help thinking.

~ 34 ~
Autumn 1724

I am now quite recovered from 'that night', which is not to say that I feel particularly well but I am, at least, as well as I was before.

Anne, naturally, did send word to Céleste and Sophia but I was able, I think, to put on a good show and we spent a most enjoyable day together, mainly discussing Sophia's forthcoming engagement. Before they left, I happened to mention how much I miss going out in the trap, especially in this glorious weather, but that Anne thinks it far too soon. A nod is as good as a wink to Céleste and I knew she'd drop it into the conversation with Anne before they left.

Which is how I came to be collected by Gabe yesterday; this time with no need of a footwarmer, extra rugs or, sadly, the honeyed port. It was so warm and sunny that only a parasol was required.

The little pony was nearly as excited as I was to be out and about, and the trap fairly sped along the lanes; for me, it was an unexpected treat. We took a tour round Thatchling, stopping only to pick up a package, then made a long loop before finishing up at Lucille's. This was what I'd been waiting for, the opportunity to find out what had happened in the wood that night after I found myself back at the Grange.

'I said to Lucille, you'll never see a more unfortunate accident than that.' Gabe shook his head slowly as I caught Lucille giving me a sideways look. 'No one deserves to die that way. If he'd jumped on it cleanly, it would've got him round the lower leg and he might have lost a foot, but he'd have survived. He must have fallen onto it somehow to get clamped like that.

I tutted as if he was telling me something I didn't already know. I was seeing again the moment Vano landed awkwardly right next to the trap, turning an ankle and overbalancing, unable to save himself. I closed my eyes to blot it out.

Gabe had found it very hard returning to camp with the body. The daughters and their husbands were young, in deep shock, and in no doubt that the fault lay with 'that little bastard'. Having persuaded Tobias to go home, he remained, explaining that he would help the travellers all he could as long as they cleared the traps.

'Lucille took them some food the next day and we wrapped the body properly for they seemed reluctant to touch him for some reason. We helped them make a pyre and they burnt all his possessions along with him – that's the custom, apparently. They were gone soon after.'

'And Doma?' I couldn't wait any longer. 'She's here?'

'Aye, course she is. The little thing was waiting for me in the wood, sitting propped against a tree. She slipped her hand in mine without a word, and we came back here.'

Lucille was smiling. 'She'll be back soon. I sent her out with the milk pail and some coin. She's a fast learner, you know.'

It wasn't long before we heard the gate swing open and Lucille went out to take the milk from her. Shyly, Doma entered, waited by the door for a second or two, then knelt by my side and rested her head on my knee. I stroked her hair and when she raised her head, we both laughed to see tears in our eyes.

'Thank you.' Her accent was near perfect.

Although old enough to be her grandparents, Gabe and Lucille had already decided that she should stay if that's what she wanted, and it was clear that the child wasn't preparing to leave. We all watched as she carefully unwrapped the package Gabe had collected from his niece, her eyes wide as she held up each new treasure; picture books and second-hand clothing.

It did my heart good to see how well things have turned out for Lucille; not only does she have the man she always wanted, but now a child she thought she'd never have. Good things do sometimes come to those who wait, and no one has waited longer than Lucille. Perhaps Melina always knew that if she kept her daughter safe in her early years, she would reap the reward.

Communication was still slow but, between the few English words that Doma had already learned and Lucille's skill with pen and paper, this is what Lucille had discovered.

Doma and her Romany mother had been living somewhere on the continent until a couple of years ago. Fairly soon after arriving in England, her mother had taken up with Vano, seduced by this handsome man who also understood and spoke her language. The relationship went down badly with both Vano's daughters and Doma.

Some months ago, Doma's mother died and in her last days she made Vano promise to provide for her daughter, knowing there was no alternative and hoping they'd learn to get along. Vano had no option but to promise; he'd witnessed the woman's gifts, and his tribe's traditional fear of the spirit world was enough to make sure he kept his word.

The night Doma absconded, therefore, was a dilemma for Vano; did he let her go and risk retribution from beyond the grave, or chance his luck on Grange land? Doma may not have understood English but she sensed that the reason he and his daughters never ventured there, may be the very reason it called to her.

And, of course, she was right.

Was the curse responsible for Vano's accident? I think not; after all, he'd shown no fear of being on Grange land the last time he was here. No, surely, it's the wood. Haven't I always known, along with Melina, Lyssa and Lucille, and who knows how many before them, that it has its own special magic? And Vano sensed it, as Zillah had, too.

* * *

It's been a while since I experienced a glimpse into the future. I remember clearly the first time it happened, well over 50 years ago, when I witnessed the murder of a priest, in vivid colour with no details spared. Since then, they've been more akin to vague portents, like the warnings prior to Tobias's beating, and nothing as clear as that first time.

Not until this morning, that is.

The young woman was clearly Doma, no longer the reticent, skinny girl of years before, but now confident and radiating good health. It looked like she was doing her rounds in the village, carrying a black bag I knew to be Melina's; the one containing her midwifery kit and anything else she might need on her visits.

I have no doubt that, in whatever time I was seeing, she also knows every inch of Fox Wood, where all the best herbs are to be found and has discovered the little spring. I feel sure that she's a friend to the animals, and there may even be some special ones watching over her. I like to think that's the case.

~ 35 ~
11th October 1725

They've all been with me recently. It's a good sign.

Bernard is in my dreams most nights, looking exactly as he did the first time I set eyes on him; his sleek, white hair falling neatly to his shoulders, dressed in his beautiful teal-blue silk doublet and breeches. The shimmering aura which had once rendered me speechless is there again, as is the twinkly-eyed smile which never failed to make my insides melt.

If he's seeing me now I wonder what he makes of this useless bag of bones. He at least had the good sense to go before he reached this stage.

I thought I saw Aphra yesterday when I woke before dawn, quite clearly standing at the foot of my bed. With head cocked to one side and hands on hips in typical pose, the expression on her face suggested that I was taking far too long. It made me smile; she never did like waiting.

Hopefully, she won't have to wait long. Satisfied that I've fulfilled my promise to Alice to the best of my ability, she can rest easy now that everything here appears settled and Oakwood Grange is safe to carry on for the foreseeable future.

Tobias and Rose wasted no time after their wedding and are already expecting their first child. He is now *de facto* master of the estate, with Anne only too willing to bow out of all responsibilities and spend more time visiting friends with the recently retired Samuel.

Charles is still living with his professor in Oxford, seemingly content to pursue an academic life rather than follow his father into the law, and no-one knows, not even Tobias, whether he ever plans to make an honest woman of the professor's daughter.

And Young Alice? I feel her grandmother's pride in the young woman she has become. Tobias once observed that, despite his sister being named for her grandmother, they had little in common. Not so now. Admiring Hendrick as she does, the girl who at one time had no thought in her head other than gowns, adornments and balls, has now begun to appreciate how other aspects of life are infinitely more fulfilling. It amuses me to remember how her grandmother's transformation was the other way round; far too serious as a young woman who only came around to fashion and balls later in life, encouraged by her second husband. Two good men bringing out the best in their women.

In the end, it was Tobias and Rose's wedding that swayed Samuel in Hendrick's favour. As Young Alice once pointed out to me, no one could fail to notice their attachment and it certainly was not lost on the guests whose nudges and winks signalled that they could clearly see what Samuel was patently ignoring. One respectable lady friend of the family, admittedly a little loose-lipped because of drink, even told Anne that she was in the market for another husband herself if Samuel banned the match for his daughter.

Luckily, Young Alice didn't have to drag Hendrick into Samuel's study. Encouraged by Rose, Tobias did that himself immediately after the wedding and then left them to get to know each other better. Samuel did come round, belatedly acknowledging the exceptional circumstances which had reduced Hendrick to a 'working man with no assets' and, finding himself in an opposition group of one, eventually gave his consent.

Unable to refuse, I have made promises to Young Alice that I won't be able to keep; it saddens me more than I can say, but it isn't in my gift to change things. I think she knows it herself. No doubt, I shall be watching from afar with her grandmother when she and Hendrick tie the knot.

Apart from Céleste and Sophia, who were here yesterday, both trying so hard to be jolly it nearly broke my heart, that promise is now the only thing that saddens me. I'm ready and happy to go, knowing that I've outlasted my usefulness here and have become a burden.

Mary has had instructions from me to leave the curtains open on the last few nights. She hasn't argued with me about the danger of draughts and has lingered and fussed around the room aimlessly until she can find nothing else to keep her before wishing me 'God Bless, Madam'.

Dawn, 12th October 1725

I know what I'm about to see before I even open my eyes, and I'll be disappointed if I'm wrong.

I'm not wrong.

The trees, now completely bare of leaves, are bent over in the teeth of a strong wind. I hear it whistling through the branches and moaning round the buildings as I watch her creep stealthily across the window sill and crouch down, ginger coat fluffed up to preserve some heat even as frost is settling on the very tips of her fur and whiskers. My eyesight is too poor to make out the nick in her ear and the missing claw, but I know they're there.

She blinks at me through the glass and I hold out a hand, but it's too much of an effort and I let it fall. Everything is now too much for me and I welcome it.

Is she here to escort me out of this life? And what comes next for me, if anything? After all these years, everything is still a mystery.

I close my eyes; Alice is with me.

Epilogue
Oakwood Grange, 2018

izzie Whittaker sat poised, pen in hand, to enter the details in the House Book. It had been many years since she'd used a fountain pen, and was never proficient it had to be said, but the gravity of the occasion and the history of the book demanded nothing less. She wasn't going to be the first to enter something in biro.

It had taken her four years to pluck up courage to get to this point, and the scrap pad in front of her was testament to how determined she was to get it right. They deserved nothing less.

Taking a moment to breathe deeply, she closed her eyes, half hoping to see the girl again. She'd seen her quite clearly last night when she'd taken the House Book from the oak chest; a young girl from the distant past, sitting at a desk and preparing to write an entry with quill and ink pot. Lizzie was now so used to these tiny snapshots of earlier times that, far from unsettling her, they gave her a deep sense of belonging.

It was time.

ROBERT JAMES WHITTAKER aged 66 years

and

EUGENIE (JANIE) FIONA WHITTAKER aged 62 years

Much loved parents to Elizabeth and Thomas, DIED TOGETHER

on March 12th 2014

The result of a tragic motoring accident in France.

With no blotting paper, Lizzie sat back and waited for it to dry, relieved that at least there were no mistakes, even if the handwriting wasn't the best.

The previous two entries were for her and Tom's births, clearly in her Mum's hand, and the one before that was when her parents bought Oakwood Grange in 1985. That entry was written by her Dad, the handwriting unmistakably that of an artist.

The tears came suddenly and she pushed her chair away quickly before they fell and ruined her work.

* * *

Downstairs, waiting for her in the kitchen, was another task she'd been putting off and she figured that now she'd made a start, she may as well get all the death-related jobs done at once.

Having read the solicitor's letter again, she laid it down next to the archive box sitting in front of her on the kitchen table. The name in bold letters on the lid read 'Mark Richardson', her mother's uncle who'd recently departed this life at the age of 91, and who was the last link to one side of her Mum's family. Initially meant for her mother, the contents ended up with Lizzie.

She drummed her fingers on the table trying to figure out why she'd been putting this off. The box had been sitting there for over a week waiting to be opened, and each time she passed it, she felt either a pull or a push she could make no sense of.

The phone came to her rescue. Fishing it out of her back pocket, she checked caller ID before answering.

'Hey, Tom. How's it going?'

'Oh, y'know...'

'That bad, eh?'

'I've just realised I fucking hate banking, I don't know what I was thinking of. Meeting after boring bloody meeting, late nights, early starts; I never get to see Billy in the week and Katya's fed up with me. Apart from that, everything's wonderful.'

Lizzie knew how much it had cost him to admit that. He knew what she thought. 'What does Katya say.'

'She's fond of quoting Polish sayings which, between you and me, I swear she makes up, the gist being 'do what makes you happy.'

'Mmm.' She paused. 'I hope you're still coming down for the weekend?'

'Absolutely, we've been looking forward to it. I'll bring the booze, Katya will bring cake and Billy will no doubt bring some germs from nursery. You've been warned.'

They signed off and Lizzie immediately began honing her argument.

Four years ago, just before the accident that threw their world into confusion, Lizzie, at 28, was already running Mallory's Literary Agency, living and working in their childhood home whilst her younger brother was in a flat in London. Now their parents were gone, Lizzie felt a significant amount of guilt for being childless, single and the sole occupant of a large country house.

Whilst others might suggest selling the house, that was never an option, for Oakwood Grange had been in their father's family for over three and a half centuries. Rob and Janie Whittaker had died only a couple of years into a retirement which was meant to last many more years, by which time they hoped one of the children would take it on for future generations.

And that will be Tom, thought Lizzie, but the trick is to convince him it will work.

What she knew was this. Tom will give up banking and the frankly obscene salary that brings him no pleasure. A country boy at heart, he, Katya and Billy will come back to the Grange; it's plenty big enough for all of them and it needs to live again as a family home. Their Dad's studio will be put to good use once more. She will become a proper Auntie.

None of this was wishful thinking. Lizzie had seen exactly how their lives will play out many a time; sometimes in dreams, but often when entering a room to find an older Billy with his toys, or in the kitchen garden where Tom's repairing the glasshouse. Recently, when clearing spiders from the studio, one vision was so vivid, it took her breath away. Where once there were easels and artwork, now there were sewing machines, masses of fabric lining the walls, beautiful cushions piled high – and Katya in her element, trademark scarf round her head, designing and creating exquisite pieces, and not just for their home.

Eventually, her resourceful brother will find something fulfilling to do, and Lizzie will then clear out and leave them to it. Mallory's Literary Agency was able to operate from anywhere.

She needed to plant the seeds of all this next weekend, and then she was banking on Katya to do the rest.

Lizzie turned back to the box sitting in front of her. The odd feeling was still there and she rested both hands on the lid.

Her condition, whatever it was, had never been properly diagnosed. 'Childhood depression creating poltergeist-like phenomena caused by an excess of energy' was the only explanation from various professionals and cranks alike. Her parents soon stopped seeking advice from people who were clearly guessing. Once Lizzie learned to control those upsetting episodes, Rob stopped worrying, and family life returned to something resembling normal. Janie was the only one she ever told about the visions and out-of-body experiences, knowing that her mother was open-minded about such things, having had experienced one or two weird moments herself in the past. Had it not been for her, there were times Lizzie thought she might have lost it completely.

She shook her head to try to stop the memory of the accident, but it was futile. Rob was already dead, horribly mangled in the car, but Janie had been thrown clear and was dying. The emergency services hadn't yet arrived and it was torture not to be able to hold her mother in her arms, but Janie knew she was there. She whispered her daughter's name over and over, and opened her eyes one last time before the light went out completely. Lizzie understood what she was trying to tell her; and promised she'd make sure he was alright.

It was a blessing Tom wasn't home at the time, for hiding her grief until the call came would have been impossible.

Enough now, she told herself, stop wallowing and get back to the job in hand. She removed the lid smartly and peered inside.

Given that Mark had little of value apart from his tiny cottage in Arnby-next-the-Sea in Norfolk and a clapped-out old car, his will was simple; he'd left it all to Tom and Lizzie. The keys were in the padded envelope right on top. There was going to have to be a discussion with Tom and Katya, but Lizzie really wanted to keep it – the cottage that is, not the car. Childhood memories of shrimping and windswept cricket on the beach with her parents, sleeping with Tom on blow-up mattresses on the living room floor next to the cats and the log burner; were those good reasons to hang on to it? Lizzie didn't know, but as a remote bolthole if ever one was needed might be a good enough reason.

Lying beneath the padded envelope was a jewellery box. A standard, Victorian mahogany affair, its contents were unsurprising for a working-class woman of that era – apart from a pretty miniature of a young man in a military uniform, and one exquisite pendant in a leather pouch. The latter looked Georgian, Lizzie thought, a beautiful blue enamel plaque encased in a finely chased gold mount, it wasn't until she turned it over that she noticed the plaited hair and realised it was perhaps a mourning piece. Unusually, the strands were alternating white and black, or dark brown, making a chequerboard effect. There were no initials to indicate who was being remembered, but there were assay marks and she made a mental note to look them up on the internet. At least that would confirm the date of the piece, and she put it round her neck as a reminder.

Inevitably, there were photo albums. Mark had given Janie the most recent ones years ago but these were really old, some going back to the 19th century. They were fascinating, and she spent the best part of an hour scrutinising faces and wishing someone had been better at writing down names and dates. One showed two young ladies, arm in arm, smiling broadly at the camera, and obviously enjoying a day at the seaside. Quite stylish, both wore pretty cream blouses, with a bow at the neck and leg o' mutton sleeves, tucked into long dark skirts with impossibly tiny waists. Rather fetching little straw boaters balanced on plenty of hair in up-dos.

Another photo, of a mother and baby, grabbed her attention. This one did have a date at least, 1901 on the reverse, and Lizzie found herself strangely invested in finding out who they were. She went back to the oak chest in the study.

Armed with all her mother's notes, Lizzie spread out the roll of paper, anchoring it down with sugar bowl and salt and pepper shakers, so she could see the whole of the family tree. As the dates matched, the photo had to be of Mark's mother and grandmother; the grandmother also being one of the girls in the other photo. Lizzie peered at the girl's face again. 'Well, hello there, Great-Great-Grandmama.'

Cross with herself that she hadn't shown much interest in all this before her mother died, Lizzie was only just beginning to realise the extent of the research and how long it must have taken Janie to find all that information in a pre-computer age. She resolved to try to pick up where her mother had left off, and see if she could get any further back than 1701, now that most records can be accessed digitally. Disappointingly, a quick check revealed no aristos in the chart but there was something interesting– Janie had underlined the name Céleste, which cropped up every now and then, even as far back as 1701. Both her mother and grandmother had Celeste as their middle name, too, although the accent had been dropped by then.

She'd got side-tracked. Quickly rolling the chart back up to make more room she concentrated on the rest of the box's contents. Several thick files housed birth, marriage and death certificates, school reports and exam certificates, old war-era ration cards and petrol coupons, obsolete bank savings books, letters; there must have been at least 60 years' worth of paperwork there. She put it all on one side to go through when she had more time.

That left only one more item at the bottom of the archive box; a small black and gold tin money box, the sort that kids used to have years ago. She could feel there was something solid inside, but no key and it was locked. It wasn't with the house and car keys and it wasn't in the now empty archive box, so there was nothing for it but to jemmy the lock with a screwdriver.

Whatever she was expecting it wasn't this; a box within a box. Her Russian grandfather would have known roughly how old it was and probably where it came from, but Lizzie could only guess. At no more than 3" x 2", it was metal, possibly gold, with beautifully painted panels on all sides and it screamed French, or possibly Italian, but whatever it was, thought Lizzie, it was fabulous.

Gingerly flipping the tiny clasp, the lid eased off perfectly, and Lizzie held her breath to see what treasure it contained.

No priceless jewels, no gold sovereigns, just a card and an unsealed envelope.

The card read: '*This little box was passed to my grandmother from her grandmother, with a note to pass it on to the eldest girl in the family for safe-keeping, or son if no daughter. No one knows why, but I'm following the tradition. The instructions are to read the contents of the little envelope, then replace it in the box but, as the paper is very old now, I've copied the message below.*

'Be Not Afraid

Be not afraid to see things others cannot,

Be not afraid to do things others cannot,

Be not afraid to feel things others cannot.

If you are in receipt of this Gift,

Use it wisely,

Use it for Good.

Know that you are not alone.

Elisabeth La Montagne 1725

Please pass it on as directed.'
It was signed by Mark's mother, in 1982.

Lizzie felt her heart racing nineteen to the dozen. For her, this scrap of paper was momentous.

She read it again; this time the 'Be Not Afraid' message striking home. Her heart rate started to slow and her eyes began to close involuntarily. Surrendering completely, the feeling was one of being enveloped by all the people she'd ever loved, and the phrase 'you are not alone' was echoing in her brain on some sort of cosmic loop.

She found herself clutching the pendant.

Elisabeth La Montagne. Reaching for the family tree again, she unrolled it and went to the earliest entry. Céleste La Montagne married Jonathon Miller in 1701 and they had one daughter, Sophia. So, was Elisabeth Céleste's mother? The date would fit.

There was something else niggling away at the back of her mind, but Lizzie couldn't quite grasp it until she went to put the House Book back in the chest. Hours later, all thought of stopping for food forgotten, she sat back on her heels and hoped more than anything that her mother was with her now.

For there it all was, just waiting for someone to connect the dots. Janie's discovery of Alice Harryman's 17th century diary had been a literary coup back in 1985, shedding light on an unknown period in the life of Aphra Behn. But what had always been more interesting to Janie was learning of Alice's life in this very house, her great friendship with Elisabeth Turner and the accusations of witchcraft levelled at Elisabeth by Alice's husband.

With little expectation, Lizzie had turned to the original House Book to check entries in the 1700's, and found what she was certain was the missing link.

Madame E. La Montagne

Sponsor to Anne and Astrea and loyal family friend, departed this life

On 12th October 1725, in her 83rd year.

In Lizzie's mind, there was no question that Elisabeth Turner and Elisabeth La Montagne were the same person; both clearly 'gifted' and with dates that matched with Alice's diary.

But what did come as a shock was to discover that Elisabeth, her ancestor, most probably died in this house, or else why would she be in the House Book?

Lizzie looked around the study; once her mother's study – and just knew.

* * *

'I thought I'd better let you know, Lizzie. Billy's got chicken pox.'

'That's alright, I've had it, so have you. How is he?'

'He's not too bad and we'd still love to come, if that's ok with you.'

'Sure. Anyway, I want you all to meet my new pet.'

'You got another dog, at last?'

'No, I will be getting another dog, but I'll let the cat settle in first.'

'It's not one of those weird ones, is it?'

'No, course not. It's a standard plain black moggy, very much like our old 'Cat', if you can remember that one. It's been hanging around the garden for the last few days and then, yesterday, it walked in with me and made itself at home. It seems I've been adopted. She's sitting right next to me now.'

'Good. I don't like to think of you on your own.'

She smiled. 'No need to worry about me – I'm not alone.'

THE END

Author's Note

This is a work of fiction.

With the exception of Aphra Behn, Thomas Culpeper, Nell Gwynn, John (Jack) Hoyle, Emily Price and George Granville, all other characters in this book are entirely fictitious. Any resemblance to persons alive or dead is a coincidence.

Similarly, Oakwood Grange and the villages of Upburton and Thatchling are a product of the author's imagination.

A Note on Aphra Behn

A phra Behn is remembered as one of the first English women to make a living from her literary writing.

Born in 1640, very little is known of her first 27 years, leading many to suspect that it was Aphra herself who was responsible for muddying the waters. Some biographers believe that she did indeed visit Surinam with her parents, her father dying *en route*, whilst others cast doubt, citing her short story 'Oroonoko' as fiction despite its billing as 'A True History'.

Her marriage is not found in any church records but it is generally accepted that Aphra married, or at least cohabited with, Johan Behn, a Dutch merchant, and that he either died in the Great Plague or they separated soon afterwards. At any rate, she was known thereafter as Mrs. Behn and reportedly lived in somewhat reduced circumstances.

Part of her life which is well documented relates to her role as a political spy for Charles II. Thomas Killigrew, a courtier who ran the Kings Playhouse (later the Theatre Royal) was instrumental in her recruitment but it was the government who treated her so shamefully that she was forced to borrow a considerable sum of money to return to England. A warrant was issued for her arrest but there's no evidence that she was ever imprisoned and the debt was eventually paid by an undisclosed source.

Around 1668/9, Aphra began writing for the King's Company and her first play, 'The Forc'd Marriage', was staged in 1670. Many more plays, novels and poetry followed throughout her life.

Aphra never remarried although it appears she was never

short of lovers. She was witty, unconventional and ambitious for literary recognition, but came in for a deal of criticism for 'writing like a man' and portraying sexual desire and even homoerotic themes in her works. A staunch Royalist with unfashionable views, she nevertheless became friends with notable writers of the day, including John Dryden and Thomas Otway, who supported her and celebrated her work.

After four years of failing health, but writing up to the very end, Aphra Behn died in poverty in April 1689 and was buried in the East Cloister of Westminster Abbey.

* * *

If any Aphra Behn scholars and purists have read this novel, I hope you can forgive some of the liberties taken with your heroine.

She is my heroine too.

Reference

'Aphra Behn – A Secret Life' by Janet Todd

'Samuel Pepys: The Unequalled Self' by Claire Tomalin, Penguin Paperback 2003

'A Visual History of Costume: The Seventeenth Century' by Valerie Cumming, Hardback 1984

'Women and Property in Early Modern England' by Dr. Amy Erickson, Paperback 1995

'A Memoir of Mrs. Behn' by Montague Summers, A University of Adelaide e-publication, updated December 2014

'The Archaeology of Folk Magic' article by Brian Hoggard 1999

'Eve's Herbs: A History of Contraception and Abortion in the West' by John Riddle, Harvard University Press, 1999

Bonus Content

Free bonus chapters to *The House Book*, revealing the backstories of Rob and Janie Whittaker, are available from the website www.susan-greenwood.co.uk. More bonus content for *An Uncertain Legacy* to follow...

If you have enjoyed reading this book, please consider leaving a review on Amazon by searching 'Recognition by Susan Greenwood'.

Thank you.